The Chief's Daughter

The Chief's Daughter

by

Dr. Kalu N. Nchege

DORRANCE PUBLISHING CO., INC.
PITTSBURGH, PENNSYLVANIA 15222

All Rights Reserved
Copyright © 2009 by Dr. Kalu N. Nchege
No part of this book may be reproduced or transmitted
in any form or by any means, electronic or mechanical,
including photocopying, recording, or by any information
storage and retrieval system without permission in
writing from the publisher.

ISBN: 978-1-4349-0134-7
Library of Congress Control Number: 2008926338

Printed in the United States of America

First Printing

For more information or to order additional books, please contact:
Dorrance Publishing Co., Inc.
701 Smithfield Street
Third Floor
Pittsburgh, Pennsylvania 15222
U.S.A.
1-800-788-7654
www.dorrancebookstore.com

Acknowledgments

I wish to thank my wife, Odester Nchege, whose contributions to this work are too many to mention.

I would like to express my deepest appreciation to my late father, Chief Ndukwe Kalu Nchege, for the inspiration of my life. He knew, and encouraged, what I was doing. He was a pillar of strength to me and to all in his family.

Thanks to my late brother George Nchege for his love, faith, and example. His encouragement led me to write this book.

Thanks to the late Dr. K.E. Ume, who encouraged me through his words of advice to put my thoughts in writing. He was a friend and a gentleman.

My thanks to all members of my family for support and encouragement, and to Nnena Ugo Nchege for the contributions and contacts she made to ensure that this book is published.

Dedication

In Memory of
Dr. Edward K. Weaver,
for hope in life.

Chapter 1

Newtown Hotel, the best in Ohadum District, Nigeria was located on the outskirts of Unaka town. As the weekend manager of the Newtown Hotel, Angelina was on duty on this Friday afternoon. She had not been at work very long when she looked up and saw an incredibly handsome man making conversation with the bartender. The young man had a perfect set of white teeth, which he flashed in a boyish smile. She drew in a breath at the sight of him. He was, to her eyes, the most attractive man she had ever seen.

When Jacob Ikonne, the hotel proprietor, looked in the direction of Angelina, she was devouring the stranger with her eyes. Jacob smiled. He knew what was going on. He kept observing his manager and the stranger exchanging smiles. Jacob noticed that when Angelina looked up, she realized that the stranger was flirtatiously looking at her with a longing that stunned her.

Jacob watched the young man motion to Angelina to come to where he was. She went to him.

"My name is Angelina Oyinatu. I'm the weekend manager at this hotel. May I help you with anything?" she asked with a smile.

"My name is Agara Aham. I would like to talk to you," he said.

"Me?" she asked in surprise.

"Yes," the young man said, looking at her.

"You said you are the weekend manager. What do you do during the week?"

"I'm a school teacher," she answered.

"Where do you teach?" he asked.

She smiled. "Unaka Elementary School." As she spoke, she noticed that Agara's glance was doing a slow scan of her from head to foot and back, lingering on her cleavage. He was using this opportunity to get an eyeful of her, and she didn't mind it at all. In the course of their conversation, Angelina found him to be twenty-five years old, four years older than she.

"Angelina," he called her. "I'm impressed by your beauty and good manners."

"Thank you. Will there be anything else?" she asked.

"Yes. Later," he answered.

Feeling pleased with what they saw in each other, they smiled, and Angelina went back to her office. Jacob smiled at her as she was coming into her office.

"Is everything okay?" Jacob asked.

"Yes," she answered.

So far, there was nothing about the young man that Angelina didn't like. For the duration of the time Agara was at the bar, he and Angelina continued to make eye contact. When she got ready to go home, Agara came to her, and shook her hand for several long seconds.

"Are you married?" he asked.

"No," she replied.

"I'm a lucky man," she heard him say as she turned to walk away. As if he changed his mind, he walked very fast and caught up with her.

"Is there anything?" she asked, scared of what she didn't know.

"Just want to walk part of the way with you," he said.

"Say it like it is, Mr. Aham," she said to him. "You want to know where I live."

He smiled. She told him that she lived at the teachers' quarters. He said good night to her and turned back. The parting smile he gave her was an indication of what he thought: This was going to be an easy conquest; the woman is willing and available.

On Saturday morning, Agara got dressed. After walking around the hotel premises to get familiar with the environment, he went inside to chat with Jacob.

"Tell me about Angelina," Agara said.

"She teaches school during the day and works as the manager on weekends. She is a fine lady. Judging from the look I observed between the two of you last night, she isn't going to rest until she finds out who you are," Jacob said.

Later in the morning, Angelina came to work at the hotel. She met Agara and Jacob chatting. She carefully ignored Agara and asked the proprietor, "Has the delivery man delivered soft drinks?"

"No, Angelina," the proprietor replied. Angelina went into her office.

"Agara, you've got Angelina's nose up in the air," Jacob told him.

"How is that?" Agara asked.

"Before she left yesterday, she said to me, 'Agara's the kind of man women would lust over, and with good reason. His eyes are very hypnotic. He looks very virile, and his smile is very sensual.'"

"I'm flattered," Agara said.

"She isn't a slut," the proprietor said. "I assure you of that."

"She might want to know what I do," Agara said.

"I'll tell her that you are a businessman or some kind of wealthy contractor, just by looking at you."

"Better still, let me deal with it," Agara said.

While Angelina was in her office, Jacob went in to chat with her. As he opened the door, Angelina smiled, sensing why the proprietor was coming—to talk. He smiled and said, "Angelina, you must like the new man in this hotel."

"He's a good looking man," she said.

"Well, let me tell you up front." Jacob paused and Angelina was ready to hear it.

"If the attention he paid you yesterday and today is any indication," Jacob said, "I'd predict that the man is after you. If you don't want to fall for him, you had better start running, and fast too."

Angelina took the hint. After she got off work in the afternoon, Agara walked around the community until he found himself at the teachers' quarters. He knocked at her door. There was no answer. He knocked again, and she asked, "Who is it?"

"Agara Aham," he answered.

Then she opened the door slightly.

"Hello, Angelina!" he greeted. His voice was smooth and appealing.

"Hello!" Angelina squeaked, surprised to see him at her door.

"Hold on a minute," she told him and closed the door. A minute or so later, when the door opened again, she asked him to come in.

She prepared a meal, which they ate.

"What are you doing in Unaka, may I know?" she asked.

"I'm just a visitor in search of an opportunity to make a living," he answered.

"Do you like teaching?" he asked.

"It's fun to work with children. I like teaching. Sometimes it can be a very challenging job."

"What do you like to do for a hobby?" she asked.

"I have worked as a mechanic in a banana plantation in the Cameroon. But I later left the job for personal reasons and moved on with my life."

After they chatted for a while, Agara thanked her for her hospitality. She invited him to come to the school on Monday for the Unaka Primary School Sports Day.

"I'll be there," he promised.

While he was walking back to the hotel, he thought about Angelina. She lived in a small house. Everything was very simplistic and elegant. The house was tidy and comfortable. The backyard was fenced. The room was furnished with a small spring bed, a table, four chairs, and two small stools. She had a picture of her parents on the wall. She loved her parents, and she was very close to her father. By her standard of living, she could not have been regarded as poverty stricken.

When she first opened the door slightly, Agara remembered her startled expression. Her eyes had been wide and round, her hair neatly plaited and piled on top of her head. As he brought his gaze to her face, a tantalizing smile escaped her lips. She finally opened the door for him to enter and they greeted as if she had known him for sometime. He admired her lovely face and her gazelle neck. The smile that followed on her face was enchanting. Even in his encounter with the girls in and around his village, Oharu, he had never come across one that looked so beautiful when she blushed. He noted her cultured tone of voice. Everything about her showed that she had a royal blood. He wondered why she was in the village instead of in the township, where she would be hobnobbing with the rich and the powerful.

On Monday, Agara met Angelina at her school. She introduced him to her friends and coworker. The sporting event was very exciting. He watched the pupils race, pole vault, hop-step and jump, and other athletic events. He also watched the lawn tennis game, which the pupils played with wooden bats. Agara enjoyed the events.

After the sporting events, Angelina invited her friend Miss Uzo and her boyfriend to the house. She told her friend that Agara was her friend. She entertained them with food and drink. They played card games and had a good time.

As Agara was about to leave, she looked at him, and he suspected that something was wrong.

"What is it?" he asked.

She didn't say, but touched his beard and mustache.

"You prefer a clean-shaven male?"

"Oh, but—"

"That's okay. You haven't hurt my feelings. It's coming off."

Agara was out to impress Angelina. The next day, he went to the marketplace and to the section where barbers cut hair. He sat on the stool, waiting for the barber who was chattering to his neighbor. When the barber saw the expression of impatience of his face, he came over to attend to him.

"Shave everything?" he asked him.

"Yes, my head and my beard," he replied.

"Would you like for me to clean your ears too and shape your eyebrows?" the barber asked.

"Would that be for extra charge?" he asked.

"A few coins more," the barber said.

When Agara hesitated, the barber's clients burst into a guffaw, and realizing that he had become the object of laughter, he shut his mouth and let the barber do his job. The barber soaped and rubbed, and before Agara could say anything, the barber had had his entire head shaved. One middle-aged man, Jon Akaji, walked into the shop and, looking at him, said, "Man, you sure got a clean shave, didn't you?"

"I sure did. Doesn't it look good?" he asked.

"It brings out the best look in you. I understand that the women are very crazy about bald-headed men. They say it's a sign of being high sexed," Jon said.

Agara grinned and said nothing.

"Come and see me sometime," Jon invited him.

"Where do you live?" Agara asked.

Jon gave him directions to his home.

"I will take you up on this invitation some day," he told Jon.

When Agara left the marketplace, he went to see Angelina.

"Agara, you have a nice haircut," Angelina said.

"Thanks," he said.

"What would you like to do?" she asked.

"Would you like to go to the hotel and play a game of ping pong?" he asked.

"I'd love it," she said.

They walked to the Newtown Hotel. While they were playing a game of ping pong, Angelina developed a cramp in her leg. Agara ran to her, his eyes filled with concern. She moaned as he applied gentle pressure to massage the muscle.

After a while, the cramp ceased and there was only the pleasant feel of Agara's hands on her leg. She looked at him and wondered what it would feel like to have his hands move up her legs and her entire body.

"Feel better?" Agara asked.

She smiled and said, "Thanks for getting the cramp out. You have great hands."

"It could have been better if it was done in private," he said jokingly.

She smiled at his insinuation.

Angelina had known Agara for three days. He had impressed her as a man. The next day she got a message from her mother, Beatrice Oyinatu. She was to come home for a mother–daughter talk. Angelina wondered if her father was sick. Nervously, she hurried home to her father's palace. As she approached her mother's room, her pace slowed.

"Hello, Mother."

"Hello, Sunshine," her mother responded. "You must have gotten my message."

"I did, Mother. That's what brought me. Is my father all right?"

"He is fine," the old lady said.

"You look apprehensive," Beatrice said. "Speak, Angelina. I'm listening."

"This won't take long, Mother," she said.

"I want to tell you about a young man I met a few days ago."

"What about him? And what is his name?"

"His name is Agara Aham. I'm in love with him. I want to marry him."

For a moment, her mother sat there as though petrified. She was speechless for a few seconds, which seemed like an eternity to Angelina. Her mother did not want to interfere where she knew it would be wise not to. She would not let anyone destroy her daughter's chance at happiness. "She is not a child," she thought.

"Do you know if he is married?" her mother asked.

"He has not talked about his girlfriends," she replied.

"I have heard what you said," the old woman said. "You are determined to marry a total stranger. As a mother, I will stand by your decision. But listen to this, my daughter. Zebulon Zimako, the rich man from Aloma, was here today. He met with your father. He is not very happy that you have continued to show lack of enthusiasm about marrying him. He talked about his plan to have an official high-society traditional engagement ceremony for you and him.

"There is no doubt that my father went along with his plan," Angelina said.

"He did." Then her mother grabbed her hand and said, "Angelina, I love you. The world has teeth; if you are not careful, they will tear you to pieces."

"Thank you, Mother, I love you too. Let me confide in you, Mother. I do not love Zebulon Zimako. I will not marry him. There is the age difference; he is thirty-seven and I'm twenty-one. My girlfriends and fellow teachers tell me that since his wife passed away three years ago, Mr. Zimako has a woman, or women, in every town in Ohadum District. He loves women of all ages, shapes, and sizes. They love him too. I do not want an overused man. Give me time to think about what you said," Angelina said. She then hugged her mother and left unhappily.

The next day, after school, Agara went to see Angelina. They went out and ate lunch at the Newtown Hotel. They enjoyed a meal of rice and stew with goat meat, fish pepper soup, and shared wine. From there, they went to the town square to watch adult women perform Kokoma dance—a purely hip dance. It was an evening of entertainment, watching the dancers trying to outdo one another in shaking their hips.

When Angelina went home that night, she began to scold herself. "Here I am, in love with a mammoth stranger I know nothing about, which says a lot about the state of my mind." She thought twice and counseled herself again. "Be careful with this man. You have no idea who he is, nor do you know anything about his background." Then her other mind said, "I don't know much about him, but I think I know enough of him to get by. The rest we're going to work on in the days ahead."

On Wednesday, Agara got ready to go and see Angelina. He stopped by Jacob's office.

"Where are you going?" Jacob asked.

"Going to visit with Angelina," Agara said.

"If you would like to take some flowers to her, you have my permission to cut some from those blooming plants and make a nice bunch."

"Thanks," Agara said. From the rose plants, Pride of Barbados, and beautiful lilies, he collected a nice bunch and took them to her.

She met him at the door and he presented the flowers to her. "Thanks for the flowers. I love them," she said.

They hugged, kissed, and sat down to chat. She prepared some snacks, which they ate, and shared orange drinks.

"Angelina, you have made quite an impression on me since the first night I set my eyes on you."

"Very well; I'm glad to hear that."

Agara got up and moved close to her. When he started holding her close, she pulled back. Looking into his sensual expression, she said, "Agara, please! I'm not ready for sex." When he did not say anything, she looked at the sad expression on his face and almost felt like crying.

"What is the matter, Angelina?" he asked in desperation.

"Well, Agara, we have known each other for only a few days and you want to bed me."

He stared at her, as her words hit him straight in the face.

"I'm not a promiscuous woman, if that is the idea you have of me."

"I do not think anything like that," he told her.

"But your action suggested it. Just because I fell in love with you within a few days of our meeting, you figured that I would be an easy lay."

"I never thought like that, Angelina."

Then he stretched his arms and she moved to him.

"Angelina, I want to make love to you," he said.

"Agara, tell me why you want to make love to me."

He paused and stared at her.

"Well, you can't say it. It must be free sex that you are used to having," she said.

"What?" he shouted.

"It must be so, Agara. Why should you spend money taking a woman out when you can have a bedmate in the house every night for free?" She looked at him and saw that he was speechless.

"Agara, I want to get to know you before we share a bed," she told him. "You will find out later that I don't do much on impulse. I like to think things through before I act."

"But you want me, Angelina, don't you?"

"You are a special friend, and you have made me feel that way. I've never felt quite that way about any man before. I know I haven't."

He felt pleased with her utterances, even though he couldn't get what he wanted at that time.

She looked at him and saw the longing in his eyes. She said, "I'll make it up to you when the time comes."

"Are you sure?" he asked.

"Yes. I'm sure. Maybe there is hope if you don't rush things."

"I will wait. But how long do you think I have to wait?"

She laughed and said, "Agara, give me time."

He was about to leave the house when he turned at the door and said, "Angelina, if I have to wait for more than the next two weeks, I may die of frustration."

"You won't die, Agara. A good relationship needs time to grow," she said, wishing him good night.

"Good night," he said, and swatted her bottom. His hand squeezed her jovially before letting go. She smiled at him. The promise excited him.

"Persistently running after you for a whole week has been a new experience in my life," he confessed. "No woman has fascinated my imagination and excited my senses as you do," he said to her in frustration.

After he left, Angelina told herself, miserably, that Agara moved around the community so cautiously that there was a total shutdown of any information that would give away his identity. He appeared tongue-tight about his personal life, and she wondered if he was married, engaged, or a confirmed bachelor. She had stopped questioning him about his family, feeling she was treading on very personal ground and had no right to continue doing so. She should hear only what he wanted to tell her. As far as she was concerned, Agara was a man who had a string of women back home. At twenty-one, here she was, gradually falling in love with a stranger, dropped, as it were, from outer space into her path.

The next day, she was so absorbed in her thoughts that she didn't hear him come in. She only realized that he was there when a gentle hand touched her shoulder and she saw his reflection behind her in the mirror, watching her. She turned around and faced him. Her pulse beat jerkily.

"You ought to knock, Agara," she said.

"I did, but you were too busy admiring yourself or were lost in thought," he whispered.

He appeared to be fighting for self-control, but could not overcome it. He started caressing her and taking her clothes off.

Suddenly, she reached for her clothes and put them back on, covering all the loveliness he thought had been his. She looked into his face and said, "Agara, I'm sorry, it isn't time yet."

"Is this your modus operandi?"

"What?"

"To lead a man on and then slap him down."

"You think it's unfair, do you?"

"Yes, I do," he replied.

"And you believe it's fair for you to flirt with me and turn me on when I have told you that we have to wait for the right time?"

"I take that to mean that you still want me."

"As much as you want me," she replied.

"Why are you holding back so firmly?" he queried her with frustration.

"Why do you want to know? You have not told me about the women in your past. Men always have it in their heads they have the right to know everything about a woman but not for the woman to know everything about them."

He stared at her, completely taken aback.

She then said, "When I'm good and ready, I will give myself to you, and not before. If you can't handle this, hit the road and don't stick around."

As if to change the subject, he said, "Your village is nice."

"Well, I like it. I was born here. Where are you heading to from Unaka?" she asked him.

"Just roaming," he replied in a rigid voice.

"So, you'll be leaving soon?"

"You will not know anything more about me than you already do," he told her. "Why am I being subjected to this cross-examination anyway?" he asked her.

Every question she asked about his background, Agara carefully wormed his way out of answering it. Never in her life had she been so furious with another human being. She stared at him and said, "I'm sorry, I didn't mean to pry. I was just interested."

He smiled at her as if he thought she was just a dull village woman with nothing better to do than meddle with people's affairs. His answer seemed to have shattered her daydream of a husband. She found that he had shut her out. He ducked questions concerning his marital status. She decided that he might open up when they were in bed together, probably after they might have made love. She had heard that men say a lot of things, some they don't mean, when they are in bed. She kept that at the back of her mind.

He kissed her good night and left in frustration. He had never met a woman so beautiful and so challenging. How could she say she wants him and still refuse to go to bed with him? He resolved to go to any lengths to have her. Overwhelmed by her beauty, he refused to think about the fact that he was a vagabond.

Chapter 2

In the morning, Agara decided to go and honor the invitation from Jon Akaji. He found his way to Jon's house. The man was a father, of whom the family saw little. He left the house soon after the sun had risen every morning and did not return until nightfall. He had a wife and eleven children, ten girls and one boy. He lived in a small village house.

As soon as dusk came, the children fought for a place on the bamboo beds. Jon could not afford to waste his small supply of lantern kerosene to lengthen the day. When one of the young ones turned over, her sisters groaned and followed suit. The boy, ninth in the list of the children, took advantage of the commotion to go outside and ease himself. He soon hurried back and, in no time at all, he had gone back to sleep.

Jon welcomed his visitor and entertained him well. At the back of his yard he had cows and goats. He told Agara that he would be taking one of the cows to the market the next day. Agara volunteered to go with him.

"I will be back in the morning to go with you," he told Jon.

After dinner and some drinks of palm wine, Agara thanked his host and went back to the hotel.

While in the hotel, his memory went back to Ozutown. He spent some time at the town market on the second day after he fled from his home, two weeks ago. At the end of that day, he had learned that a trader's skill depended not only on the goods he had to sell, but in his ability to convince the customer of his need for them. He also learned that the maxim in that market was "Ask for triple and settle for double." He would sell what he had at the highest profit.

The following morning, Agara went back to Jon's house. He asked him how much his cow was worth.

"I expect about fifty Nigerian currency (Nc) for it," Jon said.

They set out for the cattle market. Agara asked him to leave the sale of the animal to him. "I want you to watch and see how much money the animal will fetch."

From then on, Agara took over. They left early and got to the cattle market just as the place opened. They stopped near the entrance and had the cow positioned for sale.

"Why are we near this entrance?" Jon asked.

"In a market, position is very important," Agara replied. "At the entrance, many more people will have a chance to stop, view the animal, and consider what they would have to offer," Agara explained.

A moment later, a customer came around. He looked at the animal very critically, then he looked up and asked, "How much for the cow?"

"What do you have to offer?" Agara inquired.

The customer looked at the animal again and said, "50 Nc."

"I need at least 150 Nc for this valuable animal," Agara said, shaking his head.

"60 Nc," the customer said.

"No," Agara replied firmly. He looked at the customer and said, "My first offer is my best offer."

The customer shook his head, turned, and walked away.

Jon smiled at Agara's expert knowledge in dealing with awkward customers. While they were talking, another customer was examining the cow. The customer looked up and asked, "How much do you want for this scrawny animal?"

"How much do you have to offer?" Agara asked.

The customer counted 65 Nc and looked at Agara, who quickly proceeded to employ another technique. "Why do you want the cow?" Agara asked.

"I want it for milk production for my family," the customer replied.

Agara smiled and said, "This is a valuable animal that will provide your family with milk and produce another cow for you in a short period." Looking at the customer, Agara turned the animal around so that the customer could take a closer look. "Permit me to ask," Agara continued, "is the delicious milk from this hardy animal not worth the enjoyment of your precious family?"

The customer fell silent as he considered Agara's words. He then began to count more money, up to 95 Nc, and looked at Agara, who had frowned as he pretended not to consider the offer. The customer counted 100 Nc and handed it to him.

Looking at the customer, Agara said, "I will accept the offer because of the need it will serve for your cherished family."

The customer paid and hoofed his animal away.

Agara turned to Jon and said, "My strategy was to allow the customer to feel he had the better of the bargain."

After the sale and the much profit realized. Jon took his friend to a nearby restaurant and had a good meal and drink. While they ate and drank, Agara reminded himself that he was a man on the run. But the attractions of Angelina had overshadowed his reason for fleeing his home. He told Jon that Angelina had been kind to him, and that she had borne most of his financial expenses since he had been in Unaka. He had asked himself if all that she had done for him and what she was still doing weren't too good to be true. He wondered what the catch was. He had known her for only a few days.

Jon laughed and said, "If she has done as you said, it probably is true love. Through conversation with you, I know that you've had many women, but Angelina is your first love. No matter how hard you try, your feelings for her will never go away. And no matter what you do, the memory of your stay with her will stay with you. Bait the hook well and the fish will bite."

Jon called for another pot of palm wine and smoked deer meat. They ate and drank.

"Good luck," Jon wished him, and he went back to the hotel.

The next day, in the afternoon, he went back to Angelina's house to see her. Angelina did not have to work at the hotel. She was happy to see him. After having dinner, he began to flirt with her.

"Agara," she said, moaning breathlessly. She shuddered as he groaned her name, feeling the pressure of her breasts on his chest. He slid his palm down her back until it rested on the upper swell of her bottom and he pressed her against him.

"Oh, Agara!" she gasped as she moved away from him.

After a brief moment, he said, "Angelina, I love you. Being here and having you in my arms—you don't know what it's doing to me."

"I know what it's doing to me, Agara," she whispered with painful honesty.

"Then have pity on me, Angelina, and don't play with fire—it burns. I have very low resistance, and I'm likely to rape you. There's a limit to torture. I don't play games, Angelina."

"I can see that. But I hardly know you, Agara."

"Wait a minute, Angelina. You know me and I have told you everything about me." His hand was on her back, caressing her.

"Oh, no, Agara," she whispered pleasantly. "Please don't do this to me!"

Yet she wanted it to happen, as she noticed her willpower spinning away like a leaf on the harmattan wind. Last night, in a moment of loneliness, she had convinced herself she should do something wild, if for no other reason than for the sake of experience. "Why not go for that fantasy now?" she had asked herself.

She saw the plea in his eyes and was moved. She felt a deep moan of desire going through the chest pressed very intimately against her breasts. She was thrilled that she could provoke such a reaction from this virile man. She was nearly compelled to yield to his desires. But she controlled herself. It was not time; she was not good and ready yet. There are still unanswered questions about him, she thought. She pushed away from him with a determination that caused him to stumble backwards a few steps before he could regain his balance.

"Angelina, do you think I'll ever get to understand you?" he asked.

"I'm sure you will with time, the good Lord willing."

"I just hope I will not be too old and decrepit by the time 'you are good and ready,' as you said."

She laughed a little. "I promise that you will still be very active. Only death destroys hope."

He sighed in frustration.

"What is the matter?" she asked.

"I have never encountered this before."

"You mean you have never met a woman who withheld sex from you?"

"You can say that again," he said with all sincerity.

She smiled at him and said, "Good night. Sleep well."

"I know I won't sleep well tonight."

"Why won't you?"

"My libido has been seriously damaged. I'm not even sure that it will ever recover."

"It will, I know it will," she said. She decided to prepare his mind for the next stage in their relationship. "Agara," she called his name. "Tomorrow there is a marriage ceremony of one of my cousins in the village. I would like to go and watch it."

"If you want me to go with you, I will," he replied.

"Thanks for obliging me," she said.

Chapter 3

Agara met with Angelina and they went to observe the marriage ceremony, which started the day before with a public send-off for her cousin. During this activity, individuals and families presented gifts for her to take to her new home.

On this wedding day, Adanna was pampered by the older women of her family. Her hair was plaited and oiled and her body perfumed. Before she left the house, the old ladies briefly reviewed her conduct and responsibilities as a housewife, her entitlements, and privileges.

The drummers, dancers, visitors, and spectators formed in front of her father's home. As the beautiful colors of the setting sun were cast on the mango tree in front of her father's compound, Adanna suddenly emerged from among chanting women and gracefully danced to the center of the ring formed by the crowd.

After a while, the drummers and the procession started. In front of the bride's compound hall, the procession stopped. The drummers pounded loudly. Singing and dancing commenced, and Adanna staged the final departure dance, which was cheered by the crowd. She beamed with smiles, and her family became jubilant as they watched her cross the compound ritual boundary, affirming her virtuous state.

The crowd went loud with shouts of congratulations to the family. Adanna's grandfather stood in front of the compound hall and waved to the jubilant crowd, saying, "Go with pride, my granddaughter. I have washed the gourd and left no fault on it. Yes, I have raised you up without blame."

As the drumming and dancing continued, the slow moving crowd headed for the bridegroom's compound. Here, the welcome dance was staged. Breaking into radiant smiles, twice, Adanna danced round the circle formed by the crowd of spectators and participants. She was cheered by the villagers, excited family members, and friends.

Adanna began performing the arrival dance. As the singing, drumming, and dancing reached the highest crescendo of joy, the bride danced with the bridegroom, who piloted her into the house. She would not come out again until the next day.

Friends and family members were very well entertained with food and drinks. It had been a very exciting outing for Agara and Angelina. They enjoyed it. Agara went back to his room at the hotel.

Agara thought about Angelina. It was unlike him to pursue a woman for so long without success, he thought. He wondered how long this woman would sexually torment him. He could hardly sleep at night. He felt that there must be a reason why Angelina was holding back. She had taken him to watch a marriage ceremony. Why? he wondered.

He could not continue to overlook her actions. He had discovered that Angelina was not the sort of lady who would settle for a shallow relationship; she would prefer to go right to the bone and not let go. He had to make up his mind. Sex with her would carry a lot of obligations.

With renewed hope and determination, he went back to her house the next day. She opened the door for him. Angelina was full of smiles when she saw him come into the house. She also knew that his patience was running out. In no time, his fingers were smoothing down the naked skin of her abdomen. The quest went on until he encountered the band of her panties. Hooking his finger under it, he dared to discover what lay beyond. Unbearable heat consumed her.

"Agara," she cried out with fear. She pushed away from him with frantic hands. It was a revealing reaction to him. "Her maidenhead must still be intact," he surmised.

"Angelina," he moaned her name. "Will I be the first?"

"You'll find out for yourself when I'm good and ready," she said, looking into his face.

"Do you still want me?" she asked.

"I want you more than ever. You are very special to me," he said as his hand smoothed up and down her waist.

Her eyes widened at his declaration. Deep in her heart, something shook at his words; words she had not expected to hear. Her heart hammered her chest. She tried to say something, but didn't.

"The feeling I have for you," he continued, "is nothing like I have ever felt before. Your presence gives me joy and makes me smile. I'll never hurt you, Angelina. I'll wait until … when you are good and ready to give yourself to me, as you promised."

"Agara—" she called his name, searching for what to say. "We are very close friends now. You have become like the brother that I never had. What can I say? I love you. When the fruit is ripe, it falls," she told him.

"Angelina, I love you too. It is not just sex that I want from you."

"It is not just sex," she repeated.

"I go after what I want. I usually get it. But I've found that the longer I have to wait for something, the more I appreciate it," he said.

"Be patient in steadily working toward your goal," she replied.

After Agara left, she told herself that Agara was finally opening up to her. She took this as a sign that he was ready to take their relationship to the next level.

Chapter 4

The next morning, Agara was at breakfast with Jacob.

"Agara," Jacob called his name. "Be careful with Angelina."

"What do you mean?" he asked.

"Other men have fallen for her, but I haven't known her to let anyone get really close."

Agara wondered if Jacob was referring to himself, but he didn't want to find out. He had already vowed to pursue her.

Noting Agara's interest in Angelina, Jacob decided to tell him about the village celebration of the annual festival of Potompo, starting on Friday and ending on Saturday night. It would be two weeks since he arrived in Unaka. This year the celebration coincided with the harvest of the new yam and the bounty of the earth. Everybody in Unaka would be in a festive mood during the celebration.

The celebration took place at the foothills of the Unaka Sacred Forest. The sacred forest was the home of the ancestral gods, the original fatherless spirits. The belief in the originality of the fatherless gods portrayed nature's capability of producing life spontaneously. The people stood in fear of this sacred forest because of the scary tales associated with it. The forest was filled with varieties of plant life: trees with huge tropical leaves dancing in the wind, different types of flowering shrubs and thick parasitic vines that completely devoured their host trees. These trees, whispering in the harmattan winds, seemed to touch the blue sky.

At night, the forest appeared silent and mysteriously filled with gloom from the thick interlacing branches of trees overhead. During the day, the sky was totally obscured by the thick canvas of foliage overhead. Except for brief sunlight spots here and there, the forest floor was shrouded in permanent twilight. From the top of the hill, the green valleys presented a beautiful sight: wild flowers portraying the handiwork of the Supreme Creator.

According to oral history of the Potompo celebration, the nonagenarian priest of the Unaka Sacred Forest conducts the ceremony. The priest reminds the participants that it was a festival originated by women: "In the olden days, women who got married and did not get pregnant within two years were blamed for barrenness. Men accused such women of having wasted their youth. Because there was no sperm count, women had no way of exonerating themselves from the accusation.

"Participation in the celebration afforded the women an opportunity to try their luck with other men to show that, in some cases, the fault was not from the women. The period of Potompo celebration was the only time that a married woman could make love with a man other than her husband and not be accused of infidelity. Trust the power of women who collectively convinced the men of old that this celebration should take place every year.

"Potompo is a celebration of life and fecundity," the nonagenarian continued. "At some point in the celebration, participating couples make love. During last year's celebration, a married lady participated in the celebration because after bearing six girls for her husband, she became tired of asking for forgiveness for not bearing him a son. She gave birth to a son nine months after the festival ended. She wanted to prove to her husband and other gossipers that it took more than one person to make a baby.

"There was something special about making love around Iroko sacred wood fire. It made women conceive during the celebration," the priest said. "In the olden days, during this festival, a human being was sacrificed to the old gods. In time, the practice of human sacrifice stopped and a ram was substituted. In remembrance of that time, a man will be dressed in ram's skin, and a mock sacrifice made to the old gods."

Jacob made arrangements for Agara's participation in the festival. The chief of Unaka was informed that a young man by the name Agara was to be the sacrificial ram. When the chief asked for details concerning the young man, Jacob briefed him as much as he knew.

On Saturday evening, Agara stood by Jacob at a corner near the celebration field. They watched the participants as they walked to the center of the large circle that had been formed by several bonfires.

During the ceremony, Angelina danced and twirled. She looked around and didn't see Agara. "Where could he be?" she thought. She closed her eyes, wishing she could make herself disappear, sink into a deep hole and never have to come out again. She should have known that he's always been a free spirit, a man with no strings attached. The day before the final ceremony, Jacob had confided in her that Agara would be there. Her heart leaped with joy and excitement. But she never discussed this ceremony with him. She was hoping that if he wanted her as badly as he had expressed, he would have been here.

Suddenly, Agara saw Angelina join the dancing group, and he watched her as she twirled and swayed to the music and the echo of the drums. The very idea of Angelina being taken by another man during the height of the festivity, even for a moment, was more than he could stand. He decided to go for her. He had resolved to have her by any means possible. Would this be the night she would be good and ready? he wondered. He knew that this festival for the gods meant marriage. It wasn't as if marrying Angelina was a bad idea; but the thought of getting a wife in Unaka, and possibly having children here, scared him. "In any event, a scared man can't win," he reminded himself. He was hell bent on having her at any cost.

Jealousy rose and choked in his throat as Angelina danced and flirted with young men. "Tonight, the spirit of the gods will be contagious. Many people, without hesitation, will shed their clothes to escape the heat of the fires and dance more freely." He remembered Jacob's words. "Couples will go off into the shadows to honor the old gods with lovemaking," Jacob had told him. Could he stand and watch someone else take his place in Angelina's heart? No. Unless he went for her before it was too late! he thought.

Jacob took him to the cultural shrine house for dressing. The dancing continued. Moments later, the nonagenarian priest of the festival shouted so loud that the crowd scattered momentarily. He lifted his hands, as if calling on the gods for some help. A huge ram with large curved horns walked into the center of the circle toward the priest. The beast was so large that many people stared in awe. The crowd went into jubilation because the god of fertility had sent the animal for sacrifice. The drums and music went out louder and faster, and dancers performed without stopping.

The nonagenarian priest, deaf as a post, cupped a hand around his ear and signaled for the drumming, singing, and dancing to stop. He ordered the ram to be slaughtered in a ritualistic way—slashing the throat. With one stroke of the knife, blood (red dye) splashed everywhere, and the animal was taken out of view. Immediately, a real ram was substituted. Many of the women participants ran to touch the sacrificial ram at the center.

Angelina followed to touch the original ram that had been taken out of view. She was amazed to find that Agara had been so perfectly clothed and fixed in a ram's clothing that it was hard to detect who he was. The hotel proprietor had done this for her. This was the night she had looked forward to—when she would be "good and ready for him."

"Come on, the priest is calling for participants to go to the Potompo inner circle ground!" she shouted joyfully.

At this time, non-participants were left at the large circle, where they were being entertained with music and dancing. The priest gave orders that participants select their partners. As the drums pounded and the music went into the air, the couples danced and chanted, occasionally throwing their hands toward the star-quilted sky. This was the hour married women who had had no children by their husbands danced with their lovers and implored the god of fertility to favor them with fruitful mating.

The priest started murmuring some chants in a strange, melodious voice and moving clockwise around the Iroko sacred wood fire. He offered sacrifice of the fat ram and poured libation. When the gods smelled the sweet aroma of the Iroko wood and burning ram, they rejoiced and flew above the sweet smoke in the form of apparitions.

"This is to the past heroes who have ascended to be with the gods at the Sacred Forest," the priest said, pouring libation. "This is to the Supreme Creator, the most distant creator of all the gods," the priest continued as he poured more libation. "This is to the One Above who showered the gift of life upon all in the Sacred Forest," the priest concluded as he poured the rest of the palm wine to the ground.

In the third round, the drum went off, and the priest shouted loudly and clearly, "It … is … time! Couples that have been single are now married by the gods, and only death can part them," the priest declared. "Married men and women are free to choose their love for the night."

Immediately, the couples started shedding their clothes and disappearing into the shadows. Despite the occasional clouds that passed over the full moon, casting shadows of darkness, lovers had no trouble finding convenient spots.

Angelina was excited to be with Agara at this time. Agara fits in wherever he happens to be, just like a chameleon, was the first thing that came to her mind. She could not decide whether it was a trait she envied or of which she felt suspicious. She did not want to think about what he would do after this event. She wanted to enjoy this moment and worry about tomorrow later. The excitement was fast growing within her body.

Chapter 5

The participants went into jubilation when an owl, perched on a tree nearby, talked to its mate farther down the wooded area. The owl's call stirred the participants toward the brink of awareness. This was not the call of death. It came from a store of ancient knowledge that the owl is a bird of omen. The calling by one of the birds and its immediate response by the mate indicated that the moment had arrived for fruitful lovemaking.

Angelina led Agara through thick undergrowth without speaking. The only sounds were their footsteps crunching on decaying tree leaves. They stopped at a spot under a wild mango tree where Mother Nature had formed a bed of dried leaves. Agara whispered her name again and again as he shaped the outline of her hips with his palms. They kissed and kissed again. Then his voice became merely a low growl that reminded her of an animal mating sound.

He wrenched himself away to spread their wrappers over the leaves and settled her onto it. Slowly, he removed the last of her clothing to expose her slender body to the moonlight. On this celebration night, Angelina was good and ready. All the shackles had been loosened—her dismay was gone. She welcomed him, moving as he guided her with the adjustment of his own body. Under the spell of the god of fertility, and with loving looks in their eyes, they sank to the ground. He caressed her body with aggression, and under his touch, she began to writhe and twist, seeking to get closer and closer, so that he could lose himself in her.

"Please, Agara. Please!" she shouted. Never in her life had she felt such a stirring of violent emotion.

"Oh, my God," Agara groaned.

"Angelina!" he whispered.

"Never have I come across a man who could excite my body to such an astounding degree," Angelina confessed. She only knew that here, under the moonlight, she must give herself to this strange man who was claiming her. She was his and he had every right to his claim. By the same token, he belonged to her. The passion of her claim on him was as mind-shaking as his on her. She was in his arms, being crushed to his chest. She wanted Agara and desperately wanted to please him.

"Oh, the gods," he groaned. "I'm not sure I can take this."

"You'll live. I'm good and ready." Angelina breathed unsteadily. She pulled him closer and held him as he took her. She was wild. Once she gave herself, she had absolutely no inhibition.

"Angelina, my wife," he murmured as he claimed her in the timeless and most eternal of ways. When he broke through the last barrier of her innocence, a flash of pain and fear passed through her. She was caught up in the wonder of it all as wave after wave of the incredible feeling washed over her.

"Oh! Agara," she shouted. Her cry carried both rapture and panic, and he understood both.

"Am I hurting you?" he asked.

"No."

"I'm glad, baby, because I'd never do anything to hurt you—I won't."

At that moment, the world could have been extinguished, for all she cared and knew. "This has been ordained and predestined by the gods," she thought, and believed.

"I was afraid that I would not be good for you, would not satisfy you."

He stilled her lips by placing an imperative finger over them.

"You were perfect, Angelina," he assured her.

"It is you that made me perfect," she replied.

They smiled at each other, feeling absolutely happy. The next moment, Angelina was gasping at his intimate caress. He was pushing her onto her back, his lips on the hard peaks of her uptilted breasts. His tongue curled around each nipple, urging them into even tighter buds. She shivered, moaned, and turned into a bundle of aroused femininity beneath him. She was going wild again with need of him.

"Angelina, my dear," he said breathlessly.

"Yes! Yes! Agara!" she answered as she wrapped her arms around his neck.

He rolled over on his back and she landed on top of him. She straddled him and rode him slowly at first; then she turned wild as he thrust upwards with her all the way until they leaped high and soared above the clouds. Small stones and twigs dug holes through the leaves and the wrapper on the ground and into his back, but he didn't feel them. All he felt were her breasts against his chest. He tightened his arms around her. They held each other as they returned to earth. The past and the future were no longer important; only this shivering, explosive need to satisfy and be satisfied counted in this little corner of the universe.

Angelina collapsed on the soft ground and lay still, breathless. She was afraid to open her eyes; she knew she was under his spell and she dared not open her eyes and break the spell that held her. As she lay on her back, the earth spun for a moment until she regained her equilibrium. She was exhausted, but filled with ebullience. Slowly, reality returned as they lay on the ground of the Potompo field.

Agara slipped his arm around her and pulled her close as the dawn unfolded. The sunrise was pushing through the trees, and with her head on his shoulder, she wondered if anything could be better than what was happening at that moment at the field.

"You pleased me, Angelina," he whispered pleasantly.

"And you me," she expressed. "Thank you, Agara."

"Why do you thank me?" he asked.

"For being gentle, for showing me that being a woman is a cause for celebration, and above all, for being my husband."

They laughed heartily. He then said, "Angelina, things will never be the same again between us."

"Yes," she agreed very quietly. "I know it for sure."

It was the truth. She had given herself completely to this strange man and he had brought new meaning to her life. She felt that something had been radically altered in her during this celebration. She was now Mrs. Angelina Agara Aham. She was grateful. They finally fell into a deep sleep in sublime happiness and slept dreamlessly far into the morning. It was the most primitive, wonderful night they both had ever known.

The sun broke suddenly through a hole in the thick cloud cover, sending low-slung shafts of light into Angelina's eyes. She awakened him, and as they rose, they found other couples getting ready to leave the field as well.

"Agara," she called his name. "There is a man." She paused.

"Tell me about him," he said.

"The man who had wanted to marry me is away. He is a rich man. His name is Zebulon Zimako. He is popularly known as Z-man. I will tell you about him later. Don't think about him, okay?" she commanded.

He kissed her and gave her butt a husbandly pat. "All right. I will not argue with you, my dear," he said, and closed his mouth.

When they reached her home, she took her key from her handbag and opened the front door. She turned, and Agara was looking at her. His eyes and the purposeful way he moved toward her made her tremble.

Before they left the field for her house that morning, they promised each other that they would sleep. It was a worthless promise that neither could keep. His suggestion that they practice caution, in deference to her recently lost virginity, fell on deaf ears. After breakfast, they caressed and kissed with renewed vigor. His first kiss was light and questing. The next was firm and questing. Each embrace only enhanced their desire. She lifted her face up to his. She felt boneless, light as air. He bent low, his mouth closed on the nipple of her breast, while his hard and strong manhood sought and found the heart of her femininity. They tasted each other and they both groaned with the delicious pain of desire.

They showered and got dressed. She applied her makeup and arranged her hair. Jacob had invited them for lunch at the Newtown Hotel. During the meal, Jacob ordered wine. The waitress brought it to the table and Jacob opened it and handed it to Agara, who poured the contents into glasses. Agara and Angelina clinked glasses, and with Jacob too.

"You look happy, Angelina," Jacob said.

"Thanks, Jacob," she replied, then she looked at him and said, "when I looked around and didn't see Agara, I thought he wouldn't show up."

"He would have been insane not to show up," Jacob said.

"Agara, thank you for showing up at the celebration," she said.

"I had to," he said. "I was afraid that there would be many men lined up at your door begging for a date before the Potompo celebration last night," he told her.

She thanked him for the compliment.

"I would be consumed by jealousy if I had to share you with another man," Agara said. "After the lovemaking at the Potompo celebration, I would have liked to lock you away from the rest of the world, if I could," he added.

When they came back to her house, she began the mental tirade she knew she would be castigating herself with for a long time to come. Her greatest concern was that she did not go through the traditional procedure of securing parental consent before marriage. What had come over her? And where would this love and lust of the flesh lead her? she wondered.

While Agara and Angelina were at the Potompo field, news of their marriage reached the palace of Chief Oyinatu of Unaka that his daughter, Angelina, had been married to Agara, a man with no known past. It became a hot gossip item that Angelina, the daughter of Chief Oyinatu of Unaka, had rejected Z-man, the richest man in Ohadum District.

The chief frowned at the news. He then smiled with obvious reluctance. He had frowned because a girl who arranged her own marriage without the suitor first approaching the parents and kindred would likely face very serious consequences. He smiled because Angelina was his flesh and blood. She was married during a traditional festival sanctioned by the gods. As the chief's daughter, Angelina would not have to go through rituals of purification, which were intended to prevent young girls from arranging their marriage or getting pregnant out of wedlock. The chief knew he would not disown his daughter because of this incident, though very serious. Blood is thicker than water. Chief Oyinatu decided that he would sit his new son-in-law down and have a serious talk with him.

After Agara left Angelina that afternoon, she went to her father's palace. She saw the old man sitting on his armchair. Her mother was sitting beside him. She greeted them and both nodded in response. Her father was smoking a pipe tobacco. From the look on their faces, Angelina would have thought there was a death in the family if she did not know her parents.

"Sit down, Angelina," her father commanded. The old man smiled. "Listen to me, Angelina," her father began. "You must bear in mind that in this culture, who we align ourselves with is governed by who our parents are." He smiled and told her to bring Agara to the palace in the evening.

As far as she could see, it was status that mattered to her parents and not how she felt. That evening, she took her husband to the palace. At a gathering of the compound chiefs and elder statesmen, she introduced Agara as her husband. To Agara, appearing before the chiefs and elders of the community was like being in a lion's den.

"Agara, my new son-in-law," Chief Oyinatu spoke his name. "Your marriage with Angelina, though legal, was unusual for the daughter of Chief Oyinatu."

Agara looked nervous. "The proper thing would have been for Angelina's parents to conduct a background investigation of her suitor's family prior to the marriage," the chief said. "Since the gods had married both of you, neither of you could secure a separation except through death; however," the chief continued, looking at Agara, "in three days' time, I will order a group of men from this palace to accompany you to your village. The group will investigate your family background and bring back the following information: your ancestral blood line; any deed of bravery associated with your family name; whether any person in your family has suffered from insanity; whether there has been any known dishonest person in your family; whether you come from a progressive or a backward family; and any other pertinent findings that the group may get."

The old man told Agara that he was welcome to Unaka and that he should consider the chief's palace his home too. "I want both of you to know that marriage is not the difficult part. The hard part is living together."

Agara felt very uncomfortable after listening to what the chief told him. *"Living together is the hard part,"* Agara repeated in his mind.

Angelina took her husband to her room on the second floor of the chief's palace. They settled in for the night. She planned for them to spend the week here at the palace. During this time, her father would send a group to go and investigate his background, as the old man had told him.

Chief Oyinatu noticed Agara's uneasiness and suspected that something was wrong. After his new son-in-law left, the old man said, "Most people who come to settle in small villages like ours, people who are not born here, are running away from something that is chasing them. Time will tell."

Chapter 6

Agara could not sleep that night, thinking about Chief Oyinatu's ultimatum that he would order an investigation check into his background. He was worried. While he had become addicted to Angelina, he was also a fugitive.

The stigma of his background would live with him forever. It didn't matter how cleanly one lived; if one grew up as a man with no past, his morals were suspect. It was infuriating to be assigned a place at birth with no hope of changing it. This was Angelina's home. Her roots went deep. She was at the highest echelon of society and he at the lowest. What a difference!

He would have to leave this place of small-minded, bigoted people. He got busy plotting a way out of Unaka and the best possible time. He surveyed Angelina's room, located on the second floor of the building. He knew that he could escape through the only window in the room. As a plan, it had a lot of drawbacks. There would be many night watchmen around. He also noted that it would be very dangerous, since he was afraid of heights. If he was going to get away, he had to get over his fear of heights and take the risk. As with everything he did, he relied heavily on happenstance. This was the only plan he could come up with and maybe the only chance he might have to escape. He had to take the risk and run like a scalded dog. He also knew that for his plan to succeed, he would need inside help.

After breakfast the following morning, he went out on a walk that took him to the home of the head night watchman who guarded the chief's palace. After meeting with the man, Agara's plan was clarified in his mind. He would leave in the wee hours of the morning, before his wife got up. He would lay aside his fear of heights. He would make love to her, because lovemaking was an anesthetic to her. It would send her to sleep immediately. He would descend through the window to the ground outside. He would travel out of the community before anyone would notice him.

For him to climb down, he got a braided raffia palm rope. It was not long enough to reach the ground, but he could jump the rest of the height. It was late in the evening when he came back. He stood outside for quite a while, lost in thought. Then he looked up, scanning the heavens, making out the faint patterns of the stars above. He would dare to be brave tonight. To avoid risks, he would stay in bed with Angelina. "No," he thought. "Here I am again," he thought. "Angelina's beauty and gentleness are all I look at. I know I must leave her, but I will miss her and dream of her the rest of my life. She is like no other I have ever met in my community or in Ohadum District. This is an obsession. Since I met her, I have been acting like a besotted moron. Ha! I, Agara Aham, a heartbreaker! The tiger's legs are broken and the antelope is challenging him to a wrestle. Never … I have never had trouble bedding women, but Angelina was a challenge to me. How could she have managed to keep me after sleeping with her? I'm now convinced that she knows some ancient spells," he concluded.

Agara felt he had to be strong. "It is over," he thought bitterly. He wiped his streaked face on his hands and tried to pull himself together. He went upstairs and tiptoed to the entrance of their room. It was late. He paused and then pushed the door open without knocking. To his surprise, Angelina was not there. His mind relaxed. Through the small square hole of a window, he looked outside and gave a shiver of fear. The hole was wide enough to permit his whole body to go through it. The wind was mild and murmorous and full of light drizzle. It was a good omen. He secured one end of the rope, ready for action.

Agara was in their room, preparing for bed, when Angelina walked in. She had been in her mother's room. She stared at him for a few seconds and shook her head. In the short period that she had known him, he had taken her life and turned it upside down, totally altered it.

"Agara, I want to know where you have been. I want to know now." She came short of stomping her feet for emphasis, her eyes flashing with fury.

He knew how to pacify a woman in a rage. "Shhh!" he said, stopping her words by laying his index finger lengthwise over her lips. "I know what you are about to say," he whispered. He drew her close and his hand burrowed under the wrapper she wore, stroking her skin as it moved to her thighs. The appeasement was coming too quickly, faster than she was ready. He fondled her, tantalized, and tasted until her whole body began to quake. He had kindled a volcano inside her.

"Agara, I haven't forgiven you for being out all day and coming back so late at night," she said, beginning to respond to the cajoling play of his hands. The tip of his tongue brushed against the slight parting of her lips. The other hand covered her breast with a gentle pressure. The sensation going through her body made her sigh with pleasure. She didn't discourage his skilled seduction. His gentle approach never failed to result in rising desire and moans of pleasure.

When he knew that the volcano was about to erupt, he drove himself deeply inside her. The hands that gripped his hips, the thighs that enclosed his, the ragged words of love he spoke were her encouragement. His manhood drove deeper and deeper until they exploded together. When the crisis passed and they returned to the world, she drifted into a sound sleep. Agara lay quietly beside her.

His body relaxed and his mind was alert to every sound in the chief's palace. So many thoughts went through his mind. "I have to leave this village," he vowed. "But where do I go from here?" he wondered. Seconds turned into minutes, and suddenly he heard the soft chiming of the old clock downstairs. He knew it was midnight, although he did not count the chimes. It was time to go.

He got up. Confident that Angelina was fast asleep and no one else was awake, he began to move cautiously to the window. Angelina's snoring was so thunderous he feared that at any moment, she would stir and discover his plan. He looked at the woman that had been so nice to him; he felt his eyes water. He looked away and continued moving toward the window, as if he knew where he was going. But he didn't. With enormous consciousness of his environment, he took a deep breath and moved on.

At the window, he turned around and momentarily watched her sleeping soundly, her legs unconsciously spread apart. He looked away from her enticing body before he did something stupid. He stepped to the window and looked down, his nerves simmering with dread. After securing the inside part of the rope, he let the other end down. He looked down to the ground, then he looked at the rope, which now seemed to him like a spider thread that would hardly support a sparrow. But a single touch earlier had convinced him that the rope would hold him. He secured his travel bag behind him. Going down the rope, sweat dampened his body. When he finally reached the ground, his heart hammered in his chest. He paused for a moment, breathing very rapidly. The night watchman had gone to the other end of the building, supposedly on his routine patrol. "Get going before you wake up sleeping tigers," he thought, and started running as though there were monsters at his heels.

When Angelina woke up in the morning, she found her husband had disappeared like a tenant that quit without warning. She became as furious as the eagle. She found a note under Agara's pillow: "Angelina, I'm on the run. I don't know when I will return." She looked around again, feeling confused. Her eyes lit on the window and a wave of fear engulfed her. She looked out of the window and noticed that it was raining. She saw the long rope. She pulled on the rope, her hands trembling. She looked down and knew he was gone with the aid of the rope.

She suppressed a sob and sat on her bed, dejected. She then went to the bathroom and looked at herself in the mirror. She realized that her brow was creased with worry, and she relaxed it. How could this have happened? The only man she had ever loved, or came close to loving, was Agara. For only a short while, they had shared something special that led to marriage. At least to her it had been special. She had been deceived into believing all he had told her before and after the Potompo celebration. He said he loved and adored her. His words had been meaningless. She had been nothing more than a novelty to him; otherwise, why would he have snuck away like a thief in the night? "But I still love him," she thought.

She went to her mother, Beatrice, and told her what had happened. "Listen to me, Angelina. Do not cry too much. Most people are not the same at the beginning of a marriage as they are during it. Time will tell if true love exists between you and Agara." She went to the kitchen and made breakfast for her daughter.

What could have happened to the man who had made love to her with delicious tenderness? What had happened to make Agara change? she wondered. She had forgiven him for his past shortcomings. She felt tears filling her eyes and running down her cheeks. They were bitter tears for what might have been. She lay back in bed, in an exhausted, dreamlike state, and wandered back to the pleasure she had once known with him. Her head swarmed with memories of his fierce demanding body.

Although Agara had left her, she still thought that once he stopped running from whatever was pursuing him, he could be made to settle down. She believed that he was afraid of commitment and that he was one of those kinds of men who just liked to flirt. She sighed at the thought that it would take an exceptional woman to understand him or satisfy his wants and needs. "Who could do that?" she wondered.

A moment later, she began to think again. She was alone. It felt like the end of the world. Agara fled as if nothing had happened. Are all men like that? Are men truly unconcerned once they have fed a physical hunger? Then she thought that worrying about it was only going to increase her blood pressure, without solving anything. She sighed.

Chapter 7

Greed never has an end. A week before the Potompo celebration, Z-man had received a message to come to Calabar. His business partner, Obioko, had struck a deal that required a lot of investment. Obioko knew who had the money.

Z-man went to Angelina's father and told him of the deal he was going for in Calabar. He met briefly with Angelina in the conference room of the chief's palace. He told her about the investment he was pursuing. He told her that executing the project would mean money in their pocket. "Lots of it," he said.

Z-man watched tears spring from Angelina's eyes.

Composing herself and looking at Z-man in the face she asked, "Mr. Zebulon Zimako, if love interfered with your business of going to Calabar to make money, would you call off your trip?"

He thought twice. Angelina was demanding too much from him. But he had to answer the question. She was still facing him. "Our elders say that if you find what is greater than the farm, you will have to sell the yam barn. There is a lot of money to be made from the business," Z-man replied.

Angelina had got the answer. In simple, concise, understandable English, she fired back. "Z-man, the most powerful force on earth is love. I do not love you and do not wish to marry you." She dashed the tears out of her eyes with the back of her hand.

Zebulon Zimako stared at her. Coal-black eyes pierced his face. He did not believe what he heard her say, and said, "Angelina, I have the money that will make you happy. The project I'm pursuing in Calabar will make you even happier."

"My love is not for sale, Z-man. Besides, marrying for money is the hardest way to earn it. Maybe one day you will come to grips with what I said," Angelina replied.

Z-man thought it was a conversation he had heard in a dream. Disappointment hurts more than pain. His hands balled into fists, and Angelina didn't know if he was getting ready to strike her. A common cover for hurt is anger. Whatever he was going to do, she would face him. She had made her feelings known.

He got up from his seat. He felt as though the floor he was standing on had just dropped away. When would he hit the bottom? He gathered himself together and strode out the door of the chief's conference room.

Angelina slumped down on the sofa, completely tired and exhausted. She was unaware, until then, how physically drained the encounter had been. She shook her head. "Money is more important to him than me," she said, chuckling. "He already has a lot of it. He is an insatiable brute," she thought. "He has never told me that he loves me, not even to say he likes me," she thought.

Angelina's rejection was a bitter pill to swallow. Z-man felt a gnawing emptiness inside his gut. Angelina was a beautiful lady, the daughter of the most powerful chief in Ohadum District. For prestige and social status, he wanted her more than any other woman around. Since his wife died a few years ago, he did not believe any woman would reject him, the richest man in Ohadum, the owner of the largest palm produce company east of the Niger River. Leadership, popularity, and women—he had them.

Z-man hoped that she would change and that in time she would come to love him. He knew there was nothing resembling love in his heart for any woman; he just needed a companion for public show. For Angelina, a woman did not have to commit herself to a marriage because it would be beneficial to the man's honor.

Z-man's driver got the vehicle ready, and early the next morning, they left for Calabar. He met with Obioko, the man who controlled the Equatorial Guinea waters. At this time, cognac was banned from Nigeria, but it was in high demand among the elite group. Obioko briefed Z-man. Thirty canoes were needed to bring the loads of cognac to land. They had to spend three weeks arranging and waiting for the delivery.

Z-man calculated how much profit this would bring. He then left and went to check into a hotel with his mistress, Joy Nneoma. She was tall and voluptuous, with jet black hair halfway down her back. Joy thought that Z-man was not much fun to be around. The only reason she was with him was because nobody with more money had come on the scene.

Two weeks passed. Z-man and his partner spent the days visiting the various smugglers' dens dotted along the coast of the Cross River. They continued to monitor the movement of the surface boats, conveying the drinks from the water of the Equatorial Guinea. By the third week, information came to them that everything was ready. Z-man and Obioko arrived at the receiving dock by the Cross River. Here they waited patiently for the arrival of the canoes and surface boats. Minutes passed like hours.

Finally, the first surface boat anchored and the young man in charge came on land and informed Z-man and his partner that the canoe loads carrying the cognac would be arriving shortly.

As Z-man spotted the fleet of canoes silently gliding closer and closer to land, he saw himself riding high on the rising tide of prosperity. A vehicle was dispatched to alert the customs officials of the coming vehicles carrying the contraband. Bribery in this part of the world was as old as the country itself. Every business project had to give a kickback to get things done in a timely manner. This always made a project cost more than its initial estimate.

Just as quickly as lightning strikes, the goods were loaded in trucks that were already waiting. In no time, all were evacuated to the warehouse in Ohadum District. The customs officers who patrolled the road were handsomely rewarded. The drinks were sold with a huge profit. Abundance, like want, ruins many. Z-man realized so much profit that he almost went rich crazy. His dealing in Calabar was done. Now he could return home to handle his unfinished business.

Z-man returned home to learn that during the Potompo festival, held two weeks earlier, Angelina had gotten married to Agara, a young stranger from nowhere, known to no one around. He was outraged. She had delivered a slap to his face and so had Agara, who married her. "Angelina has out-foxed the fox," he thought. He almost went crazy. At night he could not sleep, thinking of Angelina's body entwined with that of the vagabond, Agara. Sometimes he thought he'd go mad thinking about it. For a few weeks, he would not go to visit his old friend, Chief Oyinatu, Angelina's father. He did not want to see her. If he saw her, he would want her more. He had to stay away before he did something to disgrace himself.

When he finally calmed down and felt in control of his temper, he went to see Angelina's father. Angelina answered the door. Their eyes met. This was the first time he had seen her since she had gotten married. They greeted each other. "I would like to speak with you, Angelina," Z-man said with an air of civility.

Angelina was surprised at his tone of voice. She had never known him to be humble. She smiled, believing that he had gotten the message that she was not the kind of woman he could trifle with.

"Where and when do you want to speak with me?" Angelina asked, ready to face him.

"In the chief's conference room," he replied calmly.

Angelina went to her room, took her time and changed dresses. She put on some makeup and checked herself in the mirror. She felt satisfied with herself and came down to meet him. When she went into the conference room, Z-man was sitting quietly. She didn't know how to take it.

Both looked at each other as if they were fighting with their eyes.

"I hear that the total stranger that you married at the Potompo festival has fled," Z-man said.

She stared at Zebulon Zimako for a few seconds. She swallowed the anger that had risen in her. She struggled to control herself and took a moment before she spoke.

"How have you been doing, Mrs. Whatshisname?"

"Agara Aham," she countered.

"Do you blame me for being upset with you, when you went behind my back and married that vagabond?"

"His name is Agara," she calmly reminded him. "Remember, Z-man, we were not even engaged. So I was free to marry whomever I wanted, and you were free to marry whomever you knew would fall for your wealth," Angelina said without hesitation.

Z-man became livid. "You aren't a good loser, Z-man," she challenged him. She rose from her seat with regal composure, proud and beautiful. She turned on the heel of her shoes and walked out of the door. She was still the daughter of Chief Oyinatu, *a brave warrior that causes an enemy village to shiver.*

Chapter 8

Time passed. Do not complain about something if you had the power to change it but did not. Z-man found out through the town gossip that Angelina was about two months pregnant. He took the news of her pregnancy no better than he did of her marrying Agara; in fact, he took it worse. The baby would have been his. He was livid. Her pregnancy had irrevocably shut him off. He knew it was the end of any relationship he could have had with her.

Agara had fled. Z-man felt that Angelina would become very lonesome and would need company desperately. He decided to try a different approach with her. He would try to reason with her. He went to her house and knocked on her door.

"Who is it?"

"It's me, Z-man. May I come in?"

"No."

"Please."

"Why?"

"I want to talk to you."

"And haul more insults? No thank you, Zebulon Zimako."

"Z-man," he reminded her.

"When and if I like." She started to close the door.

He stuck out his hand and caught it. "Let me in, Angelina."

"Not after the things you said to me last time. Just go away and leave me alone," she said.

"Forget everything I said earlier," Z-man said.

"I can't. Our elders say that the arrow that leaves the bow cannot come back," she replied.

"I never should have told you how I felt."

"Of course you should have," she replied.

Angelina stepped aside and he went in. She shut the door behind him and indicated a chair for him to sit down.

"Would you like something to drink?"

"No thanks," he said.

The room became quiet. A clock was ticking, and it seemed very loud. She took firm control of herself.

"Need I remind you, Z-man, that you haven't learned to cope with rejection? My marrying Agara while you were chasing wealth is still frustrating you."

"I'm here to apologize for my overreaction. Can you grant me one point?"

"What?"

"That my initial reaction was a little justified?"

"To each his own," she said, not ready to dispute the point.

"You look gorgeous, Angelina. You are glowing," he told her.

"Pregnant women do," she told him.

She had seen little of Z-man since his visit with her at her father's palace. He had told her off and tried to avoid her. She didn't blame him. Her marrying Agara, a poor man, and one with no known past, had made him lose face. She hoped he would still continue to be her father's family friend, but the dour expression on his face did not hold much promise of that.

"Angelina, I feel bad about that bastard knocking you up and disappearing."

"Agara did not just get me pregnant. It took both of us," she stated emphatically.

"If he knew he was on the run, he should have been wearing something, you know," he said.

The pregnancy was getting very hard on her. It was making her heave her breakfast into the water cistern every morning. It made her so tired in the evenings that even combing her hair was a big ordeal. Still, she was prepared to face Z-man.

"I don't think I would have gone for that," she cut in.

At the risk of getting him more jealous, she said, "I can remember how wonderful it felt gliding into sweet oblivion with him that night at the Potompo field."

"I would have expected any reasonably intelligent woman who is sexually active to have practiced some means of contraception while dealing with an irresponsible bastard like whatshisname," Z-man hit back. "You should have known what could happen when you engage in wild, unprotected fun. He is gone and permanently out of the picture," he scolded.

"Need I remind you, Z-man, that you cannot take back spoken words? So be careful what you say," Angelina warned.

"How are you coping with and getting used to the changes associated with pregnancy?" Z-man asked, trying to shift gears.

"How would you know about getting used to pregnancy? It is not your body that is going through all the changes; it is mine." She hadn't been able to hold down much food lately. She hadn't slept at all the night before, worrying over her pregnancy and Agara's disappearance. She had been planning what she was going to say to her parents about her pregnancy.

"When are you due?"

"Sometime in six or seven months."

"Now that Agara is gone, would you need financial assistance?" he asked, looking directly in her face.

"For what?" she asked.

"Do you plan to have an abortion?"

Angelina turned, with tears in her eyes. "No, Z-man, I believe in living with my decisions and not burying them. It seemed that destiny had brought Agara and I together for a purpose. I like to think that that purpose is the baby I'm carrying. Potompo was a celebration for fecundity," she retorted. "It was my decision to go into it with clear eyes. I'm willing to assume full responsibility for my actions that night of the celebration," she said in a shaky voice. "It's not going to be easy for me to have a baby, but I'm going to, and that's it. Can you claim to know me, Zebulon Zimako?"

"I do," he replied.

"No, you don't. You don't really know a woman until you've lived with her. You know very little of me; that's why you thought I would get rid of my baby through abortion. My baby is going to be legitimate. On the day of its birth, it will have two parents—Angelina Aham and Agara Aham. Agara may not have loved me, but I love him. On his part, it may have been a spontaneous combustion of the sexual glands. Just lust. But we were married for life."

"Would you need financial help to support the baby before and after it is born?"

Angelina felt like screaming for him to get out of her sight, but she soon calmed down. Beware of unsolicited help, she thought.

"Thank you, Z-man, I don't need your money," she said with a frown on her face.

"Why do you get irritated at everything I say?" he asked her, twisting his lips, as if he had bitten into a bitter nut.

"Because I find everything you say offensive."

"Well, Angelina, if you're ever in the market for a lover, feel free to call on me."

"Thanks," she said, and let him leave.

At nine months, Angelina gave birth to a baby girl—Sochima. meaning *only God knows*. Angelina was glad. She had Agara's baby. It was something of Agara left for her; some part of him to love, since he wasn't there.

The birth of the baby went smoothly. Sochima weighed eight pounds. The baby was just like her father. She had Agara's blue eyes, which he inherited from his biological father. For the first few days, there was a kind of pleas-

ant confusion, as family friends came to coo and marvel at the baby, leaving behind their gifts.

Zebulon Zimako, as a family friend of Chief Oyinatu, came to see the
baby. He chatted with Angelina and proposed that his son, Benjamin Okenwa
Zimako, would marry Sochima to keep his wealth and that of Chief Oyinatu
secure. Angelina smiled and accepted the early betrothal of her daughter and
Zimako's son. By this understanding, Benjamin Zimako and Sochima Agara
had been "Betrothed by Parents."

Angelina accepted the gift left by Mr. Zimako. Within a week or so, the
house grew quiet. Order was established and a routine emerged so smoothly
that one might have thought Sochima had always lived there.

Sochima was an easy baby. She did a minimal amount of crying. Breast
fed, she slept through the night. She gained weight on schedule, and sat up
when she was supposed to. Angelina, healthy and vigorous, felt she and the
baby were blessed.

Chapter 9

Two years passed and still there was no sign of Agara. Angelina weaned her daughter, Sochima, and took a leave of absence from the Ministry of Education. She went back to school to get a college degree. While she was at New State University, Mbenoha, her mother, Beatrice Oyinatu, took care of Sochima. Angelina visited her daughter on weekends and showered her with love and affection.

On a beautiful day at New State University, four years later, Angelina's mother and Sochima were there for the commencement ceremony. At the right time, Angelina switched her tassel to the other side of her cap. Her mother watched her accept the diploma with one hand and shake hands with the dean with her other hand. Within a short time, the exercises were over. Whoops of joy and congratulations rang out in the New State University air. Angelina and her relations went home happily that day. She had been awarded a Bachelor of Arts (honors) degree.

A week after graduation, she submitted her application to the Department of Education for the post of principal of Unaka Girls High School. The principal had gotten married and moved away with her husband to Chad. The vice principal was acting in her place. After one month, Angelina went back to check on the status of her application. The appointment officer was very cold to her. She later discovered that she was supposed to do something that she hadn't done. The officer would not openly tell her what it was. Delaying the offer of the job was meant to be a punishment. She was supposed to have sex with the officer in order to accelerate the processing of the application. She would not go for that.

Angelina went home dejected in spirit. Her uncle, Johnson Ikeri, came to visit with her, and she narrated her dilemma to him.

"Don't worry, Angelina," Johnson said. "I know everybody."

She prepared food for him, and after he ate, he went to the People's Social Club. There, Johnson met with somebody who knew somebody who knew somebody. On Monday of the following week, Angelina was appointed principal of Unaka Girls High School, effective immediately. She moved into the principal's house.

Sochima continued to stay with her grandmother, to allow Angelina to get settled in her job. At age five, a very smart young girl, Sochima started school. She lived with her grandmother until she was eleven. She sat for the entrance examination to Unaka Girls High School. She performed so well that she was admitted with a scholarship to this prestigious boarding school.

Time passed. Z-man learned that Angelina got the job through Moses Nduka, the police detective boss. He shook his head. "That Moses must be good at his job. I have to meet him," he thought.

Z-man continued to harass Angelina about going to bed to satisfy his ego. He tried many times to bed her, using everything from flowers to guilt, but she never surrendered to him. Before she was married, she always used the excuse to Z-man that she wouldn't do it until she was married. Z-man took it well, but when Agara had it before him, he became livid. At a certain point, she was about to shout rape. But he backed off. The more she resisted him, the more aggressive and frustrated he became.

The house of the principal of Unaka Girls High School was isolated. Angelina trusted her dog, Dragon. He was big, with large canine teeth. Before she went to bed, she would feed him and leave him in the kitchen. Angelina's uncle had warned her to keep her doors locked, with the dog inside at night. "Dragon will be no good to you if the enemy gets to him first," Johnson said.

On this night, after she had gone to bed, it must have been around one o'clock in the morning when she started hearing small drums playing ghost-like music. She became afraid and she sat up. The music stopped, but every small sound in the room became magnified in her head. Moments later, the music started again, followed by soft singing in strange dialects. She heard voices. Then everything stopped. There was silence. She must be going nuts, she thought. She tried to go back to sleep, but was awakened soon after by an odd sound in the distance. It was like a soft chant in mixed dialects: Hausa, Ibo, and Yoruba. She was scared.

"Whoever is doing this, the scoundrel will pay for it," she vowed. Then she heard footsteps, followed by a slight knock on her door. She knew it could not be the ghost of Agara coming to her. Of course not him. He will never hurt me. Even though he fled from me, he loves me and he's crazy about me, wherever he is.

She cautiously moved to the kitchen and picked up a pestle. Dragon was by her side. Slowly, she moved back to her bedroom and sat on a stool beside the bed. Dragon stood by the bed. Suddenly, she saw a hooded figure moving toward her room. A mask covered the face of the figure except for two ragged eyeholes. As if a lit object was in his mouth, he spat flames. Angelina's heart thumped in her ribcage.

"Who are you?" she asked undauntedly, holding on to Dragon's collar. The figure did not answer. As the figure advance about three feet, she knew it had become a matter of life and death. She let go of Dragon, and he leaped at the man, knocking him off balance and tearing his arm and leg. The assailant hit the dog's snout with a hammer and the animal let go with a wail of pain. The man ran out of the door and made away with blood gushing from his arm and leg.

In the morning, the police came for an investigation. The team was led by Detective Moses Nduka, a seasoned special investigator. He was the man who made it possible for Angelina to be offered the job without further delay. He questioned Angelina like a good investigator would, and Angelina was happy with him. Finally, he assured her that no one was going to hurt her. The police would be on the lookout for the assailant.

Angelina was taken to the hospital. She was trembling inside. As the principal of a school, she was known. The nurse immediately came to attend to her.

"Do the police know who did it?" the nurse asked.

"Not yet," she said. Her lips were dry and cracked. She tried to moisten them with her tongue. The nurse moved closer to clean her parched lips.

The door opened and a middle-aged man wearing a white lab coat came in.

"How are you doing, ma'am?" the doctor asked politely.

Angelina could hardly talk. She was livid. She had been sedated for a few hours because her blood pressure was very high. When she felt better, the doctor told her that she was very brave to face the assailant. "It appears the man came to rape you, and your resistance was remarkable. Lucky to be alive," the doctor said.

Angelina believed that the assailant was hired by someone, and she looked forward to finding the brain behind her being attacked.

"I appreciate the care you gave me," Angelina said to the doctor.

"That's my job," he said, smiling.

She was given a bed in a private room of the hospital. Each time she recalled the attack, she was filled with dread and her head ached. She would close her eyes and force herself to see it again: the masked creature chasing her and swinging a hammer at her, she fell on her bed and sobbed. She cried, and her pounding headache tightened like a vise. Suddenly, she rushed into the bathroom and began to retch. She had not eaten any food, and her empty stomach heaved.

The doctor checked her out and put her on tranquilizer medication. The retching subsided and she was discharged the next day. "When you go home, be sure to eat," the nurse advised. "You need your strength."

"Okay," Angelina said.

Stress and weariness were catching up with her. The absence of Agara, rearing her daughter as a single mother, and the constant sexual harassment from Z-man kept her on edge. Zebulon Zimako was mounting more pressure on her in an attempt to bed her and let her know that he could do it, despite her flamboyant slap of his face.

A few weeks passed. To take her mind away from Agara, she went to talk to her Auntie Mary. As they sat and chatted, Auntie told her that she should start going out with other men, to see what else was out there for her. "There are a lot of other fish in the sea," she said. "If you look around, you will find that there are men out there who will treat you like a lady, with respect."

Angelina had thought about this but, for some reason, felt like she would be cheating on Agara, even though she didn't know where he was. She felt her heart belonged to Agara.

"You know that Z-man is still trying to stage a comeback after getting mad with me? He was in my house yesterday," Angelina said.

"What did he have to say?" Auntie asked.

"You hardly knew Agara," he said to me.

"So, what?" I asked.

"It all happened so quickly!" he said.

"That doesn't mean it was wrong," I asserted. "I love him."

"Did he love you? If he loved you, why did he desert you?" he asked mockingly.

"My eyes filled with tears, but I didn't let them fall. Each time Z-man had a conversation with me, he would try to make me feel that I made an unpardonable mistake."

"Angelina, do you want me tell you what I think?"

"Please do," I quickly said.

"You know the old saying in this community, 'A dog does not eat its vomit.' You put him down for Agara. You should not go back to him. He will never forgive you and Agara. Instead, he will seek for revenge sooner or later."

"I have already found out from a reliable source that Z-man hired the assailant to come and frighten me in my house. I promised the man that I wouldn't make a case against him."

Chapter 10

It has been over six years since Agara fled from Unaka. Angelina was in school one day when her father sent for her. She became very apprehensive because, as our elders say, "A toad does not move to the public place during the day without a good reason. If it has not seen something, something has seen it."

When she went to the palace of her father, she saw the old man in bed.

"Sit down, my daughter," the old man commanded.

Angelina sat down, facing her father and her mother. She did not know what to expect. So many thoughts came to her mind. Would her parents still be annoyed with her for marrying without parental consent? Had they heard anything concerning the whereabouts of her husband?

Her father noticed the anxious expression on her face. "I want you to go home and think of what I can do for you before I depart from this world," the old man said to his daughter.

Angelina looked at her eighty-year-old father. A smile registered on his face. She had known her father as one who had precognition. He had always known when something was wrong with him. She started sobbing, and the old man said, "I love you, Angelina. Do as I have said."

"I love you, Father," she said as she wiped the tears from her eyes. She turned to her mother and there was a smile on her face; that made her relax. "It is for good," Angelina thought. She got up from her seat and moved to her father and held his hand. Tears sprang from her eyes, as if the man had already passed away. Her mother led her out from the sitting room to her room upstairs. The old lady told her that this was no time to ponder and cry. She should do what her father said.

Angelina quickly went to think of what she needed. She consulted one of her friends, Comfort Nnama. Comfort was the president of the CORM club—Concubines of Rich Men club. Comfort told her that three of the club members were going to London on shopping vacations with their men.

"Would you like to join us?" Comfort asked.

"That would be very exciting," Angelina replied.

The next day, Angelina went back to her father and requested to be sponsored for a vacation trip to England. Her father granted her wish and ordered that money be made available for her to take on the trip. Comfort immediately went to work and pulled the necessary strings. Within two weeks, Angelina's travel documents were ready for the trip. Money talked.

Angelina officially took time off from the School Board of Education to enable her to take the trip. She was sitting in her room one day, preparing nervously for the trip, when Z-man came to see her. He had heard about her proposed sponsored vacation. He offered to give her money for the trip, but she refused his kind gesture. "You will need all the money you can get," he told her.

She countered his arrogance. "The sun will set without your assistance, Zebulon Zimako." She did not want to be obligated to him. "No man does a woman a favor and expects nothing in return," she thought.

On the last Sunday night before her departure, Angelina's father put his hand on her head and stated, "My beautiful daughter, do not be the first to break a family tradition. You are a descendant of a long line of heroes. Be strong like your ancestors." The old man paused. "My friend, Z-man, still has his eyes on you. He's a dog. If you sleep with a dog, you will wake up full of fleas. Watch him. Your husband, Agara, deserted you. Sooner of later, he'll be back. He knows your capabilities." The octogenarian chief paused again, looked at his daughter and smiled. "There is a battle ahead. You threw a challenge to Z-man when you rejected him. Stand behind your decision. Prove that the blood of your ancestors is in you; do this by making a difference in life. I have asked the gods to take care of you and help you enjoy your trip. Enjoy it to the fullest. May the gods help you," Chief Oyinatu wished his daughter.

"Thank you, Father, I will remember your words," she promised.

After she left her parents, Angelina went to visit with Auntie. She told Auntie about her trip. "I'm afraid of meeting a man. You know what I mean, Auntie? I don't want to fall in love while I'm still married to Agara."

"Angelina," Auntie began. "I know what you mean. For some years now, I have been telling you that you are still young and beautiful. You should not sequester yourself from life. I have advised you to start seeing men. Just enjoy yourself with the man; have fun."

"I don't know of any man who will take a woman out just for fun without expecting her to jump into bed with him for a reward."

"How many men have you dated since Agara fled?"

"None."

"So how would you know that you can't have fun without falling in love?" Auntie asked.

Angelina stared at her aunt. She knew that Auntie was making sense in what she was saying.

"Angelina, think about this. Agara fled from you over six years ago and has made no contact with you. And you have been off men."

"I love him, Auntie."

"I know you do. Do you have to take off your sexuality and hang it in the closet until he returns, if ever he does?"

"The gods help me," Angelina murmured.

"Yes, you need their help to see that your sexuality is part of you, and you are going to have to come to terms with it. You feel it every day, like any normal woman would when you see a good looking man."

"Stop, Auntie! Please stop!" Angelina cried. She had taken as much as she could. Her mind was racing to her time with Agara on the celebration night.

"I pray that on this trip, Angelina, you meet a man who will be nice to you and you reciprocate the nicety. Take your fun where you find it," Auntie wished her.

"Thank you, Auntie. You will be hearing from me."

Chapter 11

On Monday morning, the vehicle took Angelina and the CORM club members to Lagos, where they would board a British Overseas Airways aircraft to London. As they were waiting for the boarding announcement, Angelina noticed an attractive young man chatting with his friends and watching her from the corner of his eyes.

The young man smiled and she smiled back. She began to watch out for him. The man was so good looking that she had a hard time concentrating on a conversation with her friends. Comfort watched Angelina as her eyes flirted with those of the man.

"What is the matter?" Comfort asked Angelina.

"My womanhood twitched instantly when I made the last eye contact with that young man."

"Don't feel bad; mine would too if I wasn't going to meet my man in London," Comfort said.

Angelina smiled when Comfort agreed with her. "That's what prolonged celibacy will do to a woman. It will make her equate everything a man does to sex," she thought. She kept looking at his thick lips and wondering how they would feel against hers. He smiled again and she smiled back.

Angelina went into the restroom to check herself out to ensure that she looked gorgeous enough to meet him formally. She was wearing a blue blouse that displayed her voluptuous breasts. When she came out, the young man looked at her and smiled. She took that to mean that he was mesmerized by her beauty. As he was trying to make up his mind to come and talk to her, the announcement came over the air for passengers traveling to London on BOA to proceed for boarding.

The group boarded the plane. Angelina found herself sitting next to the young man. There were four ladies in the group: three were members of the CORM club, which included Comfort, Lucy, and Rose. Their men were already in London transacting their business and waiting for the women to come and make them happy.

Angelina's mind started focusing on the trip. Sitting next to her was the handsome young man for whom she had been lusting. "What am I nervous about?" she thought.

About eleven thirty p.m., the plane took off. After the twin engine propeller plane steadied in the air, the young man turned to her and said, "My name is Rufus. Rufus Dibia."

She put her hand out for him to shake and make her acquaintance but, instead, he squeezed it flirtatiously. It immediately sent a warm sensation through her body. Thirty minutes later, a warning sign came up that the plane was getting into turbulence and seat belts were to stay on. Angelina's heart panicked.

"With Rufus next to me, I feel okay," she thought.

The plane steadied in the air again. She and Rufus resumed their getting more acquainted with each other.

"Glad to meet you, Mr. Dibia. I'm Angelina."

"Beautiful name for a beautiful young lady," Rufus said.

"Thanks," she replied.

Rufus was about the same age as Angelina. From his dress and look, she knew he came from money.

"So, Angelina, are you traveling alone?"

"Yes. I mean no. I'm traveling with those ladies." She pointed to Comfort, Lucy, and Rose in their seats. "They are members of the CORM club," she said.

"What is that?" Rufus asked.

"CORM stands for Concubines of Rich Men. Each of these ladies will meet her man in London. The hotel accommodations have been made and paid for," she said.

"Are you a member of the club?"

"No."

"Why are you traveling with them?"

She looked at the stranger who had attracted her, but did not feel like telling all her business to him. "It's a long story," she said. "Where are you traveling to, may I ask?"

"I'm en route to Germany, to study medicine," he replied.

"Are you going to stop briefly in London?"

"I would if I had a reason to do so. My school does not start for another month," he said, not ready to let her know he was admiring her.

During the course of their conversation, they found each other very interesting.

Rufus Dibia worked for the customs and excise of Nigeria. Within two years after graduating from high school, he had accumulated an enormous sum of money, and built a very expensive home in the township of his home town. Because he was greedy and was not sharing, like he was expected to by his supervisor, rumors of impending inquiry into his financial standing reached him. "Any grasshopper that is captured by Okpoko must be deaf," the elders said. Okpoko is a creature that warns its prey before capturing it. Rufus hurriedly arranged for his travel documents and left the country with a good sum of money.

"Where did you grow up?" he asked.

"I was born and raised in Unaka village," she began. "My father is Chief Oyinatu of Unaka. I'm principal of Unaka Girls High School."

"Wow! Beauty and brains together," he exclaimed. He smiled.

"What is the matter?" she asked.

"I'm very much impressed."

"Why?"

"You didn't seem to be interested in getting money from me, like many of the girls I have met at home. Many of them flocked to me because they knew that customs officers paraded with money in their pockets."

As the plane started on its descent, Rufus said, "Angelina, when I saw you at the departure lounge, you had on a beautiful smile. I have to admit that you had me mesmerized."

She smiled.

"It must be destiny that brought us together. I almost missed my flight because of Lagos traffic, held up from Victoria Island to the airport," he said as the tires hit the ground at Heathrow Airport.

It was morning in London when the group got off the plane. Angelina and the other members of the CORM club retrieved their luggage. She turned to Rufus and asked where he was going to stay.

"I have not made any arrangements for a hotel," he said.

"We are going to check into a hotel near Heathrow Airport. Accommodations have been reserved for us by our men," Comfort interjected.

"Is that okay with you?" Angelina asked. Her thoughts were on Rufus and a chance at happiness.

"Is that an invitation?" Rufus asked.

"If you want it to be," she said.

Rufus rebooked his flight to Germany to enable him spend a few days with Angelina.

That night, a big party was held at the hotel where they lodged. Angelina was out to enjoy herself. Since she was out of the country, her father had asked the gods to release her from her bond with Agara until she returned. It had been a long time since she spent time alone with a man, and she found herself ready for fun.

Comfort called Angelina and asked if she planned on going out to eat with them and to party later.

"I don't think so," she said.

"I don't blame you. He sure is yummy," Comfort said, laughing loudly as she gave the phone to Rose.

"Tell us about it later," Rose teased and hung up the phone.

Thirty minutes later, there was a knock on Angelina's door. It was the hotel room service man, delivering chilled red wine, on the order of Rufus Dibia. As the man shut the door behind him, there was a knock on the door. It was Rufus.

"Come in," she said excitedly.

On entering the room, Rufus opened his arms. Angelina had forgotten how wonderful it felt to be held in a man's arms. She was shivering. His scent was masculine—shaving soap and cologne filled her head. The thought of the pleasure she would give and take shook her body. He wrapped his arms around her waist and pulled her gently against his chest. Her lips parted. She had to blame this on the fact that she hadn't felt the touch of a man's lips on hers in more than six years.

He wanted her right there on the sofa. He sensed that she wanted the same thing too.

"Slow down," she said, without meaning it.

He smiled and unfastened her bra and removed the last of her underwear. Rufus looked marvelously virile as he stood naked in front of her.

"Do you really want me, Angelina?" he asked.

Her body said yes.

"I want to hear it from your beautiful, sexy mouth," he said.

"Yes, I want you."

Immediately he moved between her legs, and she looped her arms around his neck. Angelina caught herself fighting for control. She didn't want it to happen, but she was ready for it. She was a married woman who had been starving for sex. Despite her reluctance and inhibitions, the need for it continued. Angelina thought, "I will let Rufus use my body, but my love, my heart, and my soul belong to Agara, wherever he may be."

Rufus put his arms around her drawing her closer.

"I'm a married woman," she whispered to him.

He looked down when she said it.

Angelina quickly added, "Listen to me, Rufus, before you start feeling guilty." She explained to him how she got married and what happened after; that her husband deserted her, and it had been more than six years.

Rufus was a smart man. "Angelina, never feel guilty when you are caring for yourself. Can we be friends?" he asked.

She smiled.

"Is that okay?" he added.

She thought about it and decided that since she had made it known to him, she would not suffer the guilt as much as if she had kept it from him.

He went to the phone to order wine. Angelina noticed that the tension that had shown on his face when she first mentioned her marriage was beginning to lessen.

When he came back and sat down, she sat beside him. Her body against his chest, she pulled his head to her breasts; her nipples were standing at attention, screaming out to be kissed. She leaned back against the arm of the sofa and let him enjoy her nipples. He ran his hand between her legs and started panting and moaning with excitement. Soon, both of them exploded. Rufus and she were both out of breath.

They rested for a brief period, and then Angelina wanted to shower with him. As soon as she bent over to pick up the soap, he pushed into her again. They got out of the shower and dried themselves. He watched her voluptuous butt swing as she walked away.

"Angelina," he called.

She turned around and smiled.

He said, "You are beautiful."

About an hour later, she went to sleep on the sofa, resting her head on his chest. When she woke up, they had wine. With a glass of wine in her hand, Angelina looked at Rufus, who smiled flirtatiously. She put her drink on the table and moved to him. He began to kiss her. Before she knew it, she was moaning and screaming joyfully.

Later, they chatted in the usual getting-to-know-you way after a good time. Angelina learned quite a bit about him. He was twenty-eight years old, one year older than she.

She asked him if he was married, engaged, or had a girl lined up for him by his parents. He laughed and said, "None of the above."

"Why? No girl good enough for you in your village?" she asked.

He smiled and said, "I come from a small village, Amadike, Eastern Nigeria. The village was founded by two brothers and their wives, many, many years ago. There is nothing to attract outsiders to come and settle there. Consequently, there have been marriages between the original families. You can see that in the facial and body resemblance of the people; however, in recent years, some families that have been decreasing in number have adopted a plan."

"What kind of plan?" she asked.

"My grandfather told me that when he was young, his father traveled to different villages far from our village. In each occasion, he returned with a young girl, about eight or nine years old, that he had paid dowry to her parents. When the girl reached marrying age, he gave her out to one of his family's young men to marry and produce offspring."

"Did the girls ever trace their roots back to their original families?" she asked.

"Not to my knowledge," Rufus said. "The girls were so nicely treated that there would be no reason for them to think of going back to their original homes. Their descendants are all over Ohadum District and elsewhere," Rufus added.

Rufus explained that as soon as he got his degree in medicine, he would be open to a relationship, with the right woman, of course.

Angelina smiled at that and wished she had met him before Agara.

"Didn't I fall for Agara after just a short meeting? How did I know what he would be?" she thought.

After a while, Angelina was tired and told Rufus she wanted to go to bed. They slept in late. When they woke up, they went to the hotel restaurant and ate lunch. In the evening, Rufus took her to a local restaurant for dinner. The atmosphere was nice, and the lights were dim. A local jazz artist was performing. Angelina was happy.

The next day he took her shopping. He bought her expensive jewelry and clothes. "You are a pretty woman and you deserve pretty clothes," he told her. For the time they were together, she felt that Rufus was truly sincere. She liked the words he whispered when she broke down into tears when remembering what she had gone through with Agara.

The day before they parted, Rufus took Angelina out to dinner. She felt relaxed. He didn't pressure her to do anything. She believed destiny had something to do with their meeting each other. Who knew where the relationship will lead? They had a good time, and the trip was for just that.

She gave him her auntie's address, should there be any reason for him to get in touch with her. The next day, he called to tell her how much he missed her. She said that through her, he had learned how to please a woman, what to say to arouse her femininity, and that for the one week they spent together, they made the kind of love that satisfied them both.

They knew their meeting was accidental and of short duration. "There is a reason for everything," Angelina thought. "He is different from the average man I have known." He had verbalized that he was not just interested in sleeping with her, and he showed it by taking interest in the things that concerned her. In the days she was with him, she never regretted a moment. They saw each other for the one week they stayed in London, and they developed a comfortable relationship.

Chapter 12

After Rufus left London, Angelina rejoined the CORM club group.

"Aren't you going to tell us about Rufus?" Comfort asked.

"What do you want to know? That we slept together and that we made light, inconsequential conversations?" Angelina replied.

"He is gone, and with your heart, no doubt," Lucy said.

"You can say that again," she said happily.

"Let's hear it," Rose said, grinning like a Cheshire cat.

"Rufus is an angel," she said happily.

"I didn't know angels do mundane things," Comfort teased.

"Everybody wants to know my love business," she said. "Anyway, there is nothing to tell, so you might as well stop staring at me."

"Even if you want to lie about it, go ahead," Lucy said.

"You know ours already. We came with the men to have fun, give them what they want, and they provide material things for us. We are happy and they are," Comfort said.

Angelina relayed a condensed sequence of events about their meeting the first day, how they made wild, passionate love, like wild beasts, consumed by spontaneous lust. "When I saw him at the airport, I thought he looked good with clothes on, but when he completely undressed … may Kamalu, the god of Thunder, strike me blind if he was not the most sensually attractive man I had ever laid my eyes on. I could hardly think straight. He started kissing me and I went totally out of control," she shared. "I became so excited that I was panting. He put his hands on my breasts and whispered in my ears, 'Angelina, you're beautiful.' 'You're gorgeous,' I whispered back to him. He began to rub my nipples until they were standing at attention. When he entered me, I felt like a stallion was pushing into me," she concluded.

"Is it that big?" Rose asked.

"I will not talk about it anymore."

"Why?" Lucy asked.

"My mother always warned me that if something is very good, don't tell it to your best friend. She might just go for it."

"You are scared one of us may want him?" Comfort asked.

They all burst into a big laugh.

"I think Jonathan Omaka's is incomparable in size and length," Comfort boasted about her man.

Everybody roared with laughter.

"The next day, Rufus ordered flowers for me from a florist," she continued. "They were beautiful. I felt proud to know that, apart from Agara, I had somebody, even though it was a temporary affair. After we made love, I looked at him, looked at the flowers, and smiled. 'What is on your mind, Angelina?' What are you trying to do to me? I asked. 'What do you mean?' he asked, and smiled. Are you trying to make me fall in love with you? I asked. 'Angelina, you are special to me,'" he said.

I did not go any further, knowing that Agara was still there somewhere. On the last night, we went to a movie theater. We enjoyed the movie. In the morning, I followed him in the cab that took him to the airport. He was leaving, and the end of our blissfulness had come. 'I don't know when or if we will meet again,' he said. We parted with tears in our eyes. As he kissed me goodbye, he whispered in my ear, 'All good things must come to an end. Keep in touch.' His plane departed on schedule."

"We are glad you had fun with him. Before we set out from home, we had no idea how it would turn out," Lucy said.

The rest chorused, "Amen."

The next day, the group flew to New York. All four of them had money to spend. Rufus Dibia had provided adequately for Angelina, as if he had anticipated their meeting. As members of the CORM club, the women were adequately provided for.

While in New York, Rufus called from Germany. "I just wanted you to know how much I have missed you since we parted. It's night over here," he said.

"Good night, and sweet dreams," Angelina said.

"I'll be thinking of you," he said, and hung up.

A true friend is with you in bad times as well as the good times. On the third day in New York, Angelina received a telegram that said her father was seriously ill and that she should return home. She contacted Rufus, and he flew back to London to meet her. Even though he was young, he had money. She knew Rufus was a real friend. He stood by her in her hour of need.

Rufus contacted one of his friends in Nigeria, Moses Nduka. Angelina was surprised to learn that Moses was his best friend. What a small world. He told her how Moses had thwarted the efforts of Z-man, who had tried to keep her out of being appointed principal of Unaka Girls High School. He also told her that it was Z-man who hired the assailant to frighten her.

"Z-man did not intend to kill you," he said, "but to frighten you into wanting a man you could rely on near you."

"Bull crap," I screamed. "Even if it took balls to defend me, his would not be required by me."

Rufus laughed.

Moses was the head of the police detectives in Ohadum District. Through Moses, Angelina learned that her father had suffered a massive heart attack and had been hospitalized.

"Sweet Jesus," she screamed. Her father was her heart. "Dear God," she prayed. "Please spare the life of my father now. I know that all living creatures here on earth must each die at its time. But give me a chance to see him before he finally goes back to you."

She wiped her tears and began the task of assembling her things. Rufus stood by her at this time of mental and emotional crises. He helped pack her luggage and re-book her flight. She flew from London to Lagos. Three days later, she was home in Unaka.

She thought about the time she spent with Rufus, and then wrote to him:

> *Dear Special Friend, I have made it back to Nigeria. The old man was in a coma when I got to the chief's palace. He had been brought to the palace because a chief in his position in life would not be allowed to die outside his home. He never came out of the coma, and passed away a day after I returned. Thanks to God that I saw him before he left for good.*
>
> *My family stumbled through the funeral in a daze of pain and hurt. As befits a great warrior chief, the Oyinatumba of Unaka was buried with a lot of fanfare.*
>
> *Rufus, the memory of our time together would not leave me. My time with you will remain indelible in my mind.*
>
> *Love,*
> *Your Special Friend.*

Chapter 13

World War II ended in 1945. Agara was discharged from the military. He stayed in Lagos while trying to get himself adjusted to civilian life again. He decided he wasn't going back into society until he had a firm and definite vision of what he wanted.

He worked among friends at the Lagos wharf until he made enough money to buy himself a Fiat. He was thirty-seven years old; not too old, but old enough to be lonely. Since his arrival, he had not dated any woman. He had been mobbed by young women he thought viewed him only as a handsome ex-service man now driving a Fiat. He hadn't met anyone who interested him. There was something that kept him from going close to any of them: it was his wife, Angelina, the chief's daughter in Unaka.

While in the military, Agara shared his emotional feelings for Angelina with one of his close friends, Jaconda Kweku. Jaconda, too, had left a loved one behind in Ghana. He was missing her just like Agara was missing Angelina. Jaconda told him that absence was like the wind for lovers apart: it could either blow out a fire or fan the flame. They had become very good friends; the best of friends are those who have the same ailments. Agara and Jaconda would often pray together for their safe return to their wives.

On this day, Agara let his head loll back on the rocking chair. Raising the glass of beer in his hand, he took a swallow and returned to his meditations on life and its vicissitudes and sometimes unexpected events.

This night, he lay on the couch. All seemed quiet in the room. It was past midnight; nobody seemed awake, other than him. It was a good time for cogitations. He thought about the woman he left in Unaka twelve years ago. She was the only woman he had found suitable for his need—love and companionship. They were united by the gods, and only death could separate them.

While in the military, he lived in fear, never relaxing, and always at alert and aware that anything could happen anytime. That night, he closed his eyes and started dreaming about the last day before the war ended. He was in a small village that was evacuating. Some of the local people were rushing from house to house, searching for their relatives, while others loaded their possessions in baskets and boxes so heavy that they would be overtaken by the slowest armed vehicles. The people were being told that this was not the time to spend worrying about personal possessions. Those who took the warning could hear the roar of guns as the enemy was advancing. They also passed those who were slowed down by the burden of pushing and pulling their lives' possessions. He could remember young children and the aging relatives trodding along, hoping to make it to the safety camps.

He woke up. Now in his country, he had become edgy, restless, and desperate to return to his wife, Angelina. He had lost touch with the people of his village; he needed his wife to connect him, to be a bridge between him and all around him. He needed to see her, to touch her, and to feel her presence. He'd dreamed of her many a night while in the military. She was beautiful and sexy. He wondered how he could keep her from running away from him if he should find her. He had to show her that she belonged to him.

"Ya gotta do what you gotta do," Agara decided. He made up his mind to go after his wife. He would go to the Newtown Hotel and trace his way to wherever she might be. He would either find her or hear about her. "She might have married a rich trader or businessman, or a school teacher," he thought. He had never refused a challenge in his life, especially where a woman was involved.

He was at Unaka in the afternoon on the following day. Travel by road was now better than it was when he fled the community. He went to the Newtown Hotel, where he stayed the first time. Management at the hotel had not changed hands, but the old workers had been replaced. The hotel looked better than it was when he was there twelve years ago.

While in the hotel, he remembered his friend Jon Akaji, and decided to go and visit him. On his way, he stopped at the Potompo celebration field, near the Community Sacred Forest. The memory of that night with Angelina came back to him, as if it were just last night. He stood, gazing at the sacred forest, where it all began.

As he spotted the big silk cotton tree under which the priest of the ceremony stood, the memory became more intense. The tree looked the same as it did back then: tall, and seeming to touch the sky above. He remembered Angelina dancing and twirling, and how he decided to go for her there and then. A tse tse fly bit him, and he swatted it and moved on to his friend's house.

When he met Jon, the man was now seventy years old. He looked like someone slightly weathered, like a farmer coming home after hours on the farm. His hands were callused, as would be expected of one who worked hard for a living. Jon did work hard.

"How are you, my old friend, Agara?" Jon asked.

"I'm fine," Agara answered.

"Where have you been all these years?" the old man asked.

"Fighting the war," he replied.

"Can you remember how we met?" Jon asked.

"We met at the barbershop, and you invited me to your home," Agara said.

"We had a good time, didn't we?" the old man asked.

"We certainly did," Agara said with a smile. "Well, Jon, I have come to Unaka to search for my wife, Angelina."

Jon smiled, because the last thing he told Agara that day, twelve years ago, was, "Bait the hook well and the fish will bite."

Agara smiled. "Jon, your prediction was right. I went back that day and let her know how much I loved her, and that paved the way for our marriage. I have not been able to get her out of my mind since I fled. I'm here to look for her."

Jon smiled. "Agara," he called. "Angelina is still around and looking beautiful. You will find her."

"I wonder if she has remarried," Agara said.

"Listen, my friend," Jon said, "never underestimate the power of love."

Jon brought a pot of palm wine and smoked deer meat. They ate and drank.

"Good luck," Jon wished him.

Agara went back to the hotel to see the hotel proprietor, Jacob Ikonne."

Chapter 14

Last night, I lay on my bed and went to sleep, Angelina recalled. *My senses were attuned to Agara's lovemaking. I moaned softly in pleasure as his hands moved from my legs to caress my thighs. He leaned in and began to kiss me passionately. He continued the caress until he entered me hard, heavy, and hot. Finally, we collapsed together in a haze of pleasure.* Then I woke up, wondering about the dream.

Recently, every night, when I went to bed, I saw Agara's image standing before me. He would appear as if he wanted to touch me, as if he and I were communicating on some spiritual plane that was beyond my understanding. His face would glow like a distant star. I wish I had wings to fly to him. The pain becomes unbearable. How can you look through me and not see how my heart and soul yearn for you? His appearing and disappearing was irritating and unnerving. I would stretch my arms to receive him and he would be gone. I would finally fall into exhausted frustrated sleep.

Since Agara fled Unaka, I have thought about him several times. But the dream appeared like a message to me from the gods. Agara had been gone for twelve years and no one had heard from him. He had gone and had taken my heart with him.

"Agara, I feel like I'll never see you again. Will you ever hold me again? Will I ever feel you inside me again? I need you, Agara. I need to know that you still love me as I love you and as you once told me that you did," Angelina thought out loud.

It was only three months ago that she had attended a party given by the Ohadum District Board of Education. She did not want to attend the party with any man. Her auntie thought that it would be a good idea for her to be accompanied by a male. Angelina had told her that no man picks up a woman, takes her to party for fun sake, does her a favor, and expects nothing in return. She declined to go with any man. But at the party, she felt like an alien in a world made up of couples only. She felt like the world had forgotten her. She missed Agara.

Angelina prayed, "Please, God, wherever Agara may be, help him see that his daughter and I need him. Send Saint Miracle to show him the way back and Saint Help to guide him home to us."

Angelina's mother had told her that sex was more than just a physical act. It involved the heart. Yet when she fell for this stranger, she did not heed the danger signals. She was heedlessly in love with a man she probably would never see again. She recalled what a wonderful time she had with him at the ancient festival for the gods. Such a memory made her shiver. Would she ever see him again? If he did come back, would he want her like he did before? When he found out about his daughter, Sochima, would he be happy?

When things look blackest, happiness is often just around the corner. Agara had been gone as if never to return. Had Angelina considered that he might someday come back? Before her father passed away, he had told her that Agara would one day come back. How would she feel if he did come back? Angelina sighed and thought, "First catch your rabbit, then make your stew."

Chapter 15

Agara came back from his visit with Jon. As he was ordering his meal, Jacob Ikonne walked in, he was the hotel proprietor when Agara first came to Unaka. The man, like him, had aged a little. They exchanged greeting, as would be expected of old friends. In the corner at which the old man described as "your usual table," the proprietor seated him so that they could talk while he ate.

"What happened to the sweet woman you left Angelina for?" Jacob asked.

"There was no woman involved," he replied.

Jacob looked perplexed. "You didn't leave her with nowhere to go?"

He shrugged his shoulders.

"Listen, Agara. This is the old hotel proprietor you are talking to. We spent time together before you left. Don't tell me that you had nowhere to go when you left here."

Agara sighed deeply.

"I still want to know how you broke up with the sweet lady you went to live with all these years."

"No woman," he replied, not feeling like telling about his past life.

"Face it, Agara, my grandfather always said that no man with good reasoning sense ever leaves a good woman for another woman, good or otherwise. So you might as well level with me."

"I left Angelina to join the Second World War, and not for a woman. Angelina was the only woman I thought about during my career in the army," he stated.

Jacob smiled at his declaration, which was the truth.

"You say you've been gone twelve years? Knowing how she loved you, and talked about you all the time, she wouldn't mind taking you back. That's one good looking woman with big juicy tits that you can't afford to let go. Yes, good looking woman," he repeated.

"Have you slept with her?" Agara asked, wondering why he seemed so sure of what he was talking about.

"No way, man," Jacob answered, shaking his head. "Our elders say, 'Never pass excrement where you eat.' I'm no fool. My father always said that there were too many women out there for a man to make a fool of himself with one. Her father, the late chief of Unaka, was my father's kinfolk."

After his meal, Jacob gave Agara directions to Angelina's house.

When it came to dealing with women, Agara knew how to dress up and make himself desirable in their sight. The women loved him for that. Keeping up with his appearance won him the eyes and hearts of the women he came across. He came home with expensive men's cologne that was pleasurable to the nose. He maintained a well-groomed appearance. The next morning he was ready to meet Angelina. He took time to take care of himself. He wore a well-tailored African dress, nice leather sandals, and a chieftaincy hat.

Agara got to Angelina's house and knocked at the door. There was no answer. He knocked again.

Angelina peeped through the crack on the wooden door. She thought she was dreaming. "Just a minute," she said. She burst into copious tears. "Praise God, praise God," she repeated silently, eyes shut. "I've been praying for the day he'd come back. My mother is dancing in Heaven today. She surely is. Lordy! Lordy!" she cried. "Thank you, Saint Miracle and Saint Help," she said. "I can't wait to ask the millions of questions in my mind." Then she paused. "The prodigal son is back. What do I do with him? Oh, Lord! Life goes in cycles between sadness and happiness."

When she opened the door, Angelina looked at him. Recognition hit. She stood perfectly still. She didn't speak, didn't greet him. Her heart rocketed into her throat and her view blurred. She didn't know if he was real or imagined. Dizziness assailed her and she gripped the doorknob to keep from falling. When she composed herself and looked at him, she felt his eyes on her, touring, analyzing, and assessing. Their eyes met, locked, and held. For long moments, they stared at each other.

If time could stand still, in that instant, it did. Then reality came crashing back. She dragged in a breath, kept her eyes on his, her heart still hammering in her throat. The realization that he was the very last person she expected at her door at that time slammed through her and shook her to her toes. She had prepared herself to blast him away if she ever saw him again. Everything that came to her mind seemed inappropriate at that moment. Thoughts of their union at the Potompo festival came back to her as they stared at each other. Something inside her clenched; she ignored the sensation.

Agara noticed how little she had changed since he'd last seen her. She looked beautiful. When he felt the silence had taken long enough, he said, "Hello, Angelina. I'm glad to see you."

She did not respond. At first sight of him, she felt the urge to turn back. She had not seen him for twelve years, and yet looking at him standing at her door, she thought he looked as handsome as ever. She wondered how she was going to receive him. With her heart pounding in her chest like a sledgehammer, she drew on that inner reserve of courage and strength that always seemed to pull her through the rough times. She felt strong and independent. She held herself firmly in control.

"I didn't expect to see you again," she said, even though she was lying.

"Life is full of surprises," he said, trying to take control of himself.

She stepped aside to let him in. She offered him a glass of water. She was so mad at him that she could hardly speak. He had put her through the wringer, but she was not about to break down now.

"Agara, what brought you to Unaka?" she inquired. She had a way of holding his eyes and demanding an answer.

"In search of my wife," he said.

"What happened to her?"

"Well, it's a long story."

"I have time for a long story," she urged him.

"Well, I left her and joined WWII."

Angelina straightened up. "Did you make any effort to get in touch with her before you came back?"

"I wrote her three times."

"But she didn't reply to any of them, did she?"

"No, she didn't."

She knew she did not get any letters from him. Even if it is a lie that he wrote, his verbalizing the intent made her feel happy inwardly. Torn between hate for abandoning her and the equally potent need to reestablish contact with him, as if his coming had not plunged her into a state of blind panic, she dropped the glass of water she was holding. She would have gone for the strongest alcohol to equip her to face him now.

He attempted to speak, but merely stuttered and stammered like a fool. Why didn't he come out straight and tell her how much he missed her and beg her forgiveness. Then he smiled.

"How have you been, Angelina?" he asked as if they had parted on mutual grounds.

"Fine," she lied very calmly. Conflicting emotions pulled at her. Her initial impulse was to let him have it for deserting her for so many years. Then a deeper part of her felt glad that he asked. She hoped that he had realized the enormity of his desertion. How could he look her in the face and converse politely after running away from her at a time she needed him most? Just looking at him caused her mind to replay the entire event at the Potompo celebration, during which they were married. She had not really known him well when they got married. She clenched her teeth, straightened her shoulders, and readied herself to face him.

"I need to talk to you, Angelina," Agara faltered, his eyes pleading for understanding.

For a moment, Angelina was dumbfounded. What happened to the things she had planned to do or say when and if she ever saw him again?

He moved closer to her and stretched out his arms. Her eyes glared at him as surprise gave way to fury. He thought he could walk back in and wipe out with ease what he'd done to her. Her temper exploded.

"Get away from me," she warned him in a threatening voice, eyes blazing. She was fuming with anger. *He's playing you like a soccer ball,* she thought. *Don't give in to the vagabond,* she warned.

Agara was equally dumbfounded when he read the expression on her face, virtually daring him to come near her. But he ignored her and grabbed her before she could say anything else. She fought him. She tried to kick him, but he held on to her. His body against hers was hard and hot. He wanted her. Neither he nor she could pretend at that moment. But she was not ready to give in, no matter how passionately he tried to convince her that he still loved her. He had to bide his time.

On a calmer note, she asked, "Where are you staying, Mr. Agara Aham?"

"At the Newtown Hotel," he said.

"I'll meet you there. Give me time to get ready," she told him, and excused herself, shaking with anger.

"Do I wait for you to go with me?" he asked.

"Didn't you hear me say I will meet you there? Am I speaking a foreign language to you, or are you hard of hearing?" she spat out angrily.

"Angelina, please take it easy," he pleaded. He meant business.

After he left, she felt that Agara no longer had any power over her, no matter how sweet his pleading may be. She felt empty for the duration of her pregnancy. She had worked very hard to become an independent, self-reliant, confident woman. Despite the good times she shared with him, he had abandoned her and disappeared. Yet she thanked goodness, because it was during that time that she summed up courage to educationally equip herself for the future.

In the meantime, Angelina asked herself what she wanted from Agara now. Why was she going to the hotel to meet the man who left her many years ago? She reminded herself that even though he left her, he had been in her blood like a virus for all these years.

At the hotel, Agara met Jacob, the proprietor of Newtown Hotel. Agara told him of his meeting with his wife.

"Did you tell her how you feel?" Jacob asked.

"Not exactly. I tried to reintroduce myself to her," Agara replied.

"I know you don't need advice on how to let a woman know you think she's special," Jacob said softly. "Don't give up on her until you've made clear how you feel and she rejects you."

"I will do that," he said, and went back to his room.

Would she ever feel as strongly as I feel for her? Agara wondered. Doubts filled him, weighing him down like a ton of cement blocks. He stood up, not wanting to keep on agonizing over the possibility of her rejecting him. He would ask her to go out to dinner with him, and he would spill his guts over a good potent wine. He knew he had a pattern in relationships: after he slept with a woman, her days with him were numbered. As far as he was concerned, sex was merely the beginning of the end. But with Angelina, it had been different.

Chapter 16

Angelina took her time to dress up and put on her makeup. It dawned on her that Agara would sooner or later meet Sochima. She would have to tell him who Sochima was. *But when?* she asked herself. *When he found out, what would his reaction be? It would have to be later,* she decided.

Sochima was in the boarding house at Unaka Girls High School. Angelina quickly arranged for her daughter to spend the holiday with Auntie Mary while she made up her mind on how to deal with this vagabond. It was a weekend that the students were allowed to go home for the Easter holidays.

As she was going to the hotel, she was thinking what to do. Would she tell him about Sochima the next time he came to the house? No. She wasn't going to tell him. Not yet. Not until—

At the hotel, Agara hugged his wife and they kissed each other. They went to the hotel restaurant and had dinner and wine. There was a cordial atmosphere around them. Dinner over, they went to his room. He opened another bottle of wine and poured two glasses. He handed one to her.

Angelina looked at him and said, "Agara, tell me what you remember happened between us before you fled."

Before he said anything, he grabbed her hand and drew her close. He buried his face in the curve of her neck.

Angelina smiled contentedly. She felt his rock hard manhood and knew what was coming. She braced herself to face him.

"Now, my dear Angelina, what happened then is in the past," he said.

"Be careful what you tell me this time, Agara," she warned him.

"I tried to tell you then, and besides, I thought you would have known from my dialect that I was from Oharu."

"Come on, Agara! Own up that you had other things on your mind besides trying to tell me that you were a man on the run, a wanderer."

"Yes, Angelina. You fascinated me," he agreed.

"I knew I was right. All you actually had on your mind was how you could talk me into bed."

"Angelina, that wasn't the only thing on my mind," he said, taking a swallow of the wine in his glass.

"Go on, Agara. Say it."

He tried to put his arms around her waist, but she twisted away. He chuckled. "You are going to punish me, right?"

She turned and pointed to the door. "You can leave Unaka if you want. Why should I be smiling with you as my husband and friend?"

He looked hurt. "Let me tell you, Angelina, that you have beat me up enough."

"I know I haven't. If I had, I would not be sitting here with you," she said. "You didn't even have to bother coming back," she said. *Does he honestly think I should come running when he crooked his little finger?* she thought.

He got up and stared at her with his mouth open.

"Agara, I became interested in you when we first met. Soon, you frustrated my efforts to love you. The second time you came around, I put the past behind me and looked forward to a greater future."

"Oh, Angelina." Agara drew an uneven breath as the upper part of the soft mounds of her breasts were revealed. "Angelina, I'm sorry," he said.

His words produced mixed feelings in her. She was glad to see him come back, especially so that Sochima could meet her father. She could not help but remember the old saying, "Fool me once, shame on you, fool me twice … shame on me."

"Agara, I tried, believe me. I tried every way I could to forget you. It took me a long time to get the yearning for you out of my system. For a time, I convinced myself that I hated you. But when I saw you again, I knew I had been fooling myself."

"Angelina, I love you," he admitted gently. "Can we talk like grownups?" he asked, turning around to look for a place to sit down.

"Tell me about it, Agara. Tell me that you got tired of the woman you left behind." She started all over, near sobbing.

"Angelina, I deserve all this and more, but please give me a chance to talk to you. I came back because of my love for you," he said.

She was so mad at him for talking about love that she could spit fire. She then realized that arguing would not change a thing that had happened. She motioned for him to sit down next to her.

"I have been an asshole," he said.

"More than that," she interjected.

"Are you going to give me a chance to talk?"

Frustrated, Angelina ignored him, got up, and said, "Agara, there are many things we need to talk about. Right now I'm tired and need to go home."

Agara followed her home. At her door, she turned around and said, "Good night. I'll see you at the hotel tomorrow."

"Good night, Angelina."
They kissed and parted for the night.

Chapter 17

The next day, Angelina met Jacob at the hotel. They sat down to talk.

"Agara really loves you. Don't ever doubt that," Jacob began. "I know little of his life, and I know he must have come across a lot of women while he was in the military service. He must not have truly loved anyone of them; that's why he has come back to you. Talking with him earlier, I concluded that he's so much in love with you that he'd be ready to pounce and gobble you up in a moment and not even stop to spit out the bones."

She could not help but smile. "Thank you, Jacob," she said as she moved toward Agara's room.

At the entrance to his hotel room, she knocked. When he came to the door and opened it, Agara took a second look at her and smiled. She wore a beautiful dress. Half her full breasts hung out of the low-cut neckline. Agara smiled again and said, "Angelina, you look very sexy in that expensive outfit."

"Thanks," she said. "I wore it just for you."

He spread out his arms.

She slid into them. "Mother of God," she thought incredulously. "Does he have to touch me for me to fall apart?" He knows what he's doing. He always has. I shouldn't forget it." She struggled to get out of his arms, but he held her tight.

"Now, Agara, let go of me. This isn't going to work," she said, and with as much strength as she could gather, she pushed him away.

He noticed her tone of voice and decided to shift gears.

"Can we go and have dinner at the restaurant and go to the cinema theater after?" he asked.

"That's fine with me," she said.

They went to the restaurant of the Newtown Hotel and ordered their food. While they were waiting, Angelina took time to look at Agara. The streak of white in his black hair had widened, and he had lost weight, but was still as handsome as ever.

"You've got to keep moving forward," he murmured inaudibly.

"What is the matter?" she asked him.

"I'm trying to move forward, but my past keeps coming back to haunt me," he replied.

"The past is the only part of your life that you cannot change. Do you want to talk about it?" she asked.

The waiter chose that time to bring their food.

She watched Agara take a fork of goat meat into his mouth and begin to chew. She immediately sensed that something was wrong, but she would wait and see. They had dinner together, and when they were done, Agara led her outside, his hand around her waist.

They went to the Rex cinema to watch a cowboy movie. It was an erotic thriller, which added additional stimulation to Agara's libido, which was already in overdrive. Angelina, too, had been aroused by the scenes in the movie. She had also gone along with Agara's physical flirting, but that was as far as it could go.

It was late when they got to the hotel room. They sat and listened to each other's ideas, laughed at each other's jokes, and shared past heartaches. As they settled on the sofa in the parlor, Angelina wondered why she should be with him at that time of the night, alone. How could she escape him when he had been making hot since they met earlier that day.

She immediately decided it was time to go home, so Agara walked her back in silence. Before he left her, she said, "Agara, do not waste time grieving over past mistakes." She kissed him and he left.

The next day, Angelina refused to think about Agara. She did not want to go and see him after school. She had thought about him for twelve years, and when at last she had seen him again, it had been as though time had stood still; she'd been young again, trembling on the edge of love. But she was afraid that when all was said and done, a week or so later, he might get lost again. It was his turn to apologize, and she was waiting for him to sincerely do just that. She was tired of always being the one to forgive and forget her own pain so that he would not have to feel his. It had taken its toll on her and she was not about to do it again.

She needed a little time to think things over. But Agara would not give her that time. He was at her house, just as she was returning from school. She caught the anticipatory frown on his face and knew he was readying himself for a confrontation. She had learned to read him well during the short period spent with him, but she knew she wouldn't just sit around and wait for him to pounce.

He kissed her fondly and asked if they could go out and have dinner. Angelina accepted the invitation gladly, and wondered how she would deal with him at the end of the day. She also wondered what the future held for them.

After dinner, the couple went back to Angelina's house. Agara was a little hesitant to make a move, and Angelina smiled inwardly. He looked at her and she knew he had something to say.

"Angelina, have you forgotten how it was on the night we were married?" he asked very quietly.

His question triggered thoughts of her night with him and the things they did and said during the celebration. That night she had been insatiable, had initiated intimacy with a flaming passion, setting both of them on fire with shattering desire. He had known exactly what she needed and had given it to her with an eagerness that thrilled her.

"Agara," she said, "that night has come and gone. We are in a new era. I'm a different woman now, and you have no right to pursue me like this."

He sighed. "Did you think about me, Angelina, while I was gone?"

"What did you expect, Agara?" she demanded stiffly, rising from her seat and moving toward the window.

When she turned to face him, Agara said, penitently, "Angelina, I was a fugitive."

She stared at him.

"Can't you understand that?" he asked.

"Agara," she said, "tell me this: if the situation had been turned around, how would you feel?"

"I don't think I want to hear this," he replied.

Feeling frustrated by his lack of understanding, she said hotly, "Then you have the option of running away like you did before."

"Don't force me out this time, Angelina," he more or less begged her.

"If you should turn around and walk away, I will understand how you feel."

He stared at her speechless.

She then said, very forcefully, "Listen to me, Agara. I meant what I said."

"Angelina, I repeat, you shouldn't turn me away just like that. What happened on that night was just the beginning. We were married for life."

Momentarily she became quiet. Dragging up the past was just too painful. She said, "Well, Agara, it has taken me awhile to get over it. What you are doing now is opening the wound again. Please leave me alone."

Agara stepped outside to find it was already dark. He looked at his wristwatch and discovered it was past midnight. He and Angelina had been sitting, talking, laughing, and arguing for hours. When he came back inside, he saw her smiling: he was happy. He said, "Good night, Angelina."

"Good night," she said.

He went back to the hotel.

The next day, Angelina went to Auntie Mary to talk with her. She told her of her dilemma.

"I love Agara, but his appearing and disappearing and reappearing is of concern to me.

"Angelina," Auntie began. "Love is not the only ingredient in marriage. In addition to love, there is commitment, loyalty, and trust. You need to consider what he is presenting to you this time, whether you can live with it." Auntie Mary continued, "Let me add here that there is no such thing as a perfect marriage. You have to work hard at it."

Agara came back to the house in the evening. Angelina was at the door when he showed up. He kissed her and said, "I love you, Angelina."

"I love you too, Agara."

He advanced forward, and with the effortless swiftness of a jungle leopard, she found herself in his arms, and before she knew it, she was trapped. The sweeping impact of her embrace took her senses away. Agara caught her mouth, as it was turned upward, lips slightly parted in surprise. The small cry of protest went down her throat. Agara had been tired of trying to talk her back into his arms and had opted for a more direct approach. At first, he didn't ask for a response, but was bent on restating the claim he felt he had made on the night of the Potompo celebration. When Angelina resisted, he swung her around. His legs, aggressively apart, propelled her between his thighs so that she became aware of his arousal. Suddenly, her whole body began to search for something it had once known while in his arms.

"Angelina, I want you more than anything else in this universe," he said, his breathing shaky. "I have never wanted any woman the way I want you."

She closed her eyes and took a deep breath when she heard him say, "Angelina, please don't turn me away again."

He groaned when he touched her, his breath already hot and unsteady.

"I have never known such ache of need for a woman," he murmured.

He took her nipple in his mouth. It felt so wonderful that Angelina didn't want him to stop. Suddenly, she pushed him away.

"Look, Agara," she said.

He stared at her in surprise.

"All these things are happening too fast for me. You are pushing me to insanity."

"Angelina, you need to make up your mind," he said, frustrated.

Agara was right. She was confused. In the past, she dove into marriage heart first. This time, she wanted to move slowly and be sure to look before she leaped. She was trying very hard to make sure that the second time around would be done with fewer mistakes.

"Angelina, oh the gods! I want you. I can't go on like this. I'm crazy about you."

"Agara," she said, breathlessly. Her voice was unsteady.

Agara wouldn't let her finish. "Do you know what you are doing to me?"

As he held her close, a sense of the inevitability of the moment assailed her, reminding her of her emotions on that beautiful night. A thrill of desire rippled along her nerves as he took her in his arms.

"Kiss me," he demanded, pulling her close.

She looked at him, his kissable lips full and sensual and driving her crazy. The banked fire of her womanhood had heated up. She tried to ignore it.

"It's not going to work, Agara. Please, let go of me."

"What isn't going to work?" he asked, and there was no mockery in his tone of voice. He knew he could smooth things over with her. He had always done that.

"Angelina, you used to like me very much," he added.

Of course he didn't let go of her. He didn't travel this far in search of her only to be dismissed just like that.

"Agara, please stop and let us talk. You haven't cared about what I've done for the years you've been gone." She saw the change in his countenance and knew that she had voiced her mind.

"Angelina," he said, "I care about you. Whatever you believe, I always have."

He started walking toward her and was about to take her arm when she said, "Please don't." She raised her arm to ward him off. He immediately became angry.

"Is this the way you treat a brother and a husband?" he asked.

"Don't even think about getting an attitude with me. You are the one that quit me," she said, putting her hands on her hips.

He attempted to grab her hand, but she jerked away from his grasp.

"Please spare me this joke, Agara," she said angrily.

He raised his arms in defeat and backed away. "Angelina, I'm asking you to give me a second chance. Although I cannot change the past, I will work on the future," he promised.

She looked at him in surprise. "Agara, please leave," she begged him.

"I can't," he said starkly.

She burst into sobs. When she looked up and her gaze met his, she said, "Agara, by leaving me, you made a fool out of me before my parents and the community. You gave away your claim on me when you deserted me, do you understand?"

She looked away from the memories of his manly attractions, mad at herself for even bothering with the discussion.

"I want you back, Angelina. You belong to me," he added gently.

"That was a long time ago, Agara."

"For life, we belong to each other. I can't walk away without you, Angelina."

"Is it so hard now? Years ago it wasn't?" she challenged him.

"Why are you talking like that, Angelina?" he asked.

"Like what?"

"Like we never had a history with one another," he said.

"Now you think you had a history?" she replied sarcastically.

"Don't we?"

"Yes. We do. It is the kind that I would like to forget."

Then there was silence. He took her hands and looked into her face.

"Tell me, Angelina, that there is no chemistry between us now. Tell me that you don't remember that night at the Potompo field. Can you tell me, Angelina, that you don't want to feel my crotch again like you did on that night? Have you forgotten?"

He took her breasts and massaged them with lazy motions that hypnotized and seduced. From his lips flowed words in a thrilling litany that fell like love songs on her ears. She heard in his voice the agony and hunger of unfulfilled desire. He fondled her breasts and teased the crowns with his fingers. She knew then that if she didn't stop him, she would be lost. She pushed herself free of his seduction.

"No, Agara. We can't."

"Why?"

"I'm not ready for it."

While the seconds ticked by, they stared at each other.

"A man knows when he finds a good woman, Angelina," he said. "And he's a fool when he lets her go," he added.

She looked at him and smiled. "Agara, what makes you think you found a good woman?"

"Angelina, my dear, we were together for many days. I know what it was like to hold you in my arms and how you gave yourself completely to me when I needed you more than I needed any woman in my life."

Angelina had always thought herself too level-headed to be swayed by smooth talk and a seductive smile, but she was having too good a time to rebuff him. She decided to keep the conversation on a friendly and flirtatious basis. She nodded her head. She felt herself weakening, but didn't know whether to agree or disagree.

Agara continued. "Oh, yes, Angelina. You are a good woman, and my lawful wife, according to the tradition of the land."

"Agara, flattery won't get you anywhere this time around."

"Yes, it will. It did before and it will again," he said jokingly.

"I hardly knew you when it all began," she reminded him.

"Does that mean you would have let just any man make love to you at the Potompo celebration that night? Just any man, Angelina?"

It was too much for her. She lost her temper and self-control in a flash of fury. Her palm lashed out, hitting the side of his face. For a moment, silence hung between them. And then Agara said, "I deserve what came to me."

For her part, Angelina felt an instinctive urge to flee, as if her life depended on it. But pride made flight impossible. Instead, she faced the fugitive. She felt good seeing the growing frustration in him. She wanted him to realize that she was no longer ready to be taken for a ride. She was standing on her own two feet. Despite her reservations and determination not to remain in love with him, Agara had somehow managed to slip past her guard and found his way back into her heart. Staring at him, she thought she hated him. But her love for him had removed the hate. She felt that it was not an accidental encounter; the gods planned it.

She was happy to see him again, but suppressed the feeling. The mere sight of him, even after all these years, still brought a smile to her lips. She took in a breath, held it, and slowly let it go, as if letting go of the pain. While she was glad to see him again, she had to listen to caution, which said, "Go easy this time." She knew that she always felt a sort of excitement in his company, but she could not be sure of him now. Agara's expertise in bed had been very irresistible to her. Her decision this time would not depend on this sucker's good lovemaking, she wanted to know more about him. She had to go slowly, because once she'd dug her heels in, it would take a crowbar to pry them loose this time.

What a fool I have been. This is the third occasion that I'm meeting this man. If he leaves, I'll never be able to look him in the eye again, she thought. The inevitable occurred on this third night. None of her lectures to herself, and none of her mental preparation, readied her to handle the situation when the moment arrived.

She raised her face, and looking at him said, "Agara, you shouldn't have come after me again. I'm trying to move forward with my life. Can't you understand?"

They stared at each other for a moment, neither of them ready to speak.

She sighed, "I repeat, you shouldn't have come back," she admonished uneasily.

Suddenly, she began to wonder how she would end this third time of his return to her.

"I had no choice, Angelina," he stated simply.

Restlessly, her body reacting uneasily to his words. She moved one hand in an impatient arc and swung at him. He ducked the blow.

"What do you want from me this time? To just take me to bed? Is that what you need to satisfy your manly ego? If so, you can't have it. Good night, Agara," she said firmly.

Realizing that she was determined to send him away, he wished her good night and left the house, his spirit defeated.

She took another swig of her soft drink, which was laced with whisky. She undressed and crawled into bed. She had had enough of Agara. She could not sleep that night; all she could do was stare at the ceiling. She felt that Agara was being genuine, but there had been other times when she thought he was being genuine, but he had disappeared and then reappeared.

"What next?" she asked herself. "I love him, but I have no way of knowing if he has come to stay this time. I can't trust him, but I'm married to him. He just has to earn my trust this time."

Chapter 18

Friday, Angelina took a day off to stay with Agara. He came to her house, and she prepared lunch. They started chatting about different subjects. He settled down and brought out his guitar. She watched as he got himself together to entertain her. He looked over the guitar, strummed once, and adjusted two strings. He strummed again, and this time it sounded about right. He began to play soft music. He hummed for a little while at first, then he began to sing, telling her how much he missed her, how sorry he was to have abandoned her for so many years.

"The gods brought us together the first time. They have reunited us again," he sang. He was asking her to take him back as the Biblical prodigal son. He looked her in the face and said, "Angelina, I bragged about you. I did so all the time while I was in the military. You are still the most charming lady I have come across."

As he spoke, she watched him and thought of the night during Potompo festival and how it had been there with him in the woods. Never before had she known such an overwhelming desire to be possessed. She thought of what her mother had told her when she lamented the disappearance of her husband. The old lady had said, "People who care about each other always find a way back after separation. It may not be on the same terms when they left, but they will usually make something that works better." Angelina nodded her head with enthusiasm at the recollection of this advice.

Agara looked at Angelina very humbly and asked, "Can we go to the hotel?"

"Why not," she answered.

As they got settled at the hotel, he kissed her again and again, and asked, "What would you like to drink?"

"Wine," she said.

"I will take care of it," he said, grabbing her hand and pulling her close. He kissed her and brought out a bottle of wine, opened it, and filled their glasses.

She sipped her wine and sat back, relaxed on the chair. He needed the drink to be able to bare his heart. When he stretched out his hand and pulled her from her chair to the couch, she went eagerly. She threw her arms around his neck, pressing her breasts to his chest. She then pulled back and looked at him observing that his mood had changed. Something had been on his mind that he had not yet shared.

"Don't look at me like that, Agara."

"Like what?" He forced a smile.

"Like you're about to be fed to the lions."

He moved closer to her. She was determined to find out about him before it was too late. He sat down and drew her close to him.

"Stop looking like a defenseless hunted animal," she said, hoping to elicit more inner conversation.

"I want to apologize for deserting you. I promise to make it up to you. Believe me, Angelina," he stammered. Perspiration trickled down his armpit. Agara always hated to apologize for anything, even when he was wrong. This was the moment of truth.

"I could not help myself," he continued. "I remember the time you asked if someone was pursuing me. I did not reply. I want you to know that for a while, I knew no stability. I moved from one village to another, from one city to another, and from one country to the next." He paused to wipe the trickles from the corners of his eyes.

"Before we got married, I realized that as a school teacher, you were making money and I was not. Angelina, you are a woman in good social and financial position. An old man in my village always told the young men that if the woman in the house was the bread winner, the man was merely her housekeeper."

"But, Agara, I never asked you for a thing."

"That's it, Angelina. Expecting me to be mooching off you because you had it and I didn't. I grew up to learn that a man should head the family and show it by being the major provider. The man of the house, when making a decision that involves household expenditure, should back it up; otherwise, what he says is mere hot air."

Oh, God help me with this man, she prayed in her heart. "All I wanted from you was love, Agara."

"I gave it to you, verbally, spiritually, and emotionally," he declared.

"Before we were married by the gods, I did not dig deep into your past. I wanted you and didn't care who or what you were. You could have been a truck pusher at the Lagos Motor Park, or a cattle driver," she said.

"You were the daughter of the most powerful chief in the Ohadum District. I had no history behind me that was worthy of writing home about," he replied.

"Mistake. I should have tried to find out about him," Angelina said in a low tone.

"Staying with you," he continued, "meant that I would be playing your stud so that you would keep me around. I could not fall for that."

"Man's ego and pride," she thought.

Part of her wanted to put on a sexy smile, but she thought it was too soon to respond. She didn't want to have to cry again if he should disappear soon after.

"I left you and fled when your father threatened to expose my family background," Agara said. "I had no place to go when I left Unaka that morning. As a vagabond, I roamed until I found myself in Lagos."

Angelina stared at him as he continued.

"The Second World War was raging in Europe, America, and North Africa. The British colonial office was recruiting Africans into the military service. I joined the military and went to do whatever I could to help. I saw wounded soldiers and shattered bodies. It scared me. I vowed to live right. Upon my return from the war, I went through a period of rehabilitation in Lagos."

He wiped the perspiration from his face. "Angelina, I never forgot you," he assured her.

She was speechless. She waited for him to continue.

"Angelina, I'm sorry for what I have put you through. Even though my past dealings with women in my home town of Oharu sent me fleeing, you are my sunshine. I cannot live without you."

Angelina stared at him, trying to read his expression. "He has another woman, or women, in Oharu. We are married," she thought.

"Are you still mad at me?" he asked.

Her lips twitched and a slow smile spread across her face. It was like the sun coming out. She just hoped that he had confessed all his sins and was ready for absolution. She now knew who she married—a man who was crazy about sex and one who liked women in quantum and variety; a man known for his sexual conquests. They were united in marriage by the gods and only death could separate them. She had to bear with him.

"I knew you had a lot on your mind," she said, as they tried to iron out their differences. "I missed you while you kept away from me," she said.

"I missed you too, Angelina."

"Apology accepted," she said, as she remembered the first day she met him at the hotel, many years ago. She had been carried away by his charming smile.

"Where do we go from here?" he asked, waiting for her to make the decision.

"I love you, Agara," she said.

He took her hand and pulled her close to his chest. He kissed her, and she kissed him back.

After they ate supper, they sat around chatting. He opened a bottle of wine, which he said he had reserved for this particular night. He poured the wine into two glasses and they drank, praying for a better today and tomorrow.

Chapter 19

"Angelina, tell me what you remember about the time we spent together," he said, trying to be nice.

Angelina hesitated before she answered. "I remember very vividly about making love. This has been uppermost in my mind. You were my first, and it was more exciting than I ever thought it would be."

She took a sip of her wine, remembering, bringing back the old feeling again.

"I remember being so scared before the intimate contact that I was trembling," she continued. "At the same time, I was excited. I'm glad you were my first, Agara."

He smiled, and she continued. "I remember one day you asked if I had a man waiting for me. When I said I did, you became insanely jealous."

"I did not want to create an unnecessary problem for you."

"But you did, Agara," she said.

"How did I?"

"When you started coming on strong, I told my mother that I did not want the man who wanted to marry me and that I was in love with you."

"What was her reaction?"

"My mother was disappointed. She did not tell my father, because she felt there was social inequity between us. As a young lady, I grew up in my father's palace. My father and the other ruling chiefs in the various compounds believed that family name and accomplishments were often the most important considerations in marriage. In some cases, these were the only considerations." She paused. "I was young and didn't know what the old people knew. I came to quietly rebel against this belief. I no longer told my parents about you because my father would not approve of his daughter marrying a man like you. As of that time, I knew you were poor and had no known past. But I loved you. I did not care who or what you were."

She paused again and Agara stared in her face.

"My father supported Zebulon Zimako as his would-be son-in-law," she resumed. "Everybody called him Z-man. I saw him as a pompous ass and a troublemaker, intoxicated by wealth. When he approached me for marriage, I did not accept him. He took my rejection very lightly. On that day, while I was entertaining the group, Z-man's evil side surfaced. I swallowed a knot of fear that had formed in my throat and threatened to close my airway. I heard him address a man who owed him just a small amount of money. What he owed Z-man was not enough to bruise the man's self-esteem down to noth-ingness. On that day, I decided that no amount of money in this world would make me marry him. I felt that a man with such verbal abuse would invariably be tempted to follow it up with physical abuse. I made up my mind that Z-man was not my choice for a husband."

She paused again. Agara was beginning to see the strong part of her he did not know.

"My mother called me and told me that my reluctance to accept Z-man as my fiancé had prompted him to come up with a plan. To avoid my falling in love and marrying beneath my dignity, Z-man had scheduled for a traditional engagement ceremony. It was going to be a big occasion. He had proposed to hold a very high society traditional engagement ceremony that would involve known prominent men and women throughout the district and the country. It would be unprecedented."

"What was your reaction?" Agara asked.

"I felt a constriction in my chest. It squeezed my throat as well, so much that I could hardly speak. The knowledge of this arrangement behind my back put me under undue stress. I took a deep breath and calmed down. I could not think of how to get out of it. Z-man, with all his money, wanted to use the oc-casion to show off his wealth. I knew that he would not agree to postpone it. He loved being the center of attention. 'It's now or never,' I vowed. 'When does Z-man plan to carry out the engagement party?' I asked my mother. 'Two weeks after the Potompo festival,' the old lady replied. 'What is the matter?' my mother asked. 'Nothing is the matter, Mother. I'm just tired,' I lied. My head was burning with rage. After my mother left, I thought, 'This is it. I will have to come up with a plan of my own. Z-man is not going to force me into marrying him. I don't love him. But can I outfox the fox? I wondered. From that day on, my stress level increased.'"

Agara continued to listen to what he had put his wife through.

"Z-man could not believe that I would reject him with all his wealth. He moved on with his surprise plan. Occasionally, I wanted my parents to bring pressure on him to postpone the engagement party, to give me time to rethink my decision, but I knew that Z-man would not buy it. He was too intoxicated with his riches. He had become a conceited bastard, I thought. I took a deep breath. I would have to do something. May Kamalu, the god of Thunder help me," I had prayed.

Agara kissed her and smiled as she continued.

"A day after Z-man left for Calabar, on a business trip, you showed up at the Newtown Hotel in Unaka, where I was the manager."

Agara squeezed her hand and moved closer to her. She put her hand through his arm, cradling it, and rested her head on his shoulder.

"Agara, I had never met anyone like you before," she whispered. She then lifted her head from his shoulders and looked directly at him. "Agara, I loved you more during the two weeks we were together than I have ever loved anyone," she said.

There was silence as they tried to undo the twelve years of separation. They were sensing a change since they met again.

Agara got up and moved toward the window. "I wish my letters had reached you," he said. "I wrote you while in Lagos, letting you know how much I missed you; that I was going into the military and that you should pray for my safe return to you."

Angelina smiled. "At least he thought of me," she whispered.

"My mother got the information that you had joined the military. I became afraid for your life. I knew that once one joined the military, death is on the calendar. I cried, but had faith. When I didn't hear from you after the war ended, I didn't know what else to think. One day, while talking to Auntie Mary about your disappearance, she told me that she was not surprised that you ran away once you got what your heart desired. Auntie went on to say that your desertion should remind me from time to time that none of my affection or intimacy meant anything to you."

Agara shook his head on hearing that.

"I didn't believe that was the case. But after pondering over her statement, I began to wonder whether the event of the Potompo festival meant more to me than you."

Agara looked away from her.

"Then, in time, the hurt began to fade and it became easier to just let it go," she continued.

Agara shook his head.

"I love you, Agara. Six years after you fled, my father, sensing that his time was about to run out, sent me on a vacation to England." Tears sprang from her eyes as she said, "I met a man."

Agara shook his head. She did not elaborate. He thought, "Don't ask questions you don't want answers to."

"Agara, can you understand what six years of celibacy does to a human being? Even to an animal that had been caged for many years?" She paused and sobbed. "Each time I met a handsome man, I found myself wishing you were around. But you had gone on with your life. The temptation became irresistible. Agara, I love you now, and I always have, more than you can imagine."

She took another swallow of the wine and began to feel its effect. She held his hand. But it wasn't just the wine that made her hold tight to Agara. She was determined to confess her guilt to the man she loved. After she told him of her escapade in London, Agara was livid. She expected him to be if he loved her.

"I admire your honesty, Angelina," he said. "I apologize for leading you into temptation," he continued. He looked at his wife and she said, "Forgive my trespass."

Agara pulled her to him and kissed her. "The gods brought us together the first time. They separated us, but the stars have changed and we are back together for good," he whispered.

She leaned into him and felt his body, his arms tightly around her. Her body began to tremble with the same anticipation she felt at the Potompo festival, when they first came together. Like the gods had stepped in again, their years apart didn't matter anymore. He kissed her softly, and she kissed him back.

Angelina's inner turmoil was suddenly resolved, as it became clear that she couldn't let him go without making love to him. He had shown signs that he cared—he had come back to find her. She clasped her arms around his neck and gazed up at him with luminous eyes.

"Angelina, I love you with all my heart."

This was the admission she wanted to hear. His hands cupped her bottom, urging her hips against his. She tightened her arms around his neck and strained to get even closer. At their intimate touch, she cried out in a voice choked with desire. He was back after many years. Nothing mattered that moment. She clung to him as if he were the only reliable thing in her world, and they merged into a single trembling entity. For an unknown time, there was only silence in the room. They needed each other.

She took his hands and led them to her breasts, and he gently caressed them. They undressed each other and their bodies finally came together, trembling with the memory of what they had once shared together at the Potompo celebration.

When Angelina got up Agara said he was struck by her beauty. He crooked his finger, beckoning her. She moved to him and they lay back. They finally joined as one and held each other tightly, letting the twelve years of separation dissolve in their lovemaking. They spent the day making up for their years of separation.

The next morning, Angelina cooked a breakfast of fried plantains, fried yam, beef stew, and coffee. As soon as they finished eating, they made love again, a powerful confirmation of what they had shared the previous night. They showered together and got dressed. Agara held Angelina and they kissed. Her eyes brimmed with tears when they finally released each other. She smiled nervously as she wiped the tears from the corners of her eyes. She pulled back to look into his blue eyes. For the first time, she paid attention to the color of his eyes. She wondered how he had blue eyes. She did not want to pursue that now, she would find out later.

"Agara, you haven't come to let me know that you can have me whenever and wherever you want me, have you?"

"I'm here for good, Angelina."

"I'm glad you came back. Welcome back to my life."

Agara looked at her, thinking that she was still very beautiful. He had seen many beautiful women parade through his life, but none would compare to her in beauty, intelligence, confidence, passion, strength of spirit, and honesty of purpose.

"How is your father?" he asked.

"He's dead."

"Recently?" he asked.

"He passed away six years ago, and my mother passed away six months after him."

Immediately, her countenance changed. She sat on the sofa with her face in her hands. She looked distraught. Agara watched her get up and pull her father's picture from the wall. She looked at it and shook her head. "I cannot believe he's gone," she murmured. "It seems to me, even at old age, that he was here for a short time, and he's gone for a long time." Then she placed the picture back on the wall and sat back.

Agara sat beside her.

"That's life," Agara said. All he could do was look into her eyes and see the agony of loss.

"My father was a very caring man, you know?" she said, looking at Agara. "I miss him and will carry this memory for life," she said.

"I'm sorry," Agara said softly, knowing how much her parents loved her.

She felt the tears welling in her eyes and said, "Wait a minute." She excused herself and went into the bathroom. She looked herself in the mirror and was satisfied with her appearance. She pushed her breasts up to reveal more cleavage. When she joined Agara again, he kissed her fondly.

"Agara, after my mother passed away, I was looking through her box of clothing when I saw this letter from you. She opened it and read it again:

> *My dear Angelina. It has been a month, but it seems like years since I fled. I'm going into the military, WWII. I will miss you.*
> *Your husband,*
> *Agara.*

She started sobbing, and Agara held her close and kissed her. They laughed.

"Agara, join me for breakfast in the morning."

"I'll be here." He kissed her and went back to the hotel.

Chapter 20

The next morning, Angelina was up early. After they made up last night, she would have liked Agara to move into her house, but his ego would not let him reside there. Like men in the village, a man thirty years or more who lives with his parents is said to be homeless, because he has nothing to show; likewise, if he lives with a woman who is the provider, he is regarded as a kept man.

Angelina had not slept much during the night. Although she had thought of Agara and wondered how he would take the news of his daughter, Sochima, nothing had prepared her for his return. She went to Auntie Mary's house and brought Sochima home a day before she was due to go back to school. She prepared breakfast, and before the food was ready, Agara walked in. Angelina sighed. As Agara and she were at the breakfast table, she suddenly stopped talking.

"Sochima," she called.

"Coming, Mother," Sochima answered. At age eleven, Sochima had style and grace of movement. When she walked into the parlor, Agara froze. His mouth went dry. There was something about Sochima, something in her stance, in the way she moved, that reminded him of his mother, Apuna.

"My God!" Agara exclaimed. "She looks just like my mother," he shouted joyfully.

Agara's mother was beautiful. She had big brown eyes that were fringed with long eyelashes. Sochima shyly greeted her mother and the strange man in their house.

"Sochima, meet Agara, from Oharu," she introduced them.

"Agara, meet my daughter."

"Hello, Mr. Agara!"

"How are you, my little girl?"

"I'm fine, sir," Sochima responded courteously.

Agara's mind began to race and so many questions popped up in his mind. Knowing that Agara would have something to say, Angelina quickly asked Sochima to go back to her room. She smiled at Agara and started walking back to her room. She turned the doorknob and looked back. Instinctively, she smiled at Agara again, her blue eyes focusing on her father. As the door closed behind Sochima, there was a moment of silence, which was broken by Agara as he said, "I want to know about Sochima."

"Why?"

"She is our daughter."

"No!" Angelina braced herself to meet his gaze. "I don't comprehend what you mean, Agara."

"Don't you, really?" His voice was dangerous.

At that moment, Sochima came out of her room and went to play basketball with her friends who were from her school. As she was leaving the house, Agara stared at her with pleasure. She had his features and his build. No sooner has Sochima left the house than Agara rose to his feet and grabbed Angelina. He shook her hard.

"Tell me the truth, Angelina," he demanded.

"Let go of me, Agara!" She struggled to free herself.

"Not until you tell me the truth, Angelina."

His eyes burned into hers and his fingers dug into her arms. She felt as if she were drowning in the fury of his eyes. She tried to summon the strength to defy him. Her body tensed. She was ready to fight him. He saw the anger in her eyes and stood squarely to face her.

Angelina lowered her head and asked, "Can't we leave this alone?"

"No, we can't," he said, shaking his head and adding, "I want the truth now, Angelina."

"Yes," she answered. "She is our daughter."

"Have you told her about her father?"

"What difference would it have made, Agara? You left as soon as you satisfied your emotions. There was no trace of you; only memories of moments shared with you."

"Angelina, Sochima has to know her biological father," he stated emphatically, then he paused. He did not know his own biological father. His mother was not joking when she said that his real father had fled before he was born. The man had satisfied his desires with her and vamoosed. He sighed as he stared at Angelina.

"No!" she cried. "Her biological father has no love for family."

"Look, Angelina, Sochima has a right to know her real father," he said, very calmly, adding, "I feel sorry for what I put you through."

She was moved by his apologetic statement. "Agara, I wanted you as much as you wanted me. On that night of the festival, for the gods of fecundity, I threw myself on you."

Angelina was now in a dilemma. How was she to approach her daughter and say, "Sochima, Chief Oyinatu was not your father, but your grandfather."

Then she broke into tears. Sochima had learned that children traditionally bore their father's name, unless the child's mother did not know who got her pregnant. Agara pulled her into his arms and held her. Sochima had been the most important person in her life.

After Agara had put Angelina in the family way and disappeared, her father had felt very disappointed. Just before her father died, the old man had asked the gods to grant his daughter peace of mind at some point in her life. Her mother stood by her, although she was equally disappointed. The tears came again, and not realizing it, Angelina clung to Agara. She wept for the lost years, for herself, and for Sochima.

That afternoon, Angelina took Agara to her father's home. Agara recognized everywhere. She took him to the room where they slept some years ago. He immediately went straight to the window through which he escaped that night. She watched him, and shaking her head, she broke down into sobs.

"Agara, you have not come to do this to me again. Have you?"

He held her tenderly and kissed her.

"It's all right, Angelina," Agara whispered in her ear.

When he pulled her close to him, she was lost. She could feel the beat of his heart against her breasts. His body was warm against hers and his hands touched her gently.

"Tell me, Agara, that you aren't going to leave me again," she whispered against his ears.

"I'll not leave you again, Angelina," he promised.

They left her late father's home and went back to Angelina's house.

Agara thought back to how he had run away from the woman who had been so nice to him. What could he do to compensate her for the hardship of raising the child that he fathered?

"What are your plans now, Agara? Are you still on the run from your harem in Oharu?"

As if brushing away a fly, Agara swept away the second question.

"I plan to take you and our daughter back to Oharu, my hometown."

She stared at him, and all the resentment she'd felt several years ago came rushing back. He had not asked if she would be willing to go back with him. She'd hated him after he left her, and she hated him now for his uncompromising attitude. She bent her head down, unable to believe what was happening to her. When she looked up and saw him staring at her, she became very serious.

"Agara, you hurt me and my daughter very badly by running away."

"Listen, Angelina—" He shifted his weight from one foot to the next. "I never meant to hurt anyone," he said.

Angelina had no idea what miracle brought Agara back to her, but she thanked the heavens for it. Agara took her hand and stood, smoothing it with slow firm strokes, then he put his arms around her and she said, "Thank you, Agara, for coming back."

"Very well. Angelina, the pleasure is mine."

"Agara," she said, "Sochima needs to know about you. She will now know her real father. Her paternal past will no longer be unknown. You will no longer be fictitious to her."

Agara got up, held Angelina's hand, and they kissed and hugged each other.

After Agara went back to the hotel, Sochima came in and saw her mother sitting on the sofa and smiling.

"What is on your mind, Mother?" she asked.

"Something I need to talk to you about," she replied, and took a deep breath. "I want to talk about your father."

"My father? Chief Oyinatu of Unaka?" Sochima looked puzzled. "I have never heard you mention anyone else besides the late chief."

"I know, Sochima, my dear." Her palms got wet and she rubbed them on her wrapper.

"Why didn't you tell me about him before now?" Sochima asked.

"I guess because he ran away from you and me and I thought he would always remain a shadowy figure to you. If I had a picture of him, it would have been different."

"How did you meet him?" Sochima asked.

"He spent sometime here during the Potompo festival and we celebrated the occasion together."

"Did you know him well?"

"I thought I did, rather, I was just getting to know him when he left without a word. But, Sochima, your father was fun. Although I became mad at him for abandoning me when I most needed him, I never regretted the time we spent together. He was an exciting young man."

"Were you married to him? Surely not. That's why you always told me that your father was my father, as if you and I are sisters. I had been wondering about this because in this culture, children want to bear their father's family name. My grandfather, Chief Oyinatu, taught me to respect tradition."

"You are right, Sochima," her mother replied.

"My grandfather once told me a story about a young girl who unknowingly dated her half-brother. She almost married him because they bore different family names. Her mother, in a timely manner, stepped in and told her that they were related. Now I know why Grandpa told me the story. The old man knew that the truth would come out eventually, and I thank him for it," Sochima said.

"Sochima, according to the laws of the land, a child born as a result of the union between a man and a woman during the Potompo festival is not an illegitimate child. We were married by the god of fecundity. The marriage is binding for life. It does not make room for divorce." Angelina broke down and started crying. "I did not explain the circumstances surrounding your birth to you because I thought I was doing the best thing for you. I should have leveled with you. I made a mistake by thinking that there was only one chance in ten thousand that you would never meet him. It's a small world."

Sochima left the parlor and went into her room.

"I want to talk about my father," Sochima repeated and burst into sobs.

She did not stop crying or open her eyes. When Angelina walked into Sochima's room, she knew Sochima was terribly upset. It was natural that she would be. Angelina decided to let a little time go by before talking to her.

Sochima and I have always been close. This revelation isn't going to change it. She is my life; she is all that I have, Angelina told herself.

Later, Angelina went to the hotel to see Agara. There, she met Jacob. While Agara was taking a shower, she told Jacob about her meeting with Agara.

"Does Sochima know that Agara is her father?"

"Yes," she said, nodding.

"What did she say?"

"It was a shock to her, but she will get over it. Sochima did tell me that there were some questions she would like to ask her so-called-father that she had not known."

"I will come shortly and talk to her," Jacob said.

While waiting for Agara to finish showering, Angelina made up her mind that she would take him back without any reservations. "There is no garden without weeds," she told herself. But she needed time to absorb the shock of his coming back to her. When Agara finished showering and got dressed, she joined him in the room. She took another look at him and found him still very handsome. They went to the restaurant to eat.

While they were eating, she thought about Agara. His size and strength constituted an attraction to her. His eyes were large, blue, and beautiful. Sometimes his attitude gave an impression of inattention when, and in actuality, he was listening, observing, and missing nothing. She knew he was very intelligent, and had to admit the fact that every time she was with him, she saw a new part of his personality, and what she saw, she liked.

Two hours later, Jacob came to visit Angelina and talk to Sochima, as promised. He tried to choose his words carefully, because Angelina had been the most important person in Sochima's life. There was no doubt that Sochima had thought her mother was immune to any feelings of desire. To Sochima's knowledge, Angelina had not dated any man, and was always there when she needed her. All of a sudden, she has discovered that her mother was a woman of flesh and blood. She had loved someone real, not just a shadowy figure. Jacob tried to explain to her the circumstances surrounding her birth.

"Sochima," Jacob said, "your mother didn't have a chance. Agara zeroed in on her like a hawk circling a rat. Yes, they got married during the celebration for the gods. It was the tradition of the people."

While they were talking, Agara came to the house from his hotel room.

"Agara, this is our daughter, Sochima," Angelina proudly announced.

A smile flickered in Agara's eyes. He was pleased. He slapped his legs, lowered his head and shoulders, and shook with joy and laughter. Sochima stood there, looking at a complete stranger, and the father she never knew. She took one look at Agara and explored into a tantrum of sobs. Angelina stepped closer and held her until she calmed down.

Jacob said, "Sochima, say something to your father."

"I don't feel like it," she yelled.

"What is the matter, my dear? Can't we be friends?" Agara asked.

"You can be friends with the people where you have been," she said, looking at Agara as if he had dropped from the sky.

"Come here," Agara said, moving toward her.

"Leave her alone," Jacob said, walking toward them.

Sochima looked at Agara and asked, "If my mother did not take care of me, what would have happened to me?"

To bypass the explanation of his runaway and why her mother was the only one that showed up at the Parent-Teachers' Association meetings, Agara held his daughter and apologized to her for his absence from the family and asked her to forgive him. Jacob looked at Sochima, who looked very anxious, as if she had questions that she could not ask her mother.

"What is on your mind, Sochima?" Looking at Agara she asked, "Did you marry other women?" Agara thought of the old adage, "The truth sets you free."

"I had a wife before I met your mother."

Sochima looked at her mother, who looked surprised.

"This was not the time to worry about that," Angelina thought. In his hometown, he may have a harem a sultan would envy. But she would deal with that later.

"Did you have any other children that you know of?" Sochima continued her inquiry.

"No," Agara answered.

"What have you been doing?" Sochima continued asking.

"Sochima," Angelina interrupted. "Let's cut short this inquiry."

The young girl obeyed like an obedient child. After a few more minutes of crying, she happily accepted her father with a smile. Jacob invited the family to his hotel for dinner and drinks.

The following morning, Sochima knocked at her mother's door. Angelina had been crying, and she wiped the tears away with her fingertips.

"Just a minute." A minute to take a deep breath and get a grip on herself before she said, "Yes, Sochima, come in."

Sochima looked at her mother and said, "Mother, you've been crying?"

"I'm all right now."

Sochima sat beside her mother. Looking into her eyes she said, "Mother, I'm sorry that I said those things before my father came. I didn't mean any of it, at all."

"I know."

"I don't suppose you'll ever forgive me?"

Angelina drew her daughter close and said, "Of course, I will forgive you, if you'll forgive me. I'm happy that your biological father is back and that you can identify with him."

Mother and daughter put their arms around each other and everything was all right again.

Angelina cooked a delicious meal, and Agara came and shared lunch with them before they took Sochima back to school in his Fiat.

Sochima told her friends at school about her father. She was proud to have met him. Angelina went to the school the following Monday and registered her daughter as Sochima Agara Aham. The next weekend, she got permission to visit home on Saturday. On that Saturday, Angelina watched Agara playing with his daughter in the parlor. She smiled. "A man in he house makes so much difference," she thought.

Agara took them out for lunch. As they were enjoying the meal, Angelina looked up and saw that he had been staring at her.

"Did it ever occur to you that I would come back?" Agara asked.

"I guess you expected me to be a mind reader," Angelina answered humorously. "I'm glad you didn't forget me completely," she added.

She asked Agara to tell her all he could remember since he'd dumped her for another woman.

He laughed and said, "Let me make one point clear: I want you to know that I did not dump you for anyone."

"I hope that is correct, Father," Sochima said with a smile.

As far as Angelina was concerned, Agara was a handsome hunk and she knew that the rest of the female population could not be immune to his charms.

They later took Sochima back to her dormitory. She introduced her father to some of her friends. Agara then kissed her, and he and Angelina drove back home.

"This has been one of the most pleasant outings I've had in a long time. I mean it, Angelina. Believe me," Agara said.

His hands were already all over her. When it came to playing with a woman's body or mind, Agara was an expert. When he began to move away, she opened her eyes and gazed up at him hazily.

"What are you doing?" she asked.

"I'm leaving for a little while," he answered.

She sighed disgustingly. She could not disguise the disappointment on her face. She watched him open the door and leave.

What does he think I am? Angelina thought, some little girl he can command and order around? Stay here and wait for him? For what? If he thinks the next time he comes here I will be at the door to receive him, he better forget it. He left once before and did not come back.

When she heard his knock at the door, her heart jumped into her throat. He came in with a packet containing gifts of jewelry and clothing he had bought for her. He also took out a bottle of wine that he brought with him.

He told her that he had reserved the wine for this particular occasion and had looked forward to their reunion. He poured the wine and passed one to Angelina.

"To a wonderful reunion and a happy future for both of us," Agara said, lifting his glass to hers.

"Forever," she said as they clinked glasses and sipped the wine.

"Until death do us part," he said. "You like the wine?" he added.

"Very much," she said.

In a short while, Angelina realized that the wine was potent. The alcohol immediately went to her head. Agara started playing dance music on the gramophone he had brought back with him. He led her to the floor, and facing her, opened his arms. She moved into his embrace and he pressed her closer. On the dance floor, and in his arms, she believed that she died the morning he left her in Unaka and fled. She must have had a heart attack and died painlessly, because, surely, she was in heaven now.

They had settled their differences. They started a conversation about the townsfolk Agara had known years ago. Angelina informed him about who had married whom, who was divorced, who was prospering and who wasn't.

Before sundown, Z-man received the news that Agara had returned and was visiting with his wife. Z-man sent a message to Angelina to bring her husband for a visit. Agara had never met Z-man. She wondered what Z-man was up to. "Tell Z-man that we will be there tomorrow," Angelina said to the messenger.

"Agara, tomorrow we will visit with Zebulon Zimako. He is the man who wanted to marry me," Angelina said.

"I remember you mentioned his name. What kind of man is he?" Agara asked.

"He is rich. He has a hot temper. He acquired his riches in a short time."

"Did he do it legally?" Agara asked.

"Who knows? He pinches pennies, has got power, and uses it."

Agara sighed.

Angelina said, "We will overcome."

Chapter 21

For their visit to Z-man's, Angelina took time to dress herself.

Agara looked at her and smiled satisfactorily. "That's a really knockout outfit you're wearing Angelina," he complimented her.

"Thanks," she said with a smile. "I like it." It was one of the dresses Agara gave her the day before.

Agara wore an expensive wrapper and a collarless shirt. They left Unaka for Aloma in Agara's old Fiat, which poured smoke from the tailpipe. At the gate to Z-man's compound, the gatekeeper stopped Agara.

"Park your little old car outside the gate," the man commanded. "Only expensive cars are allowed beyond this point," he continued.

Reluctantly, Agara took the insult. He parked his car in the spot the gatekeeper showed him and cut off the engine, which made a loud popping sound. Agara looked at Angelina and said, "I'll have the carburetor serviced as soon as we get back."

Angelina was a strong woman. She didn't care about the car. Her mind was on the visit, which had already started badly.

The gatekeeper knew Angelina and immediately swung the gate open and ushered her and her husband into the compound. Z-man's new Mercedes Benz was parked in front of the house. When they entered the house, Z-man was chomping on a fat cigar, which he rolled from one corner of his mouth to the other.

"Welcome to my home, Angelina," Z-man said, looking at Angelina with an angelic smile and devilish eyes. He turned to look at Agara. The smile on his face was queer, as if the muscles of his face were not used to smiling and the exercise was causing him pain. On seeing Agara for the first time, Z-man became livid. "This man has no known name, money, or prestige," Z-man thought. Like a residual poison, hate and resentment crept through his body every time he remembered how stupidly confident he was that Angelina would not dare disappoint his plan. "What an idiot I was!" he thought. He had been the Goliath faced by a young David, struck down with a slingshot.

Agara looked around. Sitting in the special guest bar area were three men, each with a bottle of champagne opened in front of him. Ignoring Agara, Z-man introduced Angelina as the daughter of his good old friend Chief Oyinatu of Unaka. Agara turned to Angelina and looked at her as if to say, "I have not been introduced." She saw her husband looking at Z-man where he stood, his feet slightly apart, a stance that suggested arrogance and power.

Z-man smiled cunningly. The man was big boned and muscled, but wasn't exactly fat. "Poor fellow, sorry that I forgot to introduce you," Z-man said after a long moment. But his words were without genuine meaning, phrased in politeness and lacking in sincere apology. He stuck out his meaty hand and grabbed hold of Agara's and shook it as if he were swinging an ax. "I'm Zebulon Zimako. They call me Z-man."

"I'm glad to meet you, Mr. Z-man," Agara said.

"You should address me as sir," Z-man replied. He was arrogant, conceited, and egotistical. He then turned to his friends and, pointing a finger at Agara, said, "This is the son of a devil who got Chief Oyinatu's daughter pregnant and fled without so much as a 'Can I have the hand of your daughter in marriage.'"

"The bastard," one of them remarked.

"It is easy to judge someone when you do not know him," Angelina thought to herself.

"Should we, the friends of the late Chief Oyinatu, accept him just like that?" Z-man asked.

"No," the three men answered in unison.

Z-man had always been greedy, selfish, and proud of his accumulated riches. Yet he would give away anything he owned in exchange for Angelina's body, soul, and mind.

One of Z-man's friends, Dike, stretched out his hand and in shaking Agara's hand, gripped it like a gorilla. He said to Agara, "Mr. whatever your name is, we don't do things like that in my hometown, Mbenoha, home of the ancient brave warriors."

Agara stood there watching what was coming.

"Even though you got the girl during traditional festival, you should have been ready to come forward with the necessary dowry," Dike said.

"Under the circumstance that we got married, it was not necessary," Agara replied.

"Payment of dowry is never waived, under any circumstances," Dike said. "I have the good mind to take you out to the back of this house, out in the den of iniquity, and beat you thoroughly. And if you should get up after that, I would beat on you some more until you saw stars in your eyes," Dike continued taunting. All the men burst into laughter.

Agara felt humiliated. He was in a rage. Angelina suspected what was coming. Before she could reach out to stop him, Agara was pointing his finger at Dike.

"Back off, Dike," Agara shouted.

Dike stepped forward and confronted Agara. In the twinkle of an eye, Dike's fist had shot out and connected with Agara's jaw. It knocked him backwards, but Agara, a war veteran, had braced himself for the blow. He stayed on his feet. Dike struck him again and again.

He who seeks a quarrel will find it. Agara's instincts as a guerrilla fighter during WWII had been awakened. "Do not be a mouse, or the cat will eat you," he thought quickly and went to his attacker with a vengeance. He lunged at Dike, grabbed him by the front of his shirt, and plunged his fist into his stomach. Dike fell backwards and hit the bar table, knocking bottles of champagne down. Before Dike had a chance to recover, Agara's fist slammed into his chin. At that moments, fists and feet were flying. The two men grappled, striking stunning blows at each other, their noses bleeding and eyes bloodshot.

Angelina rushed into the two-man melee and wedged herself between them.

"Will you stop it now, both of you?" she screamed.

Angelina attempted to grab Dike's arm as he stumbled backwards, but his hand shot up to cover his stinging face. She reached for his arm again and he shook her off easily, his face mottled with rage at his being ordered to back off and having been knocked down.

Agara grabbed his wife and pulled her back. Z-man was lost in thought. The family of Chief Oyinatu had started regarding him as a would-be son-in-law when, out of nowhere, somehow, Agara snuck in when he wasn't looking, swept Angelina off her feet and married her without consulting the family. Z-man was very disappointed and bitter with Agara for succeeding where he failed. He would not forgive Agara for it.

When Angelina could not take it anymore, she lost the temper Z-man never knew she had. She was standing between the two fighters, who were panting for breath and swabbing at bleeding cuts. "My God, have both of you lost your minds? Who gave you the authority to defend my love life?" she questioned, her breath coming in angry gasps. "This is my life and I will live it my way, without interference. All of you, butt out! I'm the one who decided who I married," she said, looking at Z-man. "Let somebody hit Agara again and I will take out his eyeballs with my fingernails," she warned.

Z-man stared at her. Her unexpected violent utterances surprised everyone in the room. Z-man said, "Angelina, you have your whole life ahead of you. You have waited for this runaway bastard until he finally came back, for whatever reason."

"Mr. Z-man, I was married to this man and I'm still married to him," she declared emphatically.

"You got trapped into marrying this womanizer during the festival," Z-man said grudgingly.

"I was not trapped," she maintained. "I chose my love; I love my choice. I went to him willingly."

Agara looked at Dike and, with the fury of a WWII veteran, said, "Because I stepped into the trap which Mr. Zimako set up, I deserve the blows you gave me, and I accept them. But let me warn you that if you dare try it again, I will change you forever." Still mad as hell, Agara turned to Angelina and said, "As for you, my dear wife, I don't need you to defend me. I will fight my own battles with the enemy"; Mr. Zebulon Zimako he meant. "I now know where he stands in relation to you. I know why we came here, to meet him for the first time. I will not fight him in his house. I have seen the snake in the grass in my yard. I will keep the grass cut low so that I can see it when it raises its head."

The cold reception and remark had churned Agara's stomach. Angelina knew exactly what Agara was thinking from the looks he gave her. His were accusing eyes; warnings, if not outright threats. He was definitely displeased. She felt like an idiot to have taken him to visit the man who had wanted her for a wife and was rejected. "All I had wanted to do was to be friendly with Mr. Zimako, my late father's family friend. But in the process, I had turned Agara's life upside down," she thought.

As if to rub it in more, Z-man offered beer to Agara and wine to Angelina. Agara looked in the direction where the bottles of champagne were setting. He declined the offer unless it was champagne.

"Agara," Z-man replied, smiling proudly, "your wealth has not reach champagne level."

The other three men burst into laughter. Angelina felt the financial blow.

Agara turned to Zebulon Zimako and left him this message: "Do not make other people feel bad about your success."

Angelina looked at Z-man and said, "Agara staged a fight for love. At this time, love is more valuable than money. You are quite rich, all right, but you do not have to flaunt your wealth in my face and in that of Agara's. I am with him. Where the needle goes, the thread follows."

She felt very uneasy. Her husband had become devastated. She knew that any low-down bow delivered to Agara was also delivered to her.

The visit to Z-man's home was cut short. As they got up to go, obscenities poured from Agara's mouth. He turned and led his wife out of the house. With Agara's arm around Angelina's waist, Z-man stood looking at them as if he were watching them making love through their bedroom window.

Agara and Angelina returned to Unaka. After dinner at the Newtown Hotel restaurant, Agara took his wife home and returned to his room at the hotel.

That night he went to bed and drifted into the 'house of thought,' and stayed there, tossing and turning throughout the night. "Do not put much value on material things. They come and go. They bring joy and they bring sorrow," Agara thought when he calmed down. "Money is found in the midst of thorns," he reminded himself and shook his head. He had to make money, but how? "What a man will do is in his heart," the elders say. Agara then went to sleep.

In the morning, Angelina came to have breakfast with him at the hotel. Agara looked worried, and his wife knew a lot of things were going through his mind.

"Agara, tell me what you are thinking about," Angelina said.

"I'm thinking about the morning I attended Sunday school when I was young. The preacher had said that the meek would inherit the earth."

"The preacher was right," his wife said.

Agara sighed and said, "All that the meek ever inherited was the mess left behind by those strong and selfish enough to grab what they wanted and not care about the consequences. Mr. Zimako is rich and does not care about how he's treated others."

"I know," Angelina said. "He will reap what he has sowed."

Agara spent the day with his family in preparation for his return to Oharu. The family had lunch together, and visited with family, friends, and relatives in Unaka. Agara became very fond of his daughter. He thought back to what his friend Jaconda had told him while they were in the military: "Many people with an unhappy childhood turn out to be good with their children. They work hard to be good parents. It matters very much to them."

Agara kissed his wife and went back to the hotel.

Chapter 22

While in his room at the hotel, Agara poured himself a glass of whisky and sat on the sofa. He began to go over his early days. He remembered that when he was eleven years old, he fought with a boy, Samson, Adaku's son. Samson was three inches taller and ten pounds heavier than Agara; he was much older than Agara too. Agara beat the young boy up very badly.

For misbehavior such as this, Agara was brought to the office of the headmistress, Madam Elechi, a forty-year-old childless widow. She was famous for frightening children. Those were the days of teacher deification. At that time, being called to the office of the headmistress was dreaded. It meant that one was marked as incorrigible. "Master Aham, come to my office," the headmistress ordered him. When Madam Elechi used his last name, she meant business. She ordered him and Samson to her office and scolded them for fighting on school premises. The sound of her voice was as bad as the smell of vomit. Agara became very loud. The teacher warned them to be of good behavior. Agara went home and told his mother that he was in a fight in school and added a few details of his own, like some young boys would.

After classes at 2:30 p.m., Madam Elechi went to Agara's mother, Apuna, to inform her of the fight at school, because he had been to the office of the headmistress four times in the last month. This visit was like a visit with thunder and lightning. "As you know, Apuna," the headmistress started, "the school and the community demand obedience and good behavior from the children."

"Okay, go on," Apuna said.

"I'm afraid," Madam Elechi continued, "Agara is a friend of no one, including his schoolmates, and he must make a change and learn to grow happily. At school, Agara has fought playing soccer, he has fought when wrestling with his classmates, he has fought during boxing lessons, and he has fought during physical training exercise."

Apuna looked at the teacher as she continued without a smile.

"In class, Agara has fought with anyone who sat in front of him, beside him, or behind him. In any given week, he received more punishment than all his classmates put together." Madam Elechi went on to tell Apuna that she was a failure when it came to raising a child. "Agara is a discontented child, and discontent in a boy creates a sour man. Neither the school nor the community can afford a sour man," Madam Elechi informed Apuna.

The headmistress seized this opportunity to scream and threaten her with the consequences of raising a sour man in the village. Apuna felt like a helpless nonentity as Madam Elechi went on and on and on. She was verbally torn to pieces, embarrassed, and reduced to a frightened social outcast when Madam Elechi got through addressing her.

Apuna did not let it go at that. She was already having trouble raising Agara. She resented being told that she had been a failure in raising her son. She looked directly in the headmistress's eyes and asked, "Elechi, how many children do you have?"

"I was married five years, but had no children," Madam Elechi answered.

"Then you know nothing about children," Apuna replied angrily.

"Don't I? Have you forgotten that I was once a child myself? I have my childhood experiences on which to base my theories."

"Madam Elechi, you should not have said all that you verbalized, because you have no idea of what it takes to raise a child. It's a shame your husband didn't leave you with a baby. A child would provide such a comfort to you in your grief. As for me, I can simply say that anyone who says raising children is not the most difficult job in the world is not doing it right. I have never found a job harder than that of parenting. It baffles me." She had said these words before she realized that it was the most insincere display of pity she had known. She became ashamed of her utterances. That Elechi had no children was probably beyond her control, she thought. Tears of humiliation burned Apuna's eyes.

Agara listened to the headmistress as she puts his mother's feet to the heat. It pained his mother to see the way he was developing and it saddened him to see the pain he was causing her. From that moment, his life of chaos, terror, and insecurity escalated with each passing day.

Agara also recollected that when Samson's mother, Adaku, returned from the farm at 5:30 p.m., she learned that her son had been beaten up and decided to fight it out with Apuna. Adaku went to Apuna's home and the two women got into an argument. Adaku became very loud and flew off the handle, verbally reducing Apuna to a shocking level. "You are a whore," Adaku told her. "Can you tell this community whose son Agara is? Which man he favors?"

Apuna hit back hard and did not care for peace anymore. She unloaded on her opponent to the jeering of the crowd. "Adaku," Apuna said, "who are you to cast the first stone? You were married for two years without conceiving until the young pastor of Redemption Church started coming to your house to give you the sweet juice in the absence of your husband. Is Samson not a carbon copy of the pastor? Does that make you sinless? And does that not make Samson the son of a whore?"

There were shouts from the crowd, especially the women, urging the two of them to refrain from exposing themselves to the public. Apuna braced herself to meet Adaku. If Adaku was determined to fight, Apuna thought, she did not intend to leave herself undefended.

Adaku challenged Apuna to wrestle. Apuna's first reaction to the challenge was a loud burst of laughter, to the surprise and humiliation of Adaku. "Who gave you the nerve to challenge me, Adaku?" she asked her with an angry voice. Apuna grabbed Adaku and threw her on the ground and said to her, "Look at your face, ugly bitch!"

Adaku got up and challenged her again.

"Get up, Adaku, and let me teach you another lesson!" Apuna said after she threw her down a second time.

Adaku had asked for it, and if she discovered that her opponent would retaliate, perhaps she would be less inclined to fight, some onlookers thought. But Adaku got up, and all of a sudden looked scared. The crowd had become excited watching the wrestling match. Most of the people didn't care who threw the other on the ground. They just wanted to watch a fight.

Adaku challenged Apuna again, and for the third time was thrown down.

"Adaku, why do you keep on challenging Apuna?" asked an onlooker in the crowd that has gathered.

"You do not fight for your child because you are very strong!" Adaku replied, looking at the crowd, which had quieted. Her tone of voice was so soft that the anger in Apuna and that of the crowd melted away.

"I have to fight for him; he did not ask to get born," Adaku said, and left Apuna's place.

Agara also remembered that at age seventeen, his kindred expected him to enter into the new yam festival wrestling contest in his age group. But he did not want to do so. On the day of the competition, the chief and elders of the village were at the market square, where this annual event took place. The patriarch, the oldest man of the village, was there. This had to be an important event for the beloved man of the community to come to the market square. It was a tradition that he had witnessed with pride for many years.

Agara's refusal to participate in the contest became a transgression to hunt him throughout his life. His family viewed it as a disgrace, because this was one occasion where young men expressed the bravery of their family names. It enraged the old man of the village and the members of his family. He became ashamed and confused because he had let his family down. He now considered himself socially inept, physically awkward, and a loss to his family and the community.

Chapter 23

The next month, he disappeared from the village and was later seen at Victoria, in the Cameroon, where he took a job working in a banana plantation. After six months working there, the foreman, Mr. Sango, took a liking to him and started to groom him for a higher job because of his exceptional mechanical ability.

Mr. Sango invited him for lunch at his house. The man's daughter, Delilah, a school teacher, was there to help her mother prepare the food. Delilah, at twenty-two, was drop-dead beautiful.

The devil in Agara started working overtime. For the moment, the voice of caution warned, "Agara, do not cut down the tree that is giving you shade." Inside him, caution and the devil battled.

Every man must bear the consequences of his own actions. On this Saturday afternoon, he went to the home of the foreman. Delilah was home alone. She was gorgeously dressed, as if she knew Agara were coming. She knew she had Agara when he smiled. She returned the smile.

They were both attracted to each other. Agara, at eighteen, was a handsome young man. After a hurried lunch, she railroaded him into her room. Agara stared at her beautiful body as she slowly ran her fingers down his chest to the top of his trousers. She smiled at him and began to undo his fly buttons. He placed a hand on her thigh and she lifted up her dress to reveal that she was wearing nothing underneath.

She waited expectantly for him to move his hand, but he continued to stare. She leaned forward and pulled off his pants and got him on her bed. She climbed across him and lowered herself gently onto him. He remained still until she began to move slowly up and down. She took his other hand and placed it inside the top of her dress, shuddering when he first touched her breast. He just left it there, still not moving, even though her rhythm became faster and faster. Just when he wanted to shout out, he quickly pulled her down, kissing her roughly on the lips.

A few seconds later, he lay back, exhausted, wondering if he had hurt her, until he opened his eyes and saw the expression on her face. She sank on his shoulders, rolled to one side and fell into a deep sleep. He lay awake thinking that he might have died without ever experiencing such pleasure. An hour passed before he woke her.

This time, he did not remain motionless, his hands continually discovering different parts of her body. He found that he enjoyed the experience even more the second time.

When she got up, she smiled at him. "Am I going to see you next Saturday about the same time?" she asked, as she finally got dressed.

"What about your parents?" he asked.

"They will be gone shopping for the greater part of the day."

"I'll try," he said. He kissed her and took a circuitous track back to his apartment. When he got back, he was happy that there was no way of showing that he had lost his virginity. He was certain that it had not been Delilah's first sexual experience. He went into the bathroom to made sure there were no visible signs of his activities of the past two hours. He removed a touch of lipstick from the collar of his shirt.

Throughout the week, the thought of Delilah overwhelmed him. The forbidden fruit had been delicious, and he could hardly wait for the next time.

The following weekend, he was back, and she was there waiting for him. She took him in her arms and kissed him after he had finished doing his fly buttons. She looked in his face and asked, "Agara, do you love me?"

Agara paused, trying to come up with a convincing reply that wouldn't commit him. "You are a beautiful girl, Delilah," he said.

She began kissing him. "Do we have time?" he asked her.

"We certainly do," she said as she fell to her knees and began undoing his fly buttons.

As he kissed her, he decided that this would be the last time. Her father was his boss. He needed to be careful.

As she clipped on her bra and put her clothes back on, Delilah asked, "Same time next week?"

Before Agara could say anything, they were done and he put his trousers back on. She began to kiss him again and frowned as he pulled away from her grip. She was just about to press him when he said, "I'll see you next Saturday." He kissed her, opened the door, and left.

Just as the foreman was arranging to promote him and transfer him to the maintenance department, Delilah told her mother that she liked Agara very much. Mother's intuition told her that Agara had gone beyond just liking her daughter. Before the foreman got a chance to question Agara about his relationship with Delilah, he quit his job. He had bitten the hand that was feeding him. He ran back to Oharu.

He thought about how he was raised. He'd grown up poor, had been scorned and harassed by youngsters and adults who treated him as if he were as worthless as the teats on a boar hog. "Anyone who walks into the rain must not expect his body to remain dry," he thought. He got up and went to the bathroom. When he got back to bed, he resumed his thoughts.

Chapter 24

His greatest pleasure at nineteen years of age came from hanging around girls. Delilah had been a good teacher. He could no longer control his desires.

Mercy was sixteen years old, *sweet sixteen*. She was the daughter of Chief Agu of Agu Compound, Oharu. When Mercy's mother first saw her daughter talking to Agara near the compound hall, she became worried. The community had branded Agara the wildest flirt in town.

"Mercy," her mother called. "Stay away from Agara," she advised.

"Mother, he seems like a nice young man. He told me that he wanted to show me how much he liked me," she said.

"They all say that," her mother reassured her with a sad smile.

"They do?"

"Since the time of our ancestors!" her mother replied.

"Listen to me, Mercy," her mother said. "Very often, men make a nuisance of themselves, then go off, leaving messes behind for other people to clean up."

When Mercy opened her mouth in an attempt to say something, her mother silenced her with a touch to her lips.

"No need to lie, Mercy. I wasn't born yesterday," her mother said.

They both stared at each other.

"I said it's okay, and it is," her mother said.

Agara recalled that a couple of months later, Mercy came to visit him. It was a day most people had gone to the farm, and the afternoons were a time of day when every compound was deserted. The men and women who did not go to the farm had gone to the market in the neighboring village. Agara was now the community bad boy, the forbidden fruit, so to speak. That made him awfully exciting to the young girls. When Mercy entered his house, he pushed her flat on the bed.

"Let me go, please," she pleaded, twisting in his clasp.

Although she clawed and scratched his hand, her screams were shut off quickly when he came down hard on top of her, momentarily knocking the air out of her lungs. Tears of shocked surprise streamed from her eyes. She quickly closed her eyes to block out his presence, but shutting her eyes was no escape. Ignoring her plea, he moved on her, and she fought him with all her strength. She shrieked and screamed, hoping that someone, from somewhere, would come to her aid. No one did.

She lay there, her body his to do with as he liked. He took her like a savage. When he finished, he moved off her, looking at her with a smiling face, satisfied and proud of his conquest.

Mercy sobbed under the pain, the hurt, and the humiliation. She felt soiled and ashamed. She was too exhausted and weak to cry anymore. She lay back quietly, eyes closed. Her body was sore and bruised, and she longed to talk to somebody; perhaps her mother. She felt alone; she was lost in a strange house, with no one to help.

"What is fame, for a man may be shame for a woman. The man can have more than one wife, but the woman dare not have more than one husband," Mercy remembered her mother telling her one day. She went home and lay in bed. In her mind, she remembered the events and conversation that led to it. "Was he going to keep up interest, or was he going to do as her mother had warned—men often lose interest in girls who let them take advantage of them?" she wondered.

For years, Mercy had dreamed about how wonderful it would be to give oneself to one's husband, the man of your choice. She hadn't been sure just how it would feel, but she knew it must be beautiful. Giving, yes; but being taken? It hadn't been beautiful at all. It had been painful and ugly. She remembered looking at him, smiling when he moved off her and fixed himself, feeling satisfied. "How can a man feel satisfied taking what was not given to him," she wondered.

Mercy's parents returned from the farm. They learned that Agara had seduced their daughter. They fumed and threatened to run him out of the village. He was called before the chiefs and elders of the community for violating Mercy's virginity. The chief of the village gave him stern warning against raping girls. "Agara, you will be disgraced and banished from this village if you commit this act again." He was fined.

One day, Mercy came with Blessing, her best friend, to visit Agara. Mercy noticed the look that passed between Blessing and Agara. He could not control his physical desires. Mercy knew he would go after Blessing, and she became very upset. Mercy and Blessing left the house in a hurry.

A week later, Mercy came back to Agara's house.

"Why were you upset while your friend was here?" Agara asked her.

"I noticed the flirtatious look you gave Blessing," Mercy replied.

Agara knew that Mercy read his thoughts. He quickly asked her to go home and she left.

Another day, Blessing came back to visit Agara, and during this visit, she lost her virginity. She went home that night and could not sleep. She was worried. One of her friends had told her of the dangerous period for having sex. She couldn't remember whether she counted back fourteen days from the day that one expected her next period or fourteen days from one's last period. She was not very good in arithmetic in school, but whatever the count was, it was not the best time for this to have happened to her.

"Well," Blessing thought, "if this results in pregnancy, Agara will marry me. It is the price a man pays for exclusive sexual rights."

When Blessing went home one afternoon, her mother sat her down for a serious mother–daughter talk. Somehow, she had found out that something was going on between Agara and her.

"Listen to me," her mother said. "In this community, no one cares about what a man does. Even if he fell into excrement, he can get up, clean himself, dress up, and still play inyanga—*be a braggart*. But a lady has to guard her reputation."

"I'm listening mother."

"My dear, always bear in mind that a man will do anything, say anything, to get between a woman's legs, especially if she is halfway willing. Remember what I have said to you."

"I will," Blessing said, thinking it might be too late. Not heeding her mother's warning, she had slept with Agara again and again. What he offered was good.

A hard head carries a soft behind. Another month passed, and Blessing went back to visit Agara. She was attractively dressed. Like most men, she knew that Agara liked attractive women. She would make him desire her more than any other woman around, especially Mercy. She had known that men, in general, are sight stimulated. She was ready.

While she and Agara were greeting each other and chatting, Mercy came in the room. Mercy's countenance changed. There was a frown on her face.

Blessing noticed the frown on Mercy's face and said, "Look Mercy, if you have any problem with me, just say so. Don't bite your tongue. Come on, let's get it out."

"Yes, I do have a problem with you coming to look for me when you know I'm not in."

"Are we no longer friends?" Blessing asked defiantly.

"I've got your number, Blessing. I know how friends like you operate. Your time to play that game with Agara is up. Not this time around, Blessing."

"Is that right?" Blessing asked boldly.

"Yes, that's right," Mercy assured her.

"Mercy, you first introduced me to him. On that day, I asked you if it was all right for me to come over and you answered yes."

"I did because I thought you could be trusted as a friend."

"Well, it's too late to turn back from that hot stuff at his crotch," Blessing declared.

"Blessing, take it from me, a hard head carries a soft behind. We shall see."

Without wasting any time, Mercy gave out her warning: "Blessing, I do not want you in this house anymore."

"What is the matter, Mercy?" Agara asked as if he didn't know.

"Agara, my mother did not raise a fool. I'm not stupid. I read body language well. Blessing wants you by any means."

Agara stared at Mercy for a second and before he could say something, Blessing cut in. "If I do come back, what will happen, Mercy?"

"Thunder will strike you," Mercy said.

"If thunder strikes me," Blessing countered, "oral diarrhea will hit your stomach."

Mercy stared at Blessing and thought she had gone sex crazy.

"Mercy," Blessing addressed her, "you may not want me as a friend any longer, but I want to do it again with him, with no strings attached."

"Shut up, Blessing," Mercy shouted. She was seething.

"Mercy, you know when an African woman sees what she wants in a man she will go after it."

"Get out of here, Blessing. You are nothing more than a slimy sack of excrement," Mercy shouted. She was now jumping around as if she were in the boxing ring, about to knock the crazy sex-obsessed Blessing out. She did not notice the crowd that had swelled, anxious for the first punch.

Blessing threw that eat excrement look at Mercy and defiantly turned to Agara. "I'm leaving, but I will be back for more when we can do it without any interference from this village woman," Blessing said as she walked away, making sure to shake that which she inherited from her mother.

Enemies keep you on your toes. The worst kind of enemy is one who used to be a friend. A couple of days later, Mercy came to Agara's home and was shocked. She couldn't believe what her eyes witnessed. Agara was being straddled on the bed by her friend Blessing. He was too distracted to notice Mercy, who backed out of their sight and ran into the kitchen and grabbed a pestle.

"What the hell is going on here?" Mercy shouted.

Blessing jumped off Agara and turned to pick up her clothes, but Mercy was too quick for her. She had grabbed Blessing's panties and other clothes in one hand and held the pestle in the other, shaking with rage.

"Let me have my clothes," Blessing pleaded.

They were now in the living room and Agara was still putting his clothes on. Mercy opened the front door and screamed. In desperation, Blessing rushed to meet Mercy, who hit her with the pestle. Blessing was seeing stars. Mercy hit her again and she fell to the floor. She kicked Blessing on the butt and said, "Blessing, thunder has hit you." Agara came out and pushed Mercy away. He recovered Blessing's clothes and gave them to her as neighbors came to watch what was going on.

Mercy was livid. "Blessing, thunder has hit you today. This will tell you what happens when you're caught doing it with another woman's man."

When the excitement was over, Mercy cried for hours. She replayed the scene in her head over and over. She became so sick in her stomach that she started throwing up. Oral diarrhea had hit her.

That night, Mercy could not sleep. She and Blessing had been friends since childhood. Both of them knew each other's dirt. Now Blessing had thrown her dirt on Mercy, and she was not willing to forget it. Mercy vowed not to let Agara have it so easy with Blessing. She would make sure he paid dearly for playing with her heart. She knew that Agara was the village dog in heat, but she would not condone blatant disrespect for her.

Chapter 25

In the morning, Mercy did not bother to eat. She went back to Agara's home and prepared to face him. She knocked at the door, and Agara came out of the room and saw that she was in a bad mood. She looked up and asked, "Agara, why did you do this to me? Can you imagine how I felt watching you make love with my best friend right on the bed where you and I slept? Why Agara? Why?" she screamed, spitting in his face. Her breasts rose and fell in agitation. Breathing didn't come easily. Mercy became furious and went absolutely berserk, her blood heating up in her veins.

In a moment, cooking utensils thudded against the walls; lamps and lanterns shattered; pictures got knocked off the walls. The scream that echoed throughout the parlor seemed to have come straight out of hell and set the neighbors running to Agara's house. Mercy was screaming incoherently, yelling at Agara, who was now standing before her. He was about six inches from her and was fuming.

Mercy had gone into fighting mode. Even though she knew that she could not fight to the finish, she aimed at his face and struck at him, but he dodged the blow, which landed harmlessly on his chest. His hand grabbed her upper arms, thereby bruising her soft, tender flesh. She struggled, kicking her bare toes against his legs.

He punched the hell out of her. His punch knocked her down, leaving her breathless. Her head rocked back as she raised her eyes from the ground to look him in the face, then she managed to get back on her feet. When she thought the blows she rained on his chest did not feeze him, she aimed a fist and hit him in the face, bursting his lips and causing his nose to bleed profusely. Blood dripped from his mouth and nose to the floor. He stood over her, shaking with rage. His eyes widened as he grabbed her arms and raised them above her head. She stared at him, knowing that she was powerless.

As she sobbed, he coughed and sprayed more blood on the floor. Looking at his blood on the floor, he slapped her on the face, and tears flowed down from her eyes as pain moved through her body. When she moved to hit him, he grabbed her arms.

"Let go of me, Agara," she screamed and cried.

He did let go of her arms. Neighbors pleaded, but it was as if she didn't hear them. She was working herself into a frenzy. She stared into his eyes, eyes that threatened to swallow her up, but she would not let them deter her from facing him. His harsh voice somehow silenced her, only for a moment, even though her own anger had reached its boiling point. She swallowed a sudden flood of saliva that had filled her mouth, resulting from his abusive words.

Mercy ran into the bathroom and glanced at herself in the mirror. Her nose was still bleeding. She reached for toilet tissue and stuffed her nose with it. Her lower lip was split in two places and swollen to more than twice its normal size. She started crying again. Moments later, she came out of the bathroom and faced him.

"You'd think a man your size would have more pride than to pounce on a woman," she said, as anger replaced the humiliation she'd felt earlier. She hated it when a man tried to use physical strength to dominate her. Fighting was never her forte. Even though she was not a born fighter, she had lashed out at him.

"Beating and hurting a woman must be a trait in your family," she said as she found enough energy to face him again.

"It may be. What is yours? Tongue wagging?"

She ignored the remark. She had had enough. Her teeth were grinding so hard that she feared they would crack. She looked up and faced him. "Agara, you are nothing short of a greedy little boy who grabs for what he wants but has no right to it. You are a ruthless human being who takes what he wants by force. I only have contempt for you." With an ejaculation of rage, she struck out with fists and feet.

Agara held her arms. Fresh mucus ran from her nose and landed on his fingers. He immediately punched her in the side, causing her to fall to the ground. She promptly got up, struggled, and pulled away from him. She ran into a room and quickly shut the wooden door behind her and leaned against it. Agara followed after her. He forced his shoulder against the door. She could not hold it. She gave up, and Agara crashed into the room, sprawling awkwardly on the floor. Before she could find her way out of the room, Agara rose from the floor and got hold of her.

Mercy screamed and yelled. Muttering a curse, Agara let her go and she fell back across a stool, temporarily off balance by the fury of her momentum. She quickly got up and raised her hands to strike out again. Agara gripped her firmly by the arm and literally thrust her through the door. She crashed onto the ground outside, felt pain on her head and thought she had cracked her skull. She instantly fainted.

Agara was frightened. "If she has to be taken to the hospital, the doctor should start by amputating that tongue of hers," he thought. Mercy regained consciousness, picked up a rag and blew her nose.

She recalled that her mother often warned her that her sharp tongue would get her in trouble. Her cheek and jaw ached unbearably from the blows, but the wound to her pride stung more. No one had ever beaten her like he did. "What could I expect from Agara, an evil tempered brute, sired by God knows who? He is a cad, a chauvinist, with a low opinion of women," she thought.

The remembrance of that afternoon when he first seduced her invoked shameful memories. During the days that followed the seduction, she was reminded of him by the soreness between her legs. How could she have put herself in a position that allowed him to take advantage of her that day? No wonder he had no respect for her and treated her like his private slut. "Oh, well," she uttered. "Just because he's a man, and because he's stronger than I am, he thinks he can use my body any way he wants. No! I say. My mother always told me that if you make yourself a doormat, you will be stepped on. I will be no doormat for anyone. Not Agara's, not anyone's," she declared.

She then turned to Agara and said, "Try as you may, you will not be able to sleep with all the women you will meet."

"Why can't you be a good woman, Mercy?" he asked her.

"I will be your good woman as long as I look the other way while you sleep with every creature that has breasts. Right?" she asked.

"How dare you speak like that to me?" he threatened her.

"Are you so inconsiderate, so sex obsessed so –? Mercy was saying, when suddenly he brought his hand back and slammed it against her face. She fell against the wall and went to the floor.

Looking at her ribs, and watching her breathe, Agara must have thought that she didn't have enough air in her lungs. But she soon recovered.

"Perhaps you will learn that a fish will not get caught if it keeps its mouth shut. Besides, not all men want a woman who parrots his every opinion," he told her.

"Agara, you will be sorry. Real men do not measure their strength by hurting women," she said, sobbing bitterly. "You're nothing but a bully, Agara. A bully, you hear me? Why don't you hit me some more?" she shouted. Presenting the face of a confident woman, she stood and dared him to speak.

"A bully!" Agara growled like a ferocious dog. He wanted to stay angry with her, but he couldn't. "No one has ever called me a bully; a bully is always a coward," he thought. When she attempted to hit him again, Agara grabbed her hands.

"Okay, Mercy. I will turn you loose and I will stop being a bully on the condition that you promise not to hit or scratch me anymore," he said, and she left him and went into the room.

Agara followed her. He was touched. Taller than she, he stood looking down on her face, upturned toward his. The words that came out of his mouth had risen naturally to his lips, of their own accord.

"I'm sorry," he whispered.

"Really? Not minding the way I behaved?" she exclaimed. "Well, you have come to realize that force only gives you temporary advantage."

He ignored the second part of her statement. "Mercy, you merely exhibited the fire in you. You are the kind of woman who will not allow men walk all over you."

She may not have won the battle, but Agara recognized that she had the courage to fight back. He sighed and he went to the bathroom, and when he came back, he took a sip of whisky and resumed his thoughts of the past.

Chapter 26

News report of the fight between Agara and Mercy and the incident with Blessing reached the chief of the community. The compound chiefs and elder statesmen of Oharu met to discuss the problem Agara had created in the community. Agara was called to the market square. The community chief said, "Agara, your unwelcome approaches to the ladies of the community have been observed and viewed very seriously."

Agara tried to control himself. His head was buzzing with anger.

"You are hereby ordered to leave the village peacefully and not come back," the chief ordered.

"If I give the chief an inch, he will take a mile," Agara thought. He became a spitting, frothing creature, consumed by a maniacal temper. He looked like a snarling beast balked of its prey.

The community wondered what he was going to do next.

"A snake that does not exhibit a show of strength will be mistaken for a rope," he thought, as he fumed and assumed a wildcat look on his face. With his thumbs hooked in his belt loops, he stared in the faces of the chiefs and elders of the village. "This is my village. I was born and raised here," Agara said to the chief. "The man who will not demand his rights will be buried alive," he declared. Then he countered the threat. "Any attempt to bar me from staying in this community will result in my burning down the village."

"How do we tame this wild beast?" Chief Agu, Mercy's father, asked. "The tail does not wag the dog. Agara sure as hell will not cooperate and should be pushed out," the chief continued.

"This wildcat will be caged for the sake of public safety, especially the daughters of this village," the community chief said to the people.

Members of Bighead Age Group were raised to be tough. They were the watchdogs of the community. The group was instructed to take Agara to the boundary between Oharu and the neighboring village, Obidog.

As the group marched him along the road, Agara felt like a helpless bull being led to the abattoir, with no opportunity to escape. Looking at the group defiantly, he poured out his mind. "I hate all of you," he declared. "You are cowards."

This disclosure touched off the usual rounds of sneers and ridicule from the group, which refused to listen to him.

"I hate all of you," he snarled again.

"What can you do?" Keke, a member of the group asked.

Agara grabbed Keke's arm and the group stopped momentarily. Keke turned and threw a punch at Agara, who ducked, and the clenched fist flew over his shoulder. As Keke rocked forward, Agara landed an uppercut in his solar plexus with such force that Keke staggered backwards and collapsed on the ground, clutching his stomach.

The leader of the group helped Keke up from the group and commanded Agara to keep moving or else face the wrath of the group.

"I hate you!" he spat out, baring his teeth like a wild animal about to spring.

"He is the devil's son!" one of them remarked.

"He must be insane," another one remarked. "Just for asking him to leave the young ladies of the village, he pukes up his guts," the group member said.

At the designated place, the age group lifted Agara high up into the air and dropped him. He hit the ground with great force. While he was on the ground, they stared at him. One of them kicked him several times in the buttocks, but he did not react.

"Look at how Agara is fuming and shaking his head," one member of the group observed as he watched him lying on the ground. Then he turned to another member of the group and said, "Fire is cooking violence in his eyes; resistance is his ultimate goal."

Pain seared through Agara's head and he clamped his teeth together, wanting to cry out against the physical trauma being inflicted on him. But he was determined not to betray pain to anyone. He rose from the ground, grabbed one of the group members, and shook him like a caged lion would shake the bars of his prison. The group descended on him and he fell to the ground. When he rose to his feet, he took a stick from the roadside and started brandishing it before the group. The men battered him with sticks from tree branches. Their sticks rose and fell, rose and fell, again and again, until his back was sticky with blood. He went down again.

"Enough is enough," the group leader said.

As if to say not for me, one of them, Justus, crackling like a hen, hit him with a stick right on his temple. Justus had put his full weight into the swing that smashed Agara on his head. The stick vibrated in the young man's hand, as if wood had struck wood. Agara got up from the ground and unexpectedly threw Justus to the ground. Agara hit Justus with all the force he could muster. The young man fell to the ground and Agara spat on his face. At that moment, the challenge grew more complicated. Agara stood his ground, undaunted. Justus got up from the ground. While some of the men secured Agara on the ground, Justus, in turn, wielded a whip, the sound sickening as it made contact with bare flesh. Muscles rippled and blood flecked the ground.

Agara appeared to have passed out and Justus bent down to ascertain that he was still alive. At that moment, he regained consciousness, his vision blurred so that he could only make out the outline of the man.

"You are a coward, Justus. Let me handle you individually," Agara shouted from the ground.

He grabbed the man, and determined not to give up, clawed him mercilessly with his nails. Again the group descended on him, inflicting more cuts and deeper, more extensive injuries on him.

The leader of the group felt that the inhumane brutality had gone too far. But another member, popularly known among the group as the Tasmanian devil, TD, stepped forward and hit Agara, knocking him to the ground. The shouting and beating of Agara by TD was suddenly interrupted by a howl from a ferocious claw-footed beast of a dog. All members of the group turned to stare in horror at the menacing eyes of the fangs-bared black and white dog that looked like it had come from the depths of hell. It had paused to watch the inhumane treatment of Agara. One of its eyes was cocked at an awkward angle, as if it had been in a fight with another dog over a bitch.

In an amazing display of courage, the black and white behemoth came lumbering out of the woods, his great tongue lolling out like a rabid animal, his back littered with debris from his latest pillage. The canine beast leaped on TD, who was about to hit Agara more and more. The dog knocked TD to the ground, and the action of this wild beast scared the living daylights out of the group.

Seeing that the dog was poised to fight more, the leader of the group took off, shouting that it was the biggest, ugliest, and most frightful animal he'd ever seen. The rest followed as TD freed his leg from the jaws of the dog.

Agara sighed at the thought of the recollection. He took a sip of his hot drink and resumed his thoughts of his early days and what followed after his encounter with the Bighead Age Group.

Chapter 27

Despite his wounds and the brutality of the event, the flame of life still flickered feebly within Agara. For a while, he lay there unconscious. Flies buzzed, gathering on the raw flesh, and the sun burned down mercilessly on him. The dog licked Agara's wounds, chased the flies, and stood guard until he regained consciousness. He recognized the animal as Lion, his black and white puppy, now fully grown and very large—he had turned into a big monster. As a puppy, Agara thought Lion was a flop. But when the time came, seeing Agara in danger, the animal proved that it had what it took to be a hero.

Agara was covered with blood and was so weak that he could hardly stand. Looking almost dead, the harmattan wind rattled his teeth each time he opened his mouth. Slowly he rose to his feet. Along the road, he paced back and forth, as if he were searching for something but couldn't remember what it was. The animal followed him until he got near the village.

"Lion," he called his dog and patted him on the head. "I thought you were a flop," he said to the animal. Lion wagged its tail as if to say, "Never give up on anybody." The animal looked at his master and disappeared into the Sacred Forest, knowing that his job was done.

After Lion disappeared, Agara started experiencing some of the worst pain he had ever endured. He was now getting back to himself; he had been under the care of his guardian angel, which was residing in Lion.

Just before Agara entered the village, he paused and stood like a carved statue, with beaded sweat on his face. "Rather than yield to the community threat, it would be better that Kamalu, the Storm god, knocked me down dead," he vowed. He went back to his house madder than a rained on rooster. Each time he remembered the incident, it gnawed away at his very core.

In the next week or two, he began to feel better. The thought of the age group beating him up came back to him. Anger and bitterness tugged at his emotions. He felt severe pain and knew that it was because his anger had caused him to tense. As he tried to relax, his pain eased slightly and the action of the community was filed away in his memory bank for later reference.

Agara remembered that after Lion disappeared, every part of his body was sore. His eyelids were heavy. He was as puzzled about where the dog came from as he was about where it had gone. "Lion knew I missed him when he ran away and did not come back. Now he has come back to save my life at a point when I was on the borderline between life and death," he thought. He was grateful for the heroic performance of the angelic creature.

Six months later, Agara walked around the village dressed like a devil from the Evil Forest. "What is Agara up to?" many people wondered as they ran out to look at him. "He has been an unpredictable human being from childhood, and the fight with the age group has stirred fear in the minds of many people," some concerned village elders thought. In the next few days, there was an air of uneasiness over the community. Agara's confrontations with the age group and with the community had created an unpleasantness. Many in the village did not approve of the excessive rough handling that he received. No one wanted to go near him anymore.

A thought precedes action. Agara decided to carry out his threat. It was midnight when the wind coaxed out the first tongues of fire and blew them into billows of orange before the sleeping villagers knew they were in danger. Some residential buildings were ablaze. Knowing how vulnerable their own thatched roofs were to the fire, the neighbors picked up their children and ran out. The wind blew heedlessly and intensified the burning.

From where he was hiding, Agara watched the fierce advancing flames on the dry, close together, thatched roofs of the houses. Old men, women, and children who had vacated their homes stood watching as the harmattan wind turned the houses into a raging inferno. As the fire engulfed the houses, the women and children backed off because of the intense heat. They were shouting, screaming, and crying. There was deep and frustrated anger in the men, and the women registered perplexed frown on their faces.

"In a declared war, no cripple is left to be taken captive," Agara thought. Remembering that there was an old man crippled with arthritis living a few houses from the advancing flame, Agara kicked and pounded on the door until the entire household of the aged and crippled man woke up. It was easy to lose track of someone in the chaos of the fire, and the cries of the women and children. The community labored for hours, and finally put out the fire.

Agara had made good his threat to burn down houses in the community. To add salt to the wound, he ran to the police station and reported that the village was on fire. He also told the law enforcement officers that the community had pursued him in an attempt to catch him and throw him into the fire. Many of the police officers knew who he was.

The police officer sent to investigate the arson thought he had an opportunity before him to gain a reputation for action. He came to the village, questioned and frightened the first two old men he met. Scared of the uniformed man, the two old men talked nonstop.

"Did you see Agara set fire to the houses?" the police officer asked.

"No sir," the men answered.

Reverend Tobe arrived at the scene of interrogation. He looked at the big burly form of the policeman, who appeared like a determined man in uniform out to impress the public. "When one puts on the police uniform, the rest of the public is looked upon as inferior beings," Reverend Tobe thought.

In a moment, there was a densely packed crowd of men and women staring at the mean looking officer. The police officer looked at the clergyman and, although he did not have his ministerial robe on, the officer knew him. It dawned on the officer that he could not turn the situation into a scandal, especially with the clergyman on the scene.

Chapter 28

The officer finished his arson investigation, and the following week, Agara was arraigned before Magistrate Ofeke's court in Mbenoha, the capital city of Ohadum District. On the day of the court hearing, the compound chiefs were gorgeously dressed. Escorted by a police officer, and led by Chief Okaome of Oharu, they arrived at the court premises.

"Way them! Way them! Please," the policeman shouted courteously but firmly. At the sound of the police officer's voice, and at the sight of his uniform, the crowd parted, as if Moses were passing through the Red Sea. The police officer swept the village representatives through.

The community chief was carrying a walking stick. The speed with which he moved showed that the stick was more of an ornament than a necessity. The group walked into the courtroom, which was already full of men and women talking in very low tones. They were thinking and talking about Agara, the sex, crazy arsonist who had the guts to challenge the village. The balcony had been crammed to its utmost capacity. Just about everyone from Oharu and the neighboring villages was in court to hear the verdict. Those who did not make it to the courtroom stood with the huge crowd outside. A team of police officers was on hand in case the crowd became unruly.

While the court was waiting for Magistrate Ofeke's arrival, a police officer outside continued to announce that there were no more seats available in the courtroom. "The magistrate will be here very soon," the clerk announced, adding, "unless he gets tangled up talking with some female or another on his way through town. He draws women like flies."

The huge impatient crowd swayed to and fro, rapidly increasing their movements as more and more people piled up in and around the court building. Many stayed under the shade trees waiting to hear the verdict; others, who felt hungry, resorted to buying fast food: yam and beans with stew, fried yams and stew, and goat meat pepper soup.

Suddenly, the horn of the new Mercedes Benz blazed from afar as it was approaching the court premises. "The man we've been waiting an eternity for is finally here," the police officer controlling the crowd outside said in a low tone. The car pulled into the parking space reserved for the chief magistrate, and more people started finding a way to get closer to the courtroom.

The court clerk, who looked more like a jester, tapped a mallet on the table that served as a gavel. He then cleared his throat and announced with dignity, "Hear ye, hear ye, hear ye. The Magistrate Court of Mbenoha is now in session. Please rise." Everybody rose. "Please be seated," the magistrate said, and by then, no one was still standing.

"Let all ye who seek justice draw nigh," and in a low tone added, "and get disappointed," the clerk announced. The preliminary procedure of the court was observed.

During cross-examination, Agara and the village chiefs avoided each other's eyes. The community chief rose and stated, "About six or seven months ago, Agara threatened to burn down houses in Oharu community because the community did not want him to flirt with the women who were not his wives."

"What happened next?" the magistrate asked.

"Ten nights ago, Agara carried out his threat. It must have been around midnight when the town crier raced to my palace and announced that the home of one of the compound chiefs had burst into flames right before his very eyes. In no time at all, the community was the scene of a fantastic array of fire, which destroyed everything that was combustible. I have never seen anything like it, nor am I anxious to see anything like it again," the chief said. "As Agara was chased, he ran through the burning fire, and although his clothes caught fire and burned, his hair was not singed and his skin suffered no burns. We think he was sired by the devil himself," the chief continued. "In the other compounds, where the fire had not reached, every family member stood on watch like a falcon on its nest," Chief Okaome concluded.

The magistrate turned his attention to the verbal volley that went on between the two lawyers—for the community and for Agara. Mr. Chekalu, the lawyer for the village, possessed a quiet wit, unlike his flamboyant colleague, Mr. Kandu, attorney for Agara. When Attorney Chekalu called Agara to the stand and started putting the squeeze on him, the arsonist squealed like a little pig. No one in the courtroom ever knew the lawyer for the village as a desk pounder.

But Agara's attorney, Mr. Kandu, took the more aggressive and confrontational role. He was the lion in the courtroom, fighting for better settlement in favor of his client. He relentlessly backed his opponent into a corner from which there was no relief for him, until he gave him what he wanted for his client—acquittal.

As the court sat in silence, Agara pinned the magistrate with a furious eye. Before the chiefs knew what was going on, the smack of the gavel had gone out like a gunshot. A rush of murmuring voices broke from the crowd as the magistrate has returned a *not guilty* verdict and Agara was acquitted on all counts.

The village chief could not believe that Attorney Chekalu, who struck terror in the heart of any lying witness, lost the case. Immediately, the irate chief stood up and raised and aimed the club end of his chieftaincy walking stick at Agara's lawyer, who quickly hit the floor. Even the police and court messengers could not stop the disappointed villagers from rushing out of the courtroom.

"This is a justice system that isn't just. Magistrate Ofeke is inept, corrupt, and incompetent," Chief Okaome said to the police.

"Magistrate Ofeke is a weak and indecisive magistrate who seems to possess no guts at all to pronounce a serious judgment," Attorney Chekalu remarked to Chief Okaome.

"Magistrate Ofeke is always skeptical about being reversed on appeal; he is so insecure and fearful of criticism from the press that he would refuse to call any controversial case if a newsman was present in his court," the attorney for the village said.

"Even when a reporter slipped in unrecognized and the magistrate looked up and saw the person," Attorney Chekalu continued, "he would quickly call a recess and flee the bench."

After the court decision, Agara walked outside from the courtroom. The crowd surged forward, wanting to see the man who had defied the village. Agara went home holding his head high.

Time passed. Gossip has a way of traveling fast, especially if it has the potential for scandal. Two months after the court case, rumors intensified that Mercy was pregnant. Her father called Agara's stepfather, Tom Aham, and informed him that Mercy was pregnant. "Three months gone. Mercy is bawling her eyes out because your stepson, Agara knocked her up, and he hasn't been around to see her," Mercy's father said.

Tom Aham told Mercy's father that Agara would marry her.

Agara sipped his drink and resumed his thought of his early days. At this point, he was a rapist and an arsonist. He had defied the village and was regarded as one who had defecated at the shrine of his forefathers. He did not know what the community would do to him, but he had to wait and see.

Chapter 29

News of Mercy's pregnancy ran through the community and the whole Ohadum District faster than a flu epidemic. Stories of Agara's past history were told and retold in different villages around. In the eyes of the parents, Agara was up to no good. The raping of innocent young girls had become household gossip. Mothers now pulled their children inside and shut the door when they saw Agara coming. They forbade their daughters to talk to him.

One afternoon, the chief of Oharu was officially informed of Mercy's pregnancy. The chief ordered that Agara should be brought to the market square in the morning. He would be stripped naked, flogged, and disgraced.

Agara heard the action that was to be taken against him. That night he did not sleep. His thoughts began buzzing like a swarm of bees. He realized that everything he pursued only led to failure and disappointment. He decided that the time had come for him to leave the community and endure whatever hardship lay ahead of him. Self-preservation is the first law of nature.

He vowed to be like a bird in the bush—never to settle down in one place; never to leave a trace of his passage; and should a stranger come near him, he would fly away to another tree. Yes, he would run as fast as he could, never to stay in one place too long and to rest only when needed. Early in the morning he fled the village, trekking through bush paths and hiring cyclists to carry him when he got tired of walking.

On the evening of the second day, he reached Ozutown Community. He knew that the nearer he got to the town, the less likely it would be that he could afford the hotel bill. He found a small wayside hotel at the outskirts of the village. He went to the desk and asked if he could get a room. The man looked at him, nodded, and took a key from a hook behind him. He led his guest to an uncarpeted room.

Agara put his bag on the floor and stared at the little bed, the one chair, the small chest of drawers, and the battered table. By the time he turned to say,

"Thank you," the porter had already left. After he unpacked his belongings, he went into the bathroom and freshened up.

He woke the next morning as soon as the sun shone through the curtain-less window. It took him some time to wash from a bucket that had only a trickle of cold water. He decided against shaving. He dressed and went to the restaurant and had breakfast.

He went to the cattle market and watched the traders with fascination as they circled the animals, some prodding them, others simply offering opinions as to their worth. He looked vacantly at those who offered an opinion after examining the scrawny old cows. He watched as Mallam finally received an offer from a butcher for his cow, and he immediately accepted it without attempting to bargain. Money changed hands and the animal was marched to the abattoir for slaughter and sale of meat.

Agara heard Mallam tell his friend about the butcher. "After the slaughter and sale," Mallam began, "the butcher went into the local bar, where he downed several bottles of palm wine. He later left the bar, swaying from side to side until he got home and staggered past his wife and children. Within minutes he was snoring."

Agara felt sorry for the family of the butcher. "Drinking has never been good for anyone," he thought.

Agara spent the rest of the day walking round the market stalls, finding out what each stall had to offer. Some sold fruits and vegetables, while others specialized in household necessities. Most of them were willing to trade anything if they thought they could make a profit.

Agara enjoyed watching the different techniques the traders used when bargaining with their customers—some bullying, some cajoling, almost all lying about the provenance of their wares. Invariably, some of the customers ended up with a poor bargain.

The next day, he went back to the market and again began to walk around the stalls, watching the traders as they set out their wares in preparation for the day ahead. He listened as some of them traded by battering. He noticed that the position of a trader in the market was important. He stood mesmerized as he watched someone trade five big yam tubers for a hen, while another parted with two hens for a sleeping mat. Yet another trader received two bags of beans for a goat and a rooster for three young hens at the point of lay.

At the end of the day, Agara had learned that a trader's skill depended not only on the goods he had to sell, but also in his ability to convince the customer of his need for them. He also learned that the maxim in this market is, "Ask for triple and settle for double." He would never let his customer know what he was after—to sell one's ware at the highest profit. After he listened to a woman selling loin cloth, he also learned not to reply to a question with an answer, but with another question. Agara was happy when he left the market at the end of the day. He had learned something that would stay with him no matter where he went.

Agara saw the sun rise and set five times before he reached Unaka Community. He went to the Newtown Hotel. A blast of syncopated music from a gramophone was almost deafening. He met the hotel proprietor, Mr. Jacob Ikonne, who offered him accommodations.

That was twelve years ago.

Early this Saturday morning, Agara and Angelina went to Unaka Girls High School and picked up Sochima. She was now in her first year. Angelina prepared breakfast and the family ate together. The family spent the day together and had dinner. In the evening, Agara and his wife took their daughter back to the boarding school. He hugged Sochima and told her how much he loved her and promised to see her often.

"I love you, Father," Sochima said. "I love you too, my sunshine," he replied.

Angelina and Agara returned home. He opened a bottle of champagne and poured two glasses. They drank and felt happy at their reunion.

"Angelina," he said, "I'm leaving for my hometown, Oharu. The people of Oharu Community are judgmental and prejudiced. If you achieve a deed of bravery or you fall short of expectations, people will recall who your parents or grandparents were. In the village, whatever you are born to, you are stuck with it," he said.

His wife reminded him of the old saying, "Men and women are limited not by the place of their birth, not by the color of their skin, but by the size of their hope. Whatever may have been your past in your home, you can overcome it if you try."

Agara smiled. "You are my greatest inspiration," he said.

He kissed her and reluctantly she allowed him to go.

"Keep in touch," she said.

Each man is the architect of his own fate. He drove away with an agenda to make money, by any means possible, to take care of his family and to financially fight Zebulon Zimako, the rich man of Aloma.

"Heroes take risks," he told himself as he headed for his hometown after twelve years.

Chapter 30

Oharu is a small community. Somebody from one village finds out about something and tells somebody from another village, and then it's all over the district. Within a week after Agara returned to Oharu, news spread that the fugitive had returned. It had been more than twelve years since he fled the village. He met with his stepfather, who told him that his mother had passed away a year after he fled.

Agara returned from WWII with an accordion, gramophone, guitar, and a harmonica. Everybody in the village marveled at the instruments. On the first Saturday of the third month of his return, he was dressed in his army uniform. He swaggered around the community, saluting anything that moved. He felt happy.

It was like he was invited to perform for the entire village; to show off what he had learned while he was a vagabond. He went to the market square with his musical instruments and sat down on a three-legged stool. In no time at all, many had gathered around him. The community went wild with delight when he played a familiar tune on the harmonica. The young people, boys, and girls took to dancing.

After he took a break, he reached for his guitar. The gentle strumming of his guitar filled the air. He hummed for a little while at first and then began to sing. Boys and girls liked him for that. He taught the youngsters how to jive to western music. Agara beamed with smiles as he watched them having fun. From that day on, the musical equipments aroused a lot of excitement and appreciation when he played them.

Six months later, Agara purchased a horse. One day, the community watched him prepare to demonstrate his ability to ride his horse. As the horse saw him coming, it trotted to and fro, sniffing and whinnying, then it moved its ears and gave a little shiver with its skin, as if a fly had alighted on it. As he came near, the horse shook its mane, its nostrils widened, and it gave the ground a big tap with its hind hoof. The children and young adults watched as he vaulted into the saddle, swung his long leg over it, and secured his booted foot in the stirrup. The stallion pranced arrogantly before Agara pulled sternly on the reins. The animal responded immediately. After he got settled on the horse's back, the animal roared and strained its neck back, as if to make sure it was the owner on its back. He then went bounding around the community with a group of youngsters following him. He looked around and smiled. He was in control of the crowd that was following him.

One young boy hit the horse very hard with a rod and it suddenly took off. When Agara saw the animal was out of control, he jumped off and hit the ground. He was unable to get up until help came. He was taken to the hospital.

The nurse was there in no time to examine and administer first aid. "He got a good bang on the head," the nurse said. His bloodshot eyes were rolling around in his head and his tongue was hanging out of the corner of his mouth. He grunted when the nurse touched a swollen area above his ear. She applied a soothing balm, as directed by the attending doctor. She gave him painkillers, and, in a short while, he went to sleep. He drifted in and out for several hours. He had no point of reference with which to measure time. Gradually, he began to know when his blood pressure was being taken. When he woke up, the nurse tried to assess his injuries. His feet and legs appeared all right then, although he later became sore and a bit stiff. "My head hurts," he murmured as he rubbed the offending spot near the ear.

"Be still, Agara," the nurse commanded, halting his movement.

"I can't! It hurts," he murmured incoherently.

After two days, he was discharged from the hospital. Within a month, Agara was well again.

A leopard cannot change its spots. Some mothers became very apprehensive of him and concluded that he had come with musical instruments to lure their daughters. As the saying goes, once there is a crack in the foundation, the eyes of the people will always be focused on that crack, whether or not it is fixed. Agara fled the village more than twelve years ago because of his involvement with the women of this village. The community had not forgotten.

Chapter 31

Laziness does not breed success. In Oharu, Agara formed a company, Agarangelina Clearing Company. It operated at the Garden City wharf, Calabar Sea Port, and Lagos wharf. The company cleared goods at the wharf for importers and assisted exporters in moving their merchandise outside the country. The company included a network of smugglers. Speed and surprise were two key elements that marked the operation of his group, which consisted of Sango, Jeremy, and Jude.

Some remarkable sameness started to be noticed among the three young men. They became observant of everything that went on around them—the movement of strangers to and from the village, and being seen together most of the time. If anyone talked to them, they remained on the alert, looking at the person and through the person, as if they were on never-ending sentry duty. They appeared to have no trust for anybody.

Members of the group were in their early twenties. Before joining the group, these young men were pleasant, well spoken, and polite. After Agara recruited them into his operation and gave them lessons, they became different. With money in their pockets, their lives changed. You couldn't tell them anything.

During the day, Agara was out making financial deals, and during the night, his group was out delivering goods from the wharf. Because of this operation, danger lurked around every corner of the wharf at night. On the night of an operation, any mortal who ventured into the road leading to the wharf after dark was taking a chance of getting mugged.

Within one year, Agara was in money. He acquired a five-acre property at Mbenoha, the capital city of Ohadum District. It was for building his home. After clearing the site, he went to Unaka and brought Angelina to see the site. She was happy. After the visit, she went back to Unaka and arranged with an architect to draw the building plan for her. The following week the plan was ready, and work started at the site.

Six months later, Agara brought Angelina to Mbenoha. He took her to the proposed family home, currently under construction. Even at this stage of completion, the structure was very impressive. Angelina smiled contentedly. "It's going to be a beautiful home," she exclaimed joyfully.

"Do you like it?" he asked.

"I love it," she replied.

The workmen, without exception, had suspended their labors and were curiously looking at the beautiful woman with their boss. Angelina watched them admire her, and was pleased with their work. Agara prodded her forward over the rough ground and around piles of building materials toward the house. They picked their way through carefully. The workmen resumed the building activities, with drills whirring, saws shrilling, and hammers ringing.

Angelina looked back and smiled again at the fantastic work the men were doing. Some women were selling rice with stew, slices of fried yams, and plantains with stew, other women were selling water and palm wine to the workers.

They went inside the building and Angelina took note of the dining area, the kitchen, the master bedroom, the parlor, and the other rooms. She made note of what she wanted for the rooms. Through an opening intended for the window in the master bedroom, she looked out and was impressed with the scenery. When the tour ended, she said to Agara, "I think the house is going to be spectacular."

"I hope you will love it when it's finished."

"Of course I will. Don't you know that the fruits and vegetables one picks are the sweetest to that person?"

"I like your taste, Angelina," he said as he kissed her.

After inspecting the proposed home, Agara took his wife to Oharu Village, to watch the celebration of Girls Coming of Age. The main participants were at the age of puberty, and most of them were to be wedded that year. These soon-to-be women looked forward to the ceremony as an acceptance of the long established ceremony of passage to adulthood. Most girls did not let anything hinder them from participation, because they saw it as a ceremony of a lifetime. Organization and control of the ceremony was handled by the older women.

Personal adornment indicated an expression of artistic impulses. The girls painted their bodies with red and yellow earth hues and adorned themselves with strands and strands of colorful beads around their waists. The participating girls formed two groups, and each group selected a lead singer.

While the groups sang, shouted, and beat drums, the lead singer from each group unleashed a torrent of insulting maledictions toward the opposing group.

This ceremony was passed down from generation to generation, and no one harbored ill-feelings from the throwing of mock insults. Going through the ceremony made the participant the pride of her family and extended relatives. After the celebration, the girl went home and was gladly received because of the honor she had brought to her parents, family, and friends.

Agara and Angelina left after the celebration and went to Community Lake Resort for a picnic. It was a weekend treat for her. At the lake, they found a spot that Angelina liked. Agara began the chore of unloading the trunk of the vehicle. When he finished, he took a chilled bottle of beer and gulped it down in a few swallows.

When he looked up and saw that Angelina had stripped down to her bathing suit, the desire that stirred in him caused him to take another chilled drink. "God in heaven, she looks very sexy. The chest appendages look irresistible."

He moved to her and threw her on the sand. The sound he made were like those of a starving man who had just found sustenance. If they hadn't been interrupted by the arrival of a group that came to swim and have a picnic at the lake resort, anything could have happened.

After enjoying themselves swimming at the lake, Agara took his wife back to Unaka and returned to Oharu.

Chapter 32

By the end of the fourth year of Agara's return to Oharu, his mansion in Mbenoha was completed. The house had a huge standby electric generator since he couldn't depend on the electricity corporation of the nation (the ECN) for year-round electricity. Not long before the ECN had taken electricity to Oharu, Mbenoha, and the surrounding communities. The uninterrupted supply of electric to the communities threatened to undermine the high volume sale of electric generators. The companies marketing the generators saw their economic well-being sinking to an all-time low. The company directors met with the director of the ECN, and a blackout, at a prime time, commenced. Sale of electric generators rose and never came down again.

The backyard of the mansion sloped to a shallow creek that eventually emptied into the Cross River. At night, bullfrogs croaked hoarsely near the creek at the bottom of the property. Cicadas filled the breezeless air with their shrill soprano notes.

The front and backyard was beautified with flowering plants. Flowers of every variety bloomed in different places. Insects buzzed crazily and ecstatically around the profusion of blooming wildflowers, their colors so brilliant and rich they hurt the eyes. Each flower gave off a unique perfume.

Angelina came to visit just before the house was completed. She stood in the front yard, and looking around thought, "Flowers feed the soul." She loved her new home.

No yard in Ohadum District had greener grass than that which spread like carpet around the mansion. A well was drilled within the compound for the supply of water to the mansion. The yard was maintained by hired labor.

There was an old-fashioned swing, a hammock out back. It was made of sisal hemp and fastened to two iron poles on the back porch. Angelina had always been fond of porch swings because her father had one. She would sit on this swing and relax, listening to crickets chirping from their hideouts. Cicadas would begin their nightly concerts from the dense branches of the trees.

Success can bring envy. Agara's financial achievement brought him more hatred and jealousy from Z-man. It was a big threat to Z-man's position in society. Knowing that he had an enemy, Agara surrounded the mansion with two high walls. Tiger, a huge Saint Bernard, patrolled the inner gate, a watchman patrolled the outer gate with Python, a German shepherd that had a fearless expression. It was strong, agile, and well muscled. The inner and outer gates were locked at sundown.

Chapter 33

The mansion had been completed. Angelina resigned her appointment as principal of Unaka Girls High School and relocated to Mbenoha. Sochima was a freshman at New State University when her mother relocated to Mbenoha.

The first Saturday after Angelina relocated to Mbenoha, Sochima was home from the university for the weekend. She would go back to school after her visit.

On this Saturday, Agara gave a birthday party for Angelina at the People's Social Club. In the morning, Angelina went to the Garden City Salon and had a fantastic job done to her hair. She had a unique beauty of her own, inside and out. As she sat in the chair, one of the makeup artists worked on her. The young lady was just finishing the application of the last artful touches of makeup to her face when Justine Nkiru, the manager, entered.

"Hope everything goes well with you at your birthday party," Justine said.

"Thank you," Angelina said.

When Angelina returned home, she met Agara at the door. He took a look at her and smiled. "You look very hot and sexy in your new hairdo," he said in frank appreciation.

"Thank you," she said, giving him her most provocative smile.

He grinned back at her, flashing his even white teeth. Angelina knew that all they had to do was touch each other and the inferno would rage out of control. "Not now," she thought, patting her beautiful hair.

"Angelina," Agara called her. He handed her a package, which she hurriedly opened to find a very expensive head tie, blouse, wrapper, and shoes that matched. She looked at him and he said, "They are for you to wear tonight at your birthday party. They were made especially to complement your exquisite beauty."

Angelina put them on, looked at herself in the mirror and smiled. It was the most beautiful outfit she'd ever seen. It was gorgeous.

"I love it," she said, smiling tantalizingly.

"I'm glad you like it," he said. He grinned at her obvious fascination.

He gave his daughter, Sochima, a beautiful dress and jewelry for her to wear at her mother's birthday party. Sochima looked gorgeous.

The People's Social Club was beautifully decorated. Nnemugo, Director of Cheggs Event Planners, was in charge. Wine, champagne, and other drinks were on every table. The food was a buffet style arrangement. People were impressed with the service. Agara spent money as if it didn't matter.

The birthday had started, and by 8:00 p.m. the hall was full. It was a high-society party. When Angelina walked in, the room exploded with light and choruses of "Happy birthday to you, Angelina. We love you." Her mouth fell open in surprise and her face broke out into a jubilant smile. "Happy birthday, Angelina," Agara called out as he hugged and kissed her.

The music started and Agara led Angelina to the dance floor. Many at the party had known her. In a moment, the dance floor cleared as couples stopped to gather around the sides and watch. Angelina's hip movement was a romantic dance, which ended with many people's eyes sparkling with lust.

After the party, Angelina thanked Nnemugo for the excellent job she did. "The birthday cake was delicious," Angelina complimented her.

Agara took his wife home. It had been a very exciting and enjoyable birthday evening for her.

"Agara, I will never forget this night. Ever," she said as she catapulted herself into his arms.

Agara brought out a bottle of wine and poured two glasses. "Cheers to the woman I love," he said.

"Cheers to the man who made me a woman. I love you, Agara."

"I love you too," he said and stretched his arms.

They kissed each other. She looked into Agara's face and smiled.

"Agara, tonight is my night. I want you to make love to me all night," she said.

"What about continuing tomorrow?" he teased her.

"By tomorrow, if you still want to continue, I will be here for you," she bragged.

They went to bed and she took off her clothes and undressed him. She pulled him down on her. His body hardened with desire. He kissed her breasts with tenderness. While he was having her, she screamed with pleasure. They made love in every conceivable position known to man. When he finished with her, the memory of it never left her mind. At dawn, when the cock crowed to mark the end of their blissfulness, Agara felt like the impotent man at the pool of Bethesda.

Angelina got up and went into the bathroom. She looked at herself in the mirror and smiled. "I look like hell," she thought.

Agara had worn her out. Every muscle in her body was sore from the vigorous way he made love to her. She cleaned her face and put on some makeup. She combed her hair in some semblance of order and thereafter felt better.

She went into the kitchen and made breakfast. Sochima joined them.

"Good morning, Mother, and good morning to you too, Father," Sochima greeted. "I enjoyed myself last night. Many young people complimented me on my dress and—"

"Your beauty," her mother added. They laughed.

After breakfast, Sochima was driven back to her dormitory by her parents.

When Angelina and Agara returned home, they had dinner. Later, Agara pulled her close, kissed her, and said, "Angelina, I want to bear my mind to you."

"Please do," she said.

"I love you, my dear wife. You are a dear friend, the mother of my beautiful daughter, my mother incarnate."

Tears sprang from the corners of her eyes. She was about to say something when Agara said, "Please hold it."

"Angelina, from the very beginning, you have been the most fascinating, sexiest woman I've ever met. The way I feel about you is like nothing in my life before. I'm well acquainted with women, but none like your kind of woman; not one who is so loving and trusting, intelligent and openhearted." He paused. "I could go on and on," he added, "but I wouldn't want to make you conceited."

"Please go on. I won't be," she assured him. She needed to give him a chance to say it all.

He looked at her and said, "By birth and wealth, you belonged to the high echelon, yet you lowered yourself and became my wife. You stood firmly behind me when Z-man delivered the low blow to me in his house the day I first met him."

Tears formed in her eyes. After moments of silence, she asked Agara to excuse her. She went into the bathroom, showered, and went into her room. She put on her perfume, dressed up, and looked beautiful. She came back and rejoined him.

"Agara," she called.

"Yes, Angelina," he answered.

She drew in several deep breaths and looked him in the face. "I love you, Agara. Thank you for the flowers you brought me this morning. They are beautiful. I want to thank you for your patience with me and for showing me so much consideration. You have been very good to me and wonderful about everything. In bed, I have always enjoyed your first-in-the-morning lovemaking. I consider myself lucky to be married to you."

"Gimme a break, Angelina. I'm the one lucky to get you. Angelina, don't you have any idea how beautiful you are? Just one look at you and I was a goner."

She smiled. "Agara, when I finally decided that I was not going to marry Z-man, it was you that destiny sent to rescue me. You may not, at that time, have contemplated marriage, but I railroaded you into it. After risking your life in the military and surviving it, you came back to me, and to father our daughter."

Agara pulled her close and kissed her lips. He fumbled for her full breast, which fell into his seeking hand. He massaged it, enjoying the way its plumpness reshaped to fit his palm.

"Agara."

"What?"

"Nothing. I was just sighing your name. What you are doing feels so good."

After resting, they sat to discuss their new home.

Chapter 34

Agara's home was the best in Ohadum District. Z-man was troubled. He knew that Angelina, the daughter of the late Chief Oyinatu of Unaka, had risen to take her place in society. She was now the number one woman in Ohadum District. Instead of being happy for her, Z-man was bitter. It was tearing him up. She was to have been his wife.

Agara and Angelina discussed the furnishing of the mansion in preparation for the opening ceremony, during which Agara would be honored with a chieftaincy title. It would be a big occasion.

"Angelina," Agara called to her. "I want you prepare to go to London for a two-week vacation and to procure what is needed for the opening of our house. You will buy and ship household appliances and furniture for the mansion. This is your home to fix as you like. Angelina smiled at him. She did not make a mistake when she chose this man for a husband.

Motives are behind everything we do. Angelina quickly got in touch with Moses Nduka, head of the detective division of the police department. Moses was a very good friend of Rufus Dibia. Moses got in touch with Rufus, who had gotten his medical degree and was working in London. He gave him Angelina's flight information and the young doctor smiled.

The next week, Angelina was in London. Dr. Dibia was on an emergency call and could not meet her on arrival at the airport. She checked into the hotel near Heathrow Airport, where she had lodged several years prior.

She went into the bathroom and took off her earrings. She undressed in front of the mirror. She had been called beautiful since she was a young girl. Once she was naked, she looked at herself again in the mirror. Her body was firm and well proportioned. Her breasts were soft and rounded; her stomach flat, and legs slim. When she finished, she stepped back and evaluated herself. She looked good; not too dressy and not too casual. She wore a little makeup, just a touch of eye shadow and mascara to accentuate her eyes. She put perfume on, not too much. She was confident and ready for him. She did not want to overdo it; after all, she did not know what to expect, since it had been many years since they saw each other last. But she knew that the fire of a past love would always burn with a little flame.

She called the number that Moses had given her. Dr. Rufus Dibia came over as fast as he could. He had taken time off to help her out. He was surprisingly happy. The kiss was intimate and evocative, a mating of their mouths. Old firewood rekindles fast. They discussed her relationship with Agara. She was glad that her husband finally came back.

"What is your plan now?" she asked Rufus.

"I plan to return to Nigeria and take up an appointment with the Health Department," he said.

"I'm glad to hear that," Angelina said. "There is an opening for the post of medical director at Mbenoha General Hospital. I want you to apply for the position. I will take the application home with me," she said.

"I appreciate that," Rufus said.

"I have pulled some strings to get you hired for that position."

"Thanks," Rufus said after a moment of surprised silence.

"Do you think you will be home within one month?" Angelina asked.

"I will try," he said.

"My husband and I will be having the opening ceremony of our new home, and Agara will be honored with a chieftaincy title on that day. I look forward to seeing you then."

"That would be great," Rufus said.

She told him about their new home. During the week, they went shopping for the household items. She wanted his input on everything. Dr. Dibia helped her procure what she needed. They went from store to store and picked out the furniture she liked. She was doing just what she had dreamed of many years ago. Her wishes had been granted. She spared no expense. As the household purchases were made and shipped, Angelina could not believe she was not having some kind of bizarre dream.

The purchases arrived by air on schedule. When she came home and walked into the house, Agara was there to welcome her with open arms. She walked straight into the lovely bedroom. Her eyes surveyed it slowly, and when they came back to her husband, she looked at him flirtatiously.

"Are you ready?" Agara asked.

"For what?" she teased him.

"To try out the bed, of course," he said.

He reached for her and, within seconds, she found herself on the bed with him. He undressed her and she him. "You are lovely, Angelina. I love you," he said.

"I love you too."

The following day, Angelina sent Dr. Rufus Dibia's application for the post of medical director of Mbenoha General Hospital to Ms. Risa Ade, head of the Health Management Board of Ohadum District.

That afternoon, the Health Management Board met and approved the appointment of Dr. Dibia. Within a month, the doctor came home and assumed his position at the hospital.

Chapter 35

On this day, all the compound chiefs were invited for the opening ceremony of Agara's mansion. For the occasion, Angelina did not want to be rushed. She came back from her trip with expensive perfumes, dresses, shoes, and jewelry. She started wearing her hair in different styles—sewn, glued, stapled, you name it. Her hairdo became her thing. She had money and could afford to pay a lot to have it done for her in Garden City or Lagos. When it came to hairstyles, Angelina became the queen of the weave. She kept the other ladies of the CORM Club and the elite social club guessing what she would do next with her hair.

When she finished, she was attractively dressed. Her hair was styled to perfection. Sochima looked gorgeous. Her friends envied her beauty and social position. "You look gorgeous," Agara complimented his daughter. She was beautiful and sophisticated beyond her years.

The chiefs of Ohadum District were invited. Also at this function were the chief of police, Jones Sanuwo, the head of the detective squad, Moses Nduka, and Dr. Rufus Dibia.

People are fascinated by the rich and famous. Because Agara had acquired wealth, regardless of his past—a rapist, a fugitive, a vagabond, an arsonist—he would be honored with a chieftaincy title. Human beings appear to worship the sun on the horizon.

As the chiefs approached Agara's residence, the gatekeeper put the German shepherd on a leash and opened the first gate. He swung the second gate open and the chief's entourage was greeted immediately by the fierce baying of the huge Saint Bernard, Tiger, that kept guard in the yard at night. It was a powerful dog: tall, strong, and muscular.

The day watchman lured the nervously growling beast away from the driveway and the chiefs resumed their entry through the gates. As they proceeded toward the house, the huge dog stared balefully at them, whining and growling deeply in its throat. A quick frown descended on Agara's brow and he let the watchman know that he had misbehaved for not controlling the dog's rude actions. At the sight of a frown on Agara's face, Tiger was frightened and tucked his tail between his legs.

Chief Okaome of Oharu sat on a wooden chair, which could be called a throne. It was decorated with leopard skins. Above the chair was a mask portraying a menacing expression. The chief wore a hat with feathers of an eagle and a peacock—comprising of many colors. On each side of the chief were his messengers.

Angelina and Sochima were on the stage with Agara.

In his speech, Chief Okaome told Angelina and Agara that it was not the beautiful house that made the home, but the love inside it. He then conferred chieftaincy title on Agara, and the crowd went wild with jubilation.

The entertainment was lavish and the crowd jubilant, as if the people had forgiven Agara of his past transgressions.

At the end of it all, Agara still felt belittled. He had sent a special invitation to Zebulon Zimako of Aloma, so that he could show him that he, too, had financially arrived. But Z-man did not honor the invitation, instead, sources close to him said that when the invitation was delivered, he read it and tossed it into the trash can saying, "This occasion is 'infragig,' below my dignity."

Hearing this, Agara was infuriated.

Agara wondered what it would take to show Z-man that he was no longer the only cock crowing in the area. He, Agara, now belonged to the Nkpola Social Club, the most expensive social club in the area. Members were required to show evidence of wealth and ownership of at least one commercial building in three major cities in the country—a conspicuous consumption, which showed that the individual had the wealth.

Chapter 36

The wharf business had become very enticing. Agara was now a force to be reckoned with financially. Agarangelina Clearing Company had become known throughout Ohadum District. Agara was getting more recognition in society than Z-man. His bitterness for Agara gnawed at him. He must stop Agara forthwith.

Z-man received information through his agent, Dike, that a container load of imported ladies' shoes was arriving at the Garden City wharf on Sunday night. He invited Agara to a meeting. In a message he sent to Agara, he said, "My good friend, Agara, it is necessary that we meet face to face to discuss something, and as quickly as possible. This should be done today, at the People's Social Club."

The bait hides the hook. Agara was highly flattered, because this would be the first chance he got to talk business with Zebulon Zimako in person. "This is my chance to show Z-man that he is no longer the only rich man in Ohadum District," Agara thought. Then he warned himself as he got ready for the meeting: "Do not pet a porcupine unless you are looking for trouble."

Friday afternoon, Agara drove in his new Mercedes Benz to meet with Z-man at the People's Social Club in Garden City. Z-man's new Mercedes Benz was already at the premises of the clubhouse, and he was in the meeting room. When Agara walked into the private meeting room of the clubhouse, Z-man leaned back in his chair, raised his feet on the table and crossed one ankle over the other as Agara stared at him.

"Posture says a lot about self-confidence," Agara thought and smiled.

"Have a seat, Agara," Z-man commanded him, as if the meeting room was his private guest room.

Agara felt slighted by both Z-man's posture and his commanding tone of voice.

"Address me as Chief Agara," Agara instructed him. Z-man smiled and said, "I'm not aware that you are a chief."

Agara became furious and was about to blow his top when Z-man said, "Agara, we are not here to argue over chieftaincy titles. Your men know what you are."

During the meeting, Z-man specifically wanted the container load of imported ladies' shoes that were due at the wharf on Sunday night. Agara promised to deliver the container to him on Monday morning without fail.

For this meeting, Z-man and Agara were like two wolves dancing. Z-man knew that Agara was now a force to be reckoned with financially. He did not like that. "Agara beat me to the punch when he married Angelina; another strike against him," he thought.

Having agreed on the deal, Agara took this opportunity to let Z-man know how he felt about him. "After I reunited with my wife and daughter in Unaka," Agara said, "you invited my wife to your home and asked her to be sure to bring me along."

"Yes," Z-man answered. "I had never met you," he added.

"On arrival," Agara continued, "you proceeded to thoroughly subject me to utter ridicule in her presence and that of your visitors."

Z-man smiled mischievously, but didn't make a comment. He did not feel like dignifying the statements with a reply.

"What else, Agara, do you have on your mind?" Z-man asked.

"On the day I received my chieftaincy title," Agara said, "you were conspicuously absent."

"And so what?" Z-man asked brazenly.

Before Agara could say anything, Z-man's assistant cut in. "Watch how you talk to Zebulon Zimako," Dike warned. "Lack of respect for the elephant by a small creature like you is viewed as a sin against good manners."

"Will you shut your mouth?" Agara shouted.

"I say, let Dike continue," Z-man commanded.

"In case you have not woken up from your sleep," Dike continued, "Zebulon Zimako wants things done his way. You've gone against him by marrying Angelina, who rejected him, and you'll be brought into line, regardless of what he has to do to accomplish it. Don't think you can appeal to his conscience, because he'll have none of it."

Agara got the threat, loud and clear. "Regardless of how much power Z-man wields," Agara thought, "he is determined not to back down. He would fight me."

Without any further discussion, the meeting ended.

Sunday afternoon, Agara summoned his group: Jeremy, Sango, and Jude. He told them to be ready for an operation that evening. At the scheduled time, the group was ready. Shortly after the group went in for the operation, Jeremy lost his balance on a ladder. He held onto an overhead structure, his feet dangling in the air, feeling like he was stuck in limbo between the sky and the earth.

In a moment, a harsh, deep-throated growl rumbled menacingly from a dog in a corner of the room. The beast looked like a hundred pounds of muscle and teeth. Its lips curled back, revealing a set of fangs that could crush a man's arm very easily. The eyes were alert and fiercely intelligent, not threatening as much as giving a warning. The possibility that he's been abandoned was like a fist in the pit of the stomach, driving his breath from him. Of all the horrifying options that had crossed the young man's mind, he'd never considered just being left here to be tortured by the beast.

Suddenly, Jeremy's grip gave way and he came crashing down to the floor, roaring like a tiger caught in a trap. The noise he produced sent a loud sound throughout the building. He hollered and grabbed at the already swollen knot at the side of his head. He lay there in pain, terror, and confusion.

The German shepherd security dog launched itself in a mighty leap straight at Jeremy. The panic-stricken young man yelled for help as he frantically struggled to fend off the great jaws of the enraged savage beast. The crying voice of this boy and the barking of the dog almost commingled. Sango and Jude, who were in the adjacent building, heard Jeremy's cry for help and ran to him.

The night watchman ran to one office to phone for help. He tried to phone the police, but his trembling hand would not cooperate. Squeezing his hand into a fist and stretching his fingers, he took a deep breath and tried again. The phone rang once … twice … and the third time it was answered by a police corporal. The law enforcement officer started asking for the particulars of the armed robbers:

"Where are the armed robbers?" the police officer asked.

"Between goods shade A and goods shade B," the watchman answered.

"How many are there?"

"How should I know?" the watchman answered.

"Look, my friend, you need to answer the question if you want us to help you."

"I don't know."

"Look, what kind of nonsense answer is this?" the officer asked. "Are they carrying any guns, and what kind?"

"How should I know?" replied the night watchman.

"We are coming," the officer said, and replaced the phone.

After he called the police, the sound of his rapid, harsh breathing filled his ears. "The police are on the way; the police are on the way," the watchman repeated the silent litany over and over, at the same time praying that someone would get there before it was too late.

Scared out of his wits, and for several minutes, the night watchman blew his whistle for help and, for a brief moment, there was pandemonium. Even a wild rooster on a tree branch jumped down and released voluminous crows. Who could criticize the rooster? If you were frightened at that time of night, you would crow too. Some of the frightened wild chickens flew down from rooftops.

The group rescued Jeremy and escaped. It was a horrible night for Agara. When he came home early that morning, he felt and looked like a lunatic. Beside him, on top of a side table, was a pile of cigarette stubs in an ashtray in the hallway. With head bent low, he was deeply in thought. He had failed to deliver the promised container of merchandise to Z-man. His brain spun like a wheel. It was a letdown.

Angelina opened the door slightly and watched her husband for a moment, his head down between his palms. "Why ask a bat if he's okay when you see him hanging with its head down?" she thought. She wanted to go to him for fear that he might disappear again, then he heard her approaching only seconds before she got to him. When he looked up, the expression on his face was the most important clue to the physical and emotional strain of the previous night. She fixed breakfast for him. He ate, and soon thereafter went to his room. She allowed him to rest.

Later that morning, Sango and Jude came and told Agara that Z-man's boys had made away with the container of merchandise in question before they arrived. Jude told Agara how Z-man's boys laughed at them for their not being smart enough. Agara was mad. "Vengeance is mine," he thought.

That afternoon, Z-man's manager drove to Agara's residence for a meeting, because of Agara's no show. As the first gate swung open, Python, the German shepherd guard dog, ran to the car. The manager wound the window down and stuck out his hand in an attempt to be friendly. The beast nearly tore his arm to shreds. The dog also jumped at one of the headlights of the car and broke the glass. The manager frantically drove to the nearest dispensary and got treated by a nurse. On his way to report to Z-man, he knew Z-man would be furious. When he got to Z-man's compound and stopped the car, he knew Agara and Z-man would meet. "Oh, how I wish I could be a fly on the wall when they meet," he thought.

Agara did not regret the incident.

The manager told Z-man what had happened. Z-man was infuriated. He immediately sent for Agara to meet him at the People's Social Club.

Agara was there on time. Sitting across the table and facing each other, Zebulon Zimako and Agara stared at each other for a moment without a word.

"You are a rascal and a man without conscience, Agara," Z-man broke the silence. "You failed to make the delivery of a container load of valuable merchandise, as we agreed."

"We encountered problems, which I don't intend to go into," Agara cut in.

"It appears to me that in the treachery of your heart, you had planned beforehand to be faithless to your word of honor and to what friendly relations may have existed between us. You have also proven your abominable conduct toward me, which I did not expect—by arranging for your dog to attack my manager."

"It was an accident, simple," Agara said with a smile, as if he had not been told of the trick Z-man played on him.

"Let me assure you that if you don't make the delivery by sunup tomorrow morning, I shall be compelled to take measures that will be highly unpleasant to you."

"Will there by anything else?" Agara asked, unperturbed.

Z-man got up from his seat, opened the door and left, followed by Agara. The tension was mounting more and more. Each person was planning a new strategy.

Chapter 37

Agara got the threat from Z-man and left the People's Social Clubhouse, resolved to fight him to the end. He had failed in his promise to deliver the
agreed upon merchandise to Z-man, even though he had found out the trick
Z-man had played. Still, he was upset because it was a breach of a verbal con-
tract. He knew that Z-man would fight him with any weapon available to him.
He would also play Z-man's game.

The following night, Agara got his group assembled. He controlled his
group and the wharf just like the fallen angel, Lucifer, controlled his people
under the heavens. He and his boys made away with a sealed container and delivered it to Z-man under very inclement weather.

For Angelina, one hour stretched into two hours, late in the middle of the
night, and panic set in. She remained restless throughout the night. When she
looked out the window, thunder roared and lightning flashed in crackling arcs
and tongues. The wind was whipping and bending the banana and kola nut
trees in the backyard. The tropical rains came in a rush, with blinding sheets
hammering at the windows. The fury of the storm grew steadily.

Angelina trembled with fear—fear for the safety of her husband. She
couldn't help herself. She tried looking out of the rain-coated window, but vis-
ibility was poor. A jab of lightning exploded somewhere close by and thunder
shook the window. She heard a noise and thought there was someone in the
house, it turned out that it was the wind slamming a door. She was freaked
out. She fell onto her bed and screamed for help. When no help came, she
calmed herself and sat back on her bed. Like most nights when you are alone
and waiting for something, the night seemed about a hundred hours long.

She had a lot to think about, of course, but sitting alone, just thinking,
goes pretty slowly. It was like waiting for a surgeon's report on a life-or-death
operation. Not knowing was the worst part.

Suddenly, the front door burst open. Her first thought was that the howling wind had blown it open. A rush of moist air swept into the parlor. A flash of lightning illuminated the dark night, lingering for several seconds. When Agara stepped through the front door, the breath that had been caught in her throat was released in a joyous sigh. She raced to meet him as he came in, dripping wet.

"Where have you been?"

"A tree fell across the road and I had to walk home."

Immediately, thunder rumbled threateningly and she shivered at the violence of the storm he had walked through.

"Were you really worried about me, Angelina?"

"Of course, I was." She felt very defensive. "I'm not some kind of unfeeling beast, Agara."

He looked at her and released a smile.

"Agara," she said.

He looked at her.

"Lordy, lordy, I have never seen you look so haggard. Go and have a bath, and breakfast will be ready before you are done," she said, trying to treat him like a child in need of motherly attention.

Z-man's assistants opened the container delivered by Agara. It was full of empty cartons of toilet tissue except for one carton with twelve rolls of toilet tissue, intended for the consignee and his team to wipe their—

In no time at all, the story was being told everywhere. Z-man's name was heard in the streets, stories like that sell newspapers. Society people, wealthy people like him—anything they do comes out looking big in the news media.

Z-man had not had bad press in a long time. When this story leaked, the next day it became front page entertainment in the daily papers—*Agara Duped Zebulon Zimako, the Renowned Business Tycoon.* Z-man's face felt the scratch.

Agara had dealt him another blow. He was mad. Communities watched with eagerness what would happen next between these two crooked financial giants.

Z-man sent a message to Agara for a meeting. A couple of days passed before Agara responded. The two men met at the People's Social Club again.

"Agara," Z-man began, "you will recall that I sent for you after your failure to honor your commitment."

"I got your message," Agara said.

"And you sent me a message saying that a close relation of one of your group passed away at five o'clock, as you stated with shameful exactitude. But I discovered later that the close relation of the young man did not pass away until the next day."

Agara did not say anything, even when Z-man looked at him to see if he would defend himself. "I therefore concluded," Z-man continued, "that you had used death to deceive me."

"There was no reason for a meeting, because I had delivered a container to you. What was in it was yours," Agara reminded him.

"When we made the deal, the container was for a load of imported ladies' shoes, and not an empty one," Z-man replied. "Any impartial observer," Z-man continued, "will see that your cool, polite offer to fix the vehicle that your beast of a dog damaged is, under the present circumstances, calculated to put my anger and distrust for you to sleep."

"Okay. What else?" Agara asked arrogantly. "I do not wish to continue the meeting," Agara said, and the meeting ended with his last word. He was poised to counter any action that Z-man might take.

Very early in the morning, Agara was at home. He was in deep mediation when Angelina came near the door that opened onto the veranda. So many thoughts came to her mind. "What in heaven's name is he doing out here at 1:00 a.m. with so many cigarette butts in the ashtray and him looking so tense?" she wondered.

There was an empty bottle of whisky on the floor and another on the stool beside him, half full. "Is he communing with the gods? she wondered. She lingered, drawn to watching him as if he were some kind of mystery about to unfold. She knew she should get back to her room. He would be angry if he saw her watching him.

Chapter 38

Angelina went back to bed highly frustrated. For her, morning seemed to take forever to come. She tossed and turned on her bed. After what seemed like eternity, she finally went to sleep.

"C'mere," Agara yelled to his wife.

He was in the living room, so Angelina did not hear him when he first called to her. He was filthy drunk. When she did not respond to his call, he staggered to the door of her bedroom. There was a knock on her door. It must have been around 4:00 a.m.

"Who is it?" she asked, even though she knew. Suddenly the door swung open and Agara dashed into the room where she was lying in bed. She quickly got to her feet, seeing him in a terrible state. He was shit-faced drunk.

"I say, get your butt in bed with me," he hollered.

Angelina's eyes snapped wide open as she tried to understand what was going on. She got a grip on herself. "Never argue with a drunk or angry man," her late father used to say, she recalled.

She didn't like what she was seeing. It scared the life out of her. She wanted to get out of the house, but couldn't. She ran into another room to get away from him, but he pursued her into the room.

"What is it?" Angelina asked.

"I say, get your black butt in this bed with me," he demanded, pointing at the bed in the room. She knew that all he was verbalizing was merely liquor talking. He was beside himself.

He sat on a chair close to the door so that she couldn't leave. His fly buttons had been undone, exposing his near flaccid manhood. She looked out through the window and the stillness of the early morning was broken only by the sound of crickets. She wondered what had become of him. In the past few months, he had not bothered about having sex with her.

"Agara, I don't know where you've been or with whom." She became worried about the situation she was in now. She did not know what could have happened that would cause him to strike out at her. Suddenly, he grabbed her, pulled at her forcefully, and said, "I want you in bed, right now."

Angelina felt disgusted. "I don't want you now," she replied, scared to death.

"Why, Angelina? Why!" he shouted.

"Because you are stupidly drunk," she cried.

His head was throbbing very badly, but he felt he needed to prove a point. "You are my wife, Angelina, and I have a right to have you if and when I want."

She was now in a dilemma. She knew better than to argue with him when he got into one of his drunken moods.

Agara's eyes were shrewdly alert and chameleon-like, deepening in color when he was angry or amused, and seldom missing much. She quickly climbed over the bed so that it was between them. She faced her husband with clear eyes.

Suddenly, swift as a cat, he lunged and grabbed for her, almost jumping across the bed. She was quicker. She immediately realized that she was in a dangerous situation. She did not know what he intended to do next. She feared that if he caught her, he was likely to do anything, judging from his angry mood. She quickly jumped to the other side of the bed, keeping just out of reach.

Mad as hell, he lunged for her again and grabbed her with one hand. Panic lent her the strength to pull away from him. Confused and frightened, she bumped into a stool, and as she felt herself falling, she clutched desperately at him, causing both of them to lose their balance. She heard the air explode out of his lungs as he hit the floor, his body cushioning the impact of her own fall.

He groaned and lay still. For a moment, she could do nothing but lie there sprawled on top of him, trying to catch her breath and steady her shaking limbs. Disgust and despair ran through her, making her feel almost physically sick. She sprang to her feet. In his drunken state, he attempted to stand, but staggered and fell, hitting the linoleum covered concrete floor with his forehead. There was something shocking about the way he lay sprawled on the floor.

Angelina stood still, like a mannequin, unable to move. When her husband did not move, she cautiously moved to where he lay. Looking at his motionless body, Angelina was overwhelmed with fear.

"Oh my God!" she shouted, dramatically throwing her hands up in the air. So many thoughts raced through her mind. Her face became taut with worry. "What if Agara is badly hurt?" she thought frantically. "What if the condition gets worse? What if— How will it affect me? Oh, God," she prayed, "don't let anything happen to him. He has to be all right," she told herself. "He has to be." She paced up and down the bedroom and gave out sigh of relief when she noticed he was still breathing. She reached out to touch him, feeling the rapid pulse of blood moving through his veins as she touched his temple.

"Agara?" she shouted. "Agara, can you hear me?"

"Yes, I can hear you. Angelina. Holy saints!" he mumbled. "Head hurts."

She stared at him. "It should hurt," she said. "He smells like brewery," she told herself. She did not want to bother him anymore. It was better to leave him where he lay until he became sober. She looked at his condition, shut the door, and went into the next room.

Agara woke up later in the morning and dragged a shaky hand across his forehead. He winced at a nasty bump and realized how drunk he was earlier. Now his head was beginning to ache very badly. He did not feel ashamed of his drunken state because, according to him, many men have been known to fall under the influence of alcohol. He went into the bathroom, drenched a washcloth with cold water and wrung it out. He tilted his head to let the wash-cloth cool his face, in an attempt to rid him of his drunkenness.

Later, he moved into the kitchen, where he saw Angelina drinking coffee. "Fix me some breakfast," he said to his wife as he went into the bathroom to have his bath.

Despite the fact that she was disgusted with him, she fixed him breakfast. He ate it and then went back to bed. While in bed, he could not help but reflect on his drinking habit. "What has become of my wife?" he wondered. "Has she taken all she could from me?" These questions supplied no answers to him. He had tried to avoid alcohol, because the price he would pay for his intoxication was too high. This incident of drinking caused Angelina to be scared of him. She had never resisted his sexual approach. His thoughts soon lulled him to sleep.

While he was in bed, Angelina went to her room. "What a mockery of a marriage," she thought, as she reflected on what had happened. "A woman shouldn't require defenses against her husband; a marriage should be based on trust and respect." Her fight with him would not leave her. She had rejected his sexual advances, something that, under normal circumstances, a woman should not do to her husband. It was a connubial right. She braced herself to face him, knowing that sooner or later, he would seek to punish her. Culture and tradition forbid a woman to deny her husband sexual rights. She would make it up to him, but a few things had to change. She was not going to be his sexual slave.

When he awakened, sober, Angelina fixed lunch, which he ate, but then went back to bed. Angelina sighed, buried her face in her hands and rubbed her swollen eyes. She told herself that a woman is not a helpless, mindless creature. Unless he resorts to violence, a man cannot force her to step into his snare, much less remain there. She wished she could cut him out of her life now. She had had enough, but she knew she couldn't. Her marriage was a union by the gods; only the gods could grant separation. There would be no divorce.

She stayed in her room thinking her life over. She made it a point to stay out of his way. She heard him get up and go into the bathroom. "If he wants anything from me, he has to ask for it. I'm not going to volunteer," she told herself. Agara went into the bedroom, put on his clothes, and came out to greet her.

She was coming out of her room when he met her.

"Angelina," he said slowly, "how are you?"

"Fine," she replied, wondering what was on his mind.

"I need to talk to you," he said, very penitently.

"Can we talk after you eat?"

Tears sprang into Agara's eyes.

"I have told you how I feel, and we have said everything that needs to be said. There is no point in any more talk," Angelina said.

"I haven't said everything I need to say. I won't take up much of your time. I promise. Won't you do that much for an old friend and a husband?"

Instinct warned her to go it easy. Agara looked miserable, so downright pitiful, she simply couldn't refuse him.

"All right, but just for a minute."

"I feel I owe you an apology. Angelina, for the way I behaved. I blame alcohol for that. People have been known to do crazy things in moments of despair. Some have the good fortune of surviving such moments. I'm one of them."

"It's settled. No more apologizing," she replied with a smile, then she said, "Agara, you have to cut this drinking out or else learn how to handle it."

"Fair enough," he said.

"I brought you a peace offering," he said. Gesturing toward a package on the sofa, he said, "There is a piece of Damask loin cloth and a head tie to match for you."

She smiled and said, "Thank you."

He handed her a key to a new Mercedes Benz. "It is yours. You will drive and go where and when you want to," he said penitently.

She thanked him for the presents.

Chapter 39

He walked straight into the bedroom, leaving Angelina in the parlor. She went into her room and debated whether to join him in the master bedroom or wait in her room for him to come and search for her. She decided to stay in her room, feeling that it might not be wise to take the battle to the enemy.

At that moment, she heard the door handle turn. She sat up, head held high, and looking her best. She was not going to ask his forgiveness. When he saw her from the door, he hesitated and tried to decide what to do. At first, he could not look her in the eye because he felt very humiliated. He knew she rejected him because he was drunk. She was afraid of him. He closed the door and left. She smiled.

Moments later, he came back and opened the door. She was stretched out on the bed. He watched her for a few seconds to compose himself, and then he turned and started to walk out of the room again, as if convinced that he was not in the mood for sexual gymnastics. When he looked back, she had assumed the most exciting posture. He could not resist. She motioned for him to come to her, and he did.

Angelina sat up to address her husband. "Agara," she said, very softly, "I'm most horribly sorry for the things I said yesterday." Her voice shook. She clenched her hands together; her palms were wet.

Agara turned toward her and focus on her, as if there were nothing else in this world he wanted more to see.

"I was afraid that you wouldn't come back," she whispered.

"I almost didn't," he said ruefully. "I even expected that you would call the police if I showed up here again."

"No, Agara. I was upset." She shook her head wearily. "I want to make it up to you," she said.

"What is on your mind?" he asked.

She drew close and kissed him. "Agara," she began, "I'm asking that you stay home today and make love to me. I want to make it up to you."

With this invitation from his wife, Agara felt like he should make love to, and with, her until he pulled out his manhood. She quivered in his arms at the sudden vision of being devoured by him like a hungry animal. Both husband and wife laughed more merrily than they had done in a long time. Agara knew he was in for a challenge.

Angelina went into the kitchen and fixed their dinner. Shortly after, she came into the parlor and looking at her husband and said, "Agara, dinner is ready."

Food was now the last thing on his mind. He looked up and smiled at her. She smiled back sensually. Agara got up from the couch and headed for the bedroom.

"Where are you going?" she teased him. "I thought you said you were hungry?"

He turned around and said, "I am. Come to bed and let me show you how hungry I am."

She turned off the burner on the stove. She now felt as though she were walking into the lion's den. She had asked for it, so she would take what came to her. Suddenly, the lights went out. Angelina was going to ask the gatekeeper to turn on the electric generator, but Agara said, "Come on, Angelina. We don't need light for what we are going to do." The generator automatically kicked on.

Angelina eased into her husband's arms, meeting the hungry urgency of his need with a willingness that surprised her. But she was a hopeless romantic. While kissing her, he groaned as if he were in pain. She wound her arms around his neck and held on while she returned the kisses with everything in her. She wanted him so much. It seemed a very long time before he lifted his head. They were breathing as if they had been running.

Agara reached for a bottle of champagne and dribbled some over her breasts. The tips of her breasts were erect. Like a cat in heat, he slowly licked them clean. In a moment, he entered her and lifted her to a level of pleasure that she had never experienced. When they were exhausted, she looked at him and said, "While at Potompo field, I thought it couldn't get any better."

"I thought so myself. But now we have reached a level to which I have never been."

"Really?" she whispered, fascinated because he was far more experienced than she. She was thrilled by his amorous ways with her. She wondered how many lovers it took to teach him the erotic arts he practiced so well. He knew what to say to please a woman. This night, he had taught her a new language of love: they made love like crazy folk, and by the middle of the night, Agara looked like a man recovering from a chronic illness. By the time dawn came, Agara, the master seducer, who always breathlessly ached to take women to bed, was exhausted.

Later, she was examining her wounded face when he opened his eyes and said, "I'm sorry. I should have known the effects of alcohol. More people have drown in drink than in water. Drinking does nothing but take one on a road that leads to a dead end."

"Agara," Angelina said.

"Yes, dear," he answered.

"What is weighing you down?" she asked.

"The battle with Z-man is raging. It will be out of control soon," he said.

Angelina sighed. She looked at him and said, "Rest assured, Agara, four hands are better than two."

Chapter 40

Z-man did not like the way the last meeting with Agara ended. Agara had shown him that he was no longer obligated to him. He demanded a meeting with Agara at the People's Social Club on Wednesday. He was sitting at the private room of the club when Agara came in.

"Please have a seat," Z-man offered, as if he had invited him for a friendly meeting.

"Thanks for offering me a seat," Agara said, without meaning what he said.

"Agara," Z-man began.

"Yes, Zimako?" Agara answered.

From Agara's tone of voice, Z-man got the message that this was going to be an extraordinary meeting.

"Agara, do you need to be reminded that you have failed to make good your promise of delivering a container load of ladies' imported shoes, as agreed?"

Agara stood up to address him. "Zebulon Zimako, you changed the rules in the middle of the game. Do you want me to remind you that you had ordered your men to remove said container on that night before my boys arrived?" Did you think that I would not find out? The sky does not release its water without the ground knowing. Say what is on your mind, Zimako," Agara challenged him.

Z-man stood up to face him. Now that he knew Agara had found out what he did, an exchange of words ensued between them. Z-man was ready to fight with words.

"Agara," Z-man said, "any animal that stands higher than another one has a large stomach."

"What are you saying?" Agara asked.

"I'm ashamed to note that you need for me to explain to you what I mean," he said. "Our elders say that if one is given a proverbial message and he asks for an explanation, he should know that the dowry paid on his mother's behalf was for nothing."

Agara shook inside, but his military training kept him in control of himself. He would wait for the right moment to act.

"Z-man is the elephant and you, Agara, the ground rat," Z-man explained. "You are going to deliver a container, as agreed on before." Z-man growled at Agara as he slammed his hand against the table to emphasize his point. The force of the blow caused Agara to stare at Z-man in disgust.

"If you haven't come to terms with it, take it from me that I'm as high above you as the sky is above the earth," Z-man bragged.

Agara wondered how much more he could take before he unleashed his anger. He had been told that if the enemy hits you on one cheek, turn the other cheek and let him hit you again. "Do you let him kill you before you react?" he wondered. Devastated by anger, shame, and a blow to his ego, Agara barked out a command. "Zimako, if you don't get out of my face, lightning will strike your head right now." Before Z-man had a chance to react, Agara had slapped him across the face and sent him crashing to the floor of the clubhouse.

When he got up, he swung at Agara, who instantly ducked, causing him to lose his balance and stagger, falling to the floor again, this time to his knees. As people from the club gathered to find out what the brouhaha was all about, Agara kicked him on the bottom again and again with his boot.

Zebulon Zimako got up from the floor and saw the crowd that had gathered. He was ashamed. In anger, he swung at Agara, but missed his head. His fist hit the thin plywood paneled wall, and he shouted, "Oh my Lord!" He tried to shake out his pain. He turned around in circles, shaking his hand. He looked ridiculous.

"Slick bastard," Agara shouted loudly at Z-man.

The club members stood looking at them with their mouths hanging open and their eyes opened wide—something out of the ordinary was happening. This was humiliation to Z-man, the rich businessman, who didn't think his excrement stunk. He had been publicly put to shame again by Agara.

Looking at Z-man, Agara barked out another command: "Get out from here, you scallywag."

Amid the jeering and shouting, Z-man slowly moved to the bathroom and locked the door. "He who blows in the fire must expect sparks in his eyes," Z-man thought.

After he had stayed in there for a while, the caretaker of the clubhouse went to the door and asked, "Z-man, are you okay?" When there was no answer from within, the caretaker rattled the doorknob. "Zebulon Zimako, what is taking you so long? Is everything okay with you?" the caretaker asked again.

Z-man stared at the rattling knob as if it were a hissing snake, then he managed to say, "I'm okay." Shortly after, he opened the door and moved toward the door of the clubhouse, feeling like a wounded leopard. With his pride injured, he left the clubhouse, thinking, "Never underestimate your enemy."

Agara got in his car, happy as a lark. He drove away satisfied that he had shown his opponent that he would accept no more insults from him.

Chapter 41

When Agara drove home, he told his wife what happened at the clubhouse. She was happy to hear that her husband showed Z-man that he would not stomach any more nonsense from him. She reached in the bar cabinet and brought out champagne, and they drank to his victory at the clubhouse.

The war was on in earnest.

After the meeting with Agara, Z-man decided that he would show Agara that he, Zebulon Zimako, was not a tiger with broken legs. He was a famous man, not just a non-entity. He tried to enumerate in his mind the strikes against Agara. Agara had snatched Angelina from him; he had delivered an empty container to him, causing him to make bad press; he had been publicly disgraced at the People's Social Club, physically assaulted, and verbally abused him. And Agara was now richer than he.

He that is full of himself is empty. "Famous men have power," Z-man boasted to himself. "If you try to work against them, they will use every means in their power to stop you. Powerful men play dirty; the more powerful, the more unscrupulous and ruthless. I have the money and the power to ensure that things are done my way. But Agara is a power to be reckoned with now," he reminded himself.

Z-man invited the chief of police, Jones Sanuwo, for a meeting at his mansion. The police chief knew that Z-man had been as prominent a man as you could find in all the villages that made up Ohadum District. If anyone wanted a political or promotional favor, Z-man knew whom to ask. He was known throughout the district as a take-charge kind of man whose laugh echoed throughout the communities around. He owed Z-man one; his position as COP came by Z-man's influence.

The COP had heard about the treatment Agara gave him at the clubhouse. Z-man was out for revenge. During the meeting with the COP, Z-man demanded that Agara's wharf operation be stopped, thereby stopping him from making more money. He wanted to show Agara that by disagreeing with him, he was kicking against bricks; by marrying Angelina, who rejected his bid to marry her, he, Agara, was doomed to fail in any deal he entered into.

After meeting with Z-man, the COP instituted appropriate major changes in the workforce. He reconstituted the corrupt police department and appointed a new police officer to be in charge of the wharf area. He reconfirmed Moses Nduka as head of the detectives. He also called a top level management meeting of the police department. During the meeting, he received a briefing on Agara's history and past activities.

"Agara is a water snake. He has an unusual way of attracting his prey. He has been a sex crazy man since his youthful days," one of the officers said.

"Since his wealth exploded, he has been known to enter into a bar and flash wads of high denomination currency notes, buy rounds of drinks for as many people as would be in the bar at the time, and brag about his expensive cars and costly jewelry. He has flashed his newfound fortune until the people of his community have become tired of their new celebrity," another one said.

"Agara has torn the wharf apart. At night, like a maniac he has roared up and down the highway leading to the wharf, terrorizing every living thing along the road," a third officer said.

At the end of the meeting, Z-man instructed his men to attack Agara on Friday night while on his way to the Garden City wharf. He meant to go for the jugular. "Agara, like a nail that is sticking up, must be hammered down," he said. He told his men that they would be protected by the police boss.

Chapter 42

On Thursday afternoon, Angelina sat in her room thinking about the nightmarish dreams she had been having recently. She believed that some dreams are portent. She had narrated her dreams to Agara. While taking a nap in the afternoon, she had a vivid and unforgettable dream. She was bathed in perspiration. She screamed and shouted loudly, tossing and turning. Agara tried to calm his wife down, to assure her that the dream bore no relation to reality.

"Nothing more than just a dream," Agara said.

Angelina could not rid herself of the conviction that somehow she had witnessed a preview of her husband being attacked. Despite the dream, Agara left for the People's Social Club in the early part of the evening. It must have been around midnight when Angelina fell into a deep, troubled sleep. She was dreaming a most terrible and unnatural dream. She saw a pool of blood and a gathering of people, but she did not see the bloods source. She woke up and felt indescribable terror. Slowly, she dragged herself to the kitchen, feeling like one who had just recovered from a malarial illness, which had left her very weak and tired in both body and soul.

She made herself a cup of coffee and drank it, then she went back to bed. She lay awake, listening—there is nothing so tiring as to lie awake listening for a sound that never comes.

She got up and went to the window and looked outside. The forest noises flowed softly back to her, as if the inhabitants of the night had let out a collective sigh. At the same time, her breath exploded through her tight lips to join them. Crickets were chirping in the shadows behind the huge kola nut tree. She didn't know whether to cry or laugh. Agara was a curious mixture of a man: one moment he was as hard as iron and drove her to hate him, the next he showed her an unexpected caring side of his nature, which disarmed her.

In the early hours of the morning, Agara went into the house quietly. He wandered restlessly through the house, like a prowling animal. Angelina heard his footsteps. She felt happy. Angelina found that after years of marriage, she was trapped. She was dependent on him, and no matter how strong willed he was, Agara was dependent on her too. She needed to care for him. Sometimes she couldn't quite understand who needed the other more. They had become locked in roles of mutual dependency. She told him of the terrible dreams she'd had, but he told her that it was just her subconscious working overtime.

In the morning, Angelina got herself dressed and ready to walk to the home of Chankola, the diviner. Chankola is descended from a long line of medicine men. He was born in Oharu Village, and could never be certain of the exact date of his birth, as his family kept no records. But he knew he was roughly a year younger than his sister and a year older than his brother, who was now eighty.

Angelina did not tell Agara. She would seek relief from her despair. Chankola's divination was known throughout the surrounding villages. It had been told and retold in market places. He was also known as a man with the power to deal with, and protect against, evil men and spirits.

Throughout the greater part of the day, it had been raining very hard. Even under the umbrella, Angelina got drenched. "Rain never melted anyone," she thought. The rain left her shivering when she reached the home of the diviner. She stepped onto the veranda, eager to be out of the rain. She knocked at the door and stepped aside to wait. As a jagged electric knife of brilliance sliced the sky, a man appeared at the door, and Angelina was ushered in.

"Come inside out of the rain," the voice said.

As Angelina stepped into the house, Chankola came out smelling as if he'd rolled in a dead skunk. There was a large earthenware pot covered with dust in one corner and filled with all kinds of feathers: peacock, parrot, eagle, vulture, and kite.

On the walls of the room hung bunches of dried herbs and flowers, used for healing purposes. Not only did he tell the future, Chankola also made a living selling medicinal herbs. Angelina thought the seer used some of the herbs to cast his spells too.

Chankola spoke in a clear bell like voice. Angelina turned so that he couldn't see the tears that had filled her eyes. She presented him with a rooster. Sitting on a stool and facing the statue of his shrine, the old man lifted the rooster by the wings and bent the head at the neck region, so that he was holding the head under its wing.

Speaking in a low tone, he cut the throat with a knife, blood spurting onto his shrine, which represented some ancestral gods that he consulted. He would not fail to do this for fear of a curse from the ancestral deities.

When he released the rooster, it fluttered its wings, staggered forward, backward, and finally rested on its back and pedaled its legs in the air. Angelina closed her eyes and made a face like one who had just eaten bitternut.

As the rooster kicked its legs and fluttered its wings, there were feathers flying in all directions. Angelina used her wrist to wipe her eyes, which were dripping with tears at the sight of the chicken's blood, then she pulled a feather that had gone into her mouth.

The old man sat down and got ready to listen to his client. In an uncontrollable burst, he coughed several times into the tortoise shell by his side. It was his sputum container.

"Woman," Chankola said and smiled. "I know why you are here."

Angelina hoped that she would leave the place relieved from fear.

"Agara!" Chankola spat his name like venom, and hastened to shake the bell that summoned the spirits to action. In front of the seer was a large calabash, a gourd with the inner pulp cleaned out and used as a water pot. The pot contained water that was imbued with supernatural power. Before he would say anything to his client, Chankola peered into the gourd of water; this made the villagers refer to him also as "the man with the magic eye." Peeping into the calabash, the man with "the gift of seeing" watched the spirit gods talk to him.

"Angelina," Chankola called. "Listen to what the gods say about your husband, Agara:

"Agara Aham was born in Oharu, Nigeria. He was six months old when his mother, Apuna, watched him double his fists, as if ready to fight. His mother smiled and said, 'My baby, are you worried about the struggle you know must lay ahead in this world?' Between his spell cries, the baby turned out to be a charming little one. His mother loved and pampered him."

Angelina was anxious to hear more.

"At twelve months," Chankola continued, "Apuna was feeding Agara when the child bit her finger. She became worried, because it is a bad omen in Ohadum District for a child to bite the finger that feeds him. To add to his mother's worries," the seer said, "Agara's first tooth appeared in the upper jaw. She believed that a normal child cuts the first tooth in the lower jaw. No one knew what Agara would turn out to be, considering the doubling of the fist, biting the finger that was feeding him, and cutting the first tooth in the upper jaw. These were considered unusual in the development of a child from Ohadum District.

"Agara was circumcised when he was five years old, rather late," Chankola said. "His mother had felt unsure of his survival. Before the old woman who conducted the operation embarked on it, she examined the genital organ to see if it was all right to perform the surgery. During the operation, the foreskin on the penis was removed. Immediately after the procedure, the area was red and tender. Under normal circumstances, the tenderness was gone within a couple of weeks or so after the operation; but in Agara's case, the circumcision caused an infection. He suffered a lot of pain; however, after a month or so, healing took place and the scab that had formed by the incision came off. From then on, the young boy grew conscious of his male organ."

Chankola turned and looked at Angelina, who was feeling very uneasy. "Do you want to know more?" the seer asked.

"I do," Angelina answered.

The man with the magic eye looked into the water pot and continued. "By age six, Agara had become a loud-mouthed terror, smart and tough. Like many other children of his age, he was in primary school, although he appeared more mature than his age."

Angelina wondered what was coming next.

"Angelina," Chankola continued. "Agara's early life alienated him from the people of the village. I, who knows many present things by divine gift from the gods, have little knowledge of things of the future; therefore, I do not know whether he will be alive after the sun sets on—" He looked at her and stopped. "I can only tell you what the gods have told me."

Chankola coughed several times and took a break to dip his snuff. Minutes later, which seemed like an eternity to Angelina, Chankola held up a fist and lifted up a finger to summarize:

"One," he said, holding up his index finger, "your husband's past has been filled with dangerous adventures. He set himself against the people of this clan and thought he could get away with it. He believed that no adversity could defeat him during his youthful days. Two." The next finger joined its sister and formed a twin spire pointing toward the ceiling. "There are a lot of flaws and faults in his life, and I see nothing but a struggle and tragedy, unless—"

His voice was harsh, but Angelina's eyes were angry, as she chewed on her lower lips. She continued listening to the seer.

"Three." The third finger sprang up. "Agara's mother gave birth to a sour creature. Angelina, your husband is carrying a foreign blood in him," the seer said and took a break.

When he finished his break, he peered into the water pot, then he looked at Angelina and said, "The gods are determining whether I should tell you more."

"Please tell them that I need to hear it all. My curiosity has been aroused," Angelina said.

Chankola looked into the water pot again and said, "The gods need more coins."

Angelina met the demands of the man with the gift of seeing, and he continued.

"This is the story of Agara's birth as revealed to me by the gods," Chankola began. "It was the month of November. The harmattan nights were cool. The days were hot, with the winds blowing from the north, carrying with them sand and dirt," he said. "At the Garden City wharf, the men were busy off-loading the heavy construction equipment from the ship. Taking a break in the evening, Mr. Sweetman, the captain of the ship, walked into the Garden City Nightclub. He and his crewmen had finished work for the day." After coughing for a moment, Chankola continued. "Francis Hardface, proprietor of the nightclub, welcomed them with drinks on the house. The sailors had a wonderful evening. Mr. Hardface extended an invitation to Mr. Sweetman and his crew to come to his house the next day. Francis's family entertained the visitors with food and drinks," Chankola said. "They were served by Mr. Hardface's nineteen-year-old daughter, Apuna, *too beautiful to go out into the sun*. Apuna's one of those women too beautiful for her own good. 'Who cooked this delicious pepper soup?' Sweetman asked. Apuna smiled and said, 'I did. Do you like it?' 'It's good. Would you bring me some tomorrow?' Sweetman asked. "As he was leaving, Mr. Sweetman invited Mr. Hardface and his family to the ship the next day. Mrs. Hardface was indisposed and could not go. Mr. Hardface and his daughter went. She took a pot of fish pepper soup to Sweetman.

"After the visit to the ship, Sweetman gave Mr. Hardface expensive drinks. He gave Apuna expensive perfumes and necklaces. He also asked Apuna for more soup. The next day, Apuna visited Sweetman. When she left him, her maidenhead was no longer intact. Mr. Sweetman gave her more gifts. For the next ten days, Apuna was very pleasing to Sweetman. After two weeks at the wharf," Chankola said, "the ship was put to sea again. On Apuna's last visit to Sweetman, he kissed her and handed her parting gifts of jewelry. Apuna's face crumpled as the man who had made her a woman bade her good-bye. Her friends had warned her that once the man left, she'd never see him again. And they were to be proven right, because Apuna never saw Sweetman again. In December of that year, Apuna got married to Tom Aham, but Sweetman had fathered Agara and gone back to sea.

"When Apuna found that she was pregnant," Chankola continued, "she had expected it to be the end of her relationship with Tom Aham. She was almost certain that the news would send Tom fleeing. But on the contrary, Tom responded with an abrupt proposal of marriage. He wanted her and he wanted the baby. When she pressed him, he could not be dissuaded. 'Apuna,' he said, 'you are simply the most beautiful woman I've ever seen. Up close, she was so beautiful that Tom stared at her like a fool. He treated her sweetly and worshipped the ground she walked on.

"'There will be a lot of talk about us,' Apuna said to Tom. 'Gossip is a favorite form of entertainment in Ohadum District,' Tom replied. 'If it isn't us they talk about, it will be somebody else.' Apuna smiled and said, 'Tom, I love you.' 'I love you too,' Tom replied. Tom was ten years older than Apuna," Chankola continued. "Both were happily married. Tom loved his wife. He was proud of her beauty, and his peers were jealous of him. Tom was a rich trader by standards at the time. He tried, by all means, to keep his wife looking beautiful."

"So, what happened?" Angelina asked inquisitively.

Chankola took another break. Angelina was getting restless. She needed to know all about her husband's past.

"I'm ready to hear more about him," she said.

When the diviner came back from his snuff break he looked into his water pot and then looked at Angelina. "I see another face," Chankola said.

"Who is that?" Angelina asked.

"Mercy is her name."

"Is she Agara's wife?"

"The picture is not quite clear now," the diviner said.

The gods knew Angelina was rich and wanted to get as much money out of her as possible.

"More coins are needed to get the gods to show clearly and to talk," the man with the magic eye said.

Angelina complied immediately.

"Now I can see clearly," Chankola said with a smile.

"Mercy didn't love Agara any more than he did her," the old man said.

"Did they have children?"

"Mercy and Agara made love, but it was many months after before she got pregnant. She later claimed that the baby she was carrying was Agara's."

"Why?" Angelina asked.

"Her father, Chief Agu, was rich. He did not want to hear of the scandal that his daughter, Mercy, was caught screwing around."

"What kind of woman was she?" Angelina asked.

The diviner looked into the water pot and said, "Everybody in the village knew that Mercy wasn't all that discriminatory as to whom she slept with."

"Why was Agara singled out?"

Chankola smiled. The story was getting more interesting. He looked at his client and said, "At this time, Tom Aham's trading business was not doing very well. Mercy's father had money. Tom needed money to buy his wife expensive clothes and jewelry in order to maintain her standard of living. The chief bribed him with a handsome amount for him to persuade Agara to admit fathering the baby."

"Did Tom do it?" Angelina asked.

"Tom talked Agara into admitting guilt. He told Agara that since he had slept with Mercy, the baby was just as likely his as it was anybody's and that he couldn't prove otherwise."

"What happened next?" Angelina asked.

"That first week when Agara returned from Unaka, after he had been gone for twelve years," Chankola said, "Mercy was visiting from the Cameroon. She told Agara that the baby was not his and that after he fled the village, the baby's father showed up and claimed the child at birth."

"Where is Mercy now?" she asked.

"She went back to her husband in the Cameroon," Chankola said. He continued, "Angelina, do not blame Agara for this. At that time, there was nothing he could have done about it. In this community, it is a woman's word that matters when it comes to fathering a child. The case is closed."

Angelina was happy at learning more information about her husband's sex life. She could understand where her husband inherited blue eyes.

"Listen to this," Chankola said, looking at his client's face. "From his late teen years, Agara has been a womanizer."

Angelina twisted her lips, as one who has just bitten into bitter nut.

The old man looked at his client and said, "Agara loves you with all his heart. He needs you for survival."

"What do I do?" Angelina asked.

"He has led a fast life with women and is trying very hard to distance himself from them, but they keep coming back now that he has a promising financial future. He does not want any other woman but you. His enemy plans to get to him through one of his former women. Can you trust him?"

"What do the gods suggest to me?"

"You are a strong, smart woman. You can deal with it."

"How?" she asked.

"Trust. No human being is perfect."

"I know," Angelina said, thinking back. "What about his rivals?"

"One of them is after him, but the man cannot get to him unless—" Chankola stopped speaking abruptly.

"Unless what?" Angelina screamed.

"I cannot see the gods. They are gone. Be of good courage, woman, and go home. Remember, no harm can come to anybody unless his personal god, *guardian angel,* sanctions it," Chankola concluded.

As she left the house of the soothsayer, she wondered if it was cruel of him to have talked to her so strongly about her husband.

But he loves you with all his heart. He needs you for survival, the diviner said. "That's good to know," Angelina said with a smile. She decided she would find out who the women were who had been in Agara's past, or still were in his present. She already knew the man who was his rival.

As Angelina neared home, she noticed that the sky was starting to look ominous. High-banked clouds were moving in the sky. The heat was oppressive and made worse by the hovering thunderstorm. She arrived home just before the clouds parted and dropped their contents in one vast sheet of water.

Agara was in the house. She kissed him and told him how happy she was to see him. She prepared a delicious lunch and they happily enjoyed it. Angelina looked at her husband and wondered if there were people who were not superstitious, especially when Chankola's divination had been found to be true.

Chapter 43

Beware of danger signals. Friday afternoon, the phone rang and Angelina picked it up. Agara was in the bedroom.

"Hello!" she said nervously.

"Do not allow Agara to go to the wharf today," a voice said, and the phone went dead.

"Hello! Hello!" Angelina cried, frightened by the unidentified caller. She nervously hung up, missing the first time before she fumbled the receiver back into the cradle. She got to her feet and ran into her room, shut the door, and flung herself on the bed.

Agara was still in the bedroom. He was in pain. "Death is the only real cure to pain," he thought. Z-man had been a pain in his rear end and a thorn in his flesh. The man had on several occasions, verbally reduced him to his lowest level of existence because of Angelina. The battle was on and something had to give.

After several minutes, Angelina went into the master bedroom and saw Agara sitting on the armchair. He wore a chieftaincy dress with the shirttail over a pair of trousers. He lit his pipe and puffed a big cloud of smoke. He looked at his wife and smiled.

"Give the snake the right of way," Angelina thought. Hesitating at first, she went to him and implored him not to venture out that afternoon. "Agara, you are not going out this afternoon, are you?" she asked. Unknowingly, her voice had risen to a scream.

Agara frowned and looked at her fiercely. She moved back, as if going to shut the door to bar his way.

"It is very kind of you, Angelina, to be concerned about me," he stammered. "But I have a business to attend to this afternoon."

She stared at him helplessly, and then turned round, her hand covering her face, as she thought. "If only I could stop him! If only I could make him change his mind! If only—"

He glanced at her, smiled, and rising like Samson in his blindness, walked toward the door.

Minutes later, he came back to the parlor. Angelina watched him surveying the living room as if afraid he might never see it again. His eyes moved in an affectionate sweep over his aged possessions: the mouth organ hanging on the wall, the gramophone and the guitar he brought back with him from World War Two. By now, Angelina's heart was pounding, her body shaking, and tears were wetting her cheeks. The house was quiet except for the humming of the ugly old wall clock, which now pointed to the hour. Agara then stood still and took a look around, hardly seeing anything.

"I'm imploring you not to venture out. Life is for the living," Angelina pleaded with him.

"Yes, I have also heard and said many of those pithy sayings, including *strike while the iron is hot*. Angelina, my mind is made up," he said.

Dreams come true. Many are terrifying. No matter what she said, and no matter how she tried to say it, it appeared she could not come up with a plausible reason to keep him from going out. None are as blind as those who will not see, Angelina thought, wishing she had the courage to say the aphorism out loud.

Angelina again pleaded with her husband to call off his activity that evening. He brushed her aside. Unable to dissuade him from continuing with his plan, she turned back and went into her room. She then turned and watched him as he opened the door to go out.

To Agara's utter surprise, Lion, the same ferocious claw-footed beast of a dog that once came to his rescue during an encounter with his Bighead age group, stood facing him. He wondered where the dog came from. The beast had not been seen since the last time it saved his life. Now it had come back. "Why?" Agara mused.

He got the message clearly but would not accept it. The black and white dog was determined not to allow him to leave the house, let alone go to the wharf. He bent down and attempted to give the animal an affectionate pat on the head. The angelic creature did not respond. When he tried to push the animal to the side, because it was blocking the door, Lion growled and bared his large canine teeth. Agara became perplexed. The animal looked up at him beseechingly, as if trying to tell him that something was wrong. As he tried to push Lion to the side again, the beast growled and threatened to bite him. Agara stepped back into the house.

Angelina came back to him. "Agara," she called. "Guardian angels are heavenly beings that act as God's messengers. They are meant to perform good deeds. Very often, they issue warning messages, which we heed or reject and suffer the consequences."

Agara's heart was pounding in his ribcage, but he was listening.

"Like the story in the Bible about the destruction of Sodom and Gomorrah," she continued, "the angels warned the people. Animals play their part as guardian angels. These special guardians often send warnings of danger to individuals through encounters with spirits of protection residing in them."

Agara looked at his wife and looked at Lion, who had quieted. In a moment, he decided that the animal would not bar him from his activity that afternoon. As he stepped out of the door, Lion moved to bar him again, but on seeing the frown on his master's face, moved away, looking back and wagging its tail, as if to say, "Be warned. Fools rush in where angels fear to tread."

As Agara approached the gate, Lion disappeared. It had given its warning. The Saint Bernard stretched across the inner gate of the compound. "Tiger!" he called the other dog by its name, but it would not budge. He bent low to pat it on the head, and the beast of a dog growled fiercely, baring its large teeth. Agara had known the dog to snarl, but never at him. He was perplexed. Tiger was determined not to let this sour man pass through the gate. Sure enough, Agara was determined not to bow before the threat of his own dog. At that moment, Agara thought of the old saying, "The death that will kill a puppy does not allow its eyes to open." He turned toward the house and saw Angelina standing in front of the building, watching the drama unfold. Agara looked at Tiger, sitting tight by the gate. "Get out of my way," he shouted to the huge Saint Bernard. The angelic messenger of a dog looked up at him, as if wondering, "It would be utterly useless to keep a dog if you had to bark yourself." The animal got up and moved to the side.

Immediately, Python, the German shepherd, went berserk, hurdled over the gate, and stood there looking up at Agara and wagging its tail. "Python," he called the dog, but got no response. It was unusual for the dog not respond to him.

As Angelina started to walk toward the gate, she saw Python move out of Agara's way. Miraculously, Lion had come back. Tiger, Python, and Lion, all three dogs, were now standing side by side at the gate. Agara looked at the animals, looked at his wife, and smiled, as if to say, "I hear you loud and clear."

Angelina opened her arms and received her husband. They kissed each other and went back into the house. Lion disappeared; Tiger and Python took their places again in the yard.

Agara reached into the liquor cabinet and took out a bottle of whisky. Angelina watched him go to the backyard. She followed him. He sat on the hammock, slung by cords from iron posts on the porch. It was one of his favorite spots at the back of the mansion. His wife sat on a chair next to him. He opened the bottle, threw his head back and took a long pull from the bottle. He made a face as the burning liquor went down.

He offered the drink to his wife and she boldly took hold of it, threw her head back like her husband did, and took a large swallow. She immediately started coughing and sputtering, her eyes tearing and her insides flaming. Agara climbed out of the hammock and took the bottle from her as she bent at the waist to cough. He thumped her back with his open palm. She slowly straightened, drying her weeping eyes with the handkerchief he gave her.

"Agara," she said, "I don't know what you saw in me, why you married me, ran away, and then came back to me. You had so many other women to choose from. It is because of me that Z-man wants to destroy you. It would be unbecoming of me to let your enemy annihilate you. In dealing with Z-man, I have resolved that both of us will float or sink together," she vowed. "Bear with me," she said. "I, too, have my shortcomings."

He was touched by her words. He kissed her tenderly. She then went into the house to arrange for dinner. Agara threw his head back, listening to the cicadas singing cheerfully and the bullfrogs croaking mournfully down at the creek. Later, his wife came back and announced that dinner was ready. They went in and ate.

Friday night, Z-man restlessly waited to hear from his men who had gone after Agara. There was no report from them. Throughout the night, he got no report from the police either. He was mad. In the morning, he had a meeting with the Chief of Police, who told him that according to information from Agara's boys, no wharf activity was planned for the Garden City wharf.

"What next?" Z-man thought.

Chapter 44

Two weeks passed. Agara had become a formidable financial threat to Z-man. On this day, Agara was dressed to go out.

"Where are you going?" Angelina asked, bent on knowing his movements. After her visit to the home of the diviner, and the canine angelic warnings, she was prepared to ward off any evil.

"Going to a business meeting," he replied.

His tone of voice sounded unusual. Angelina reached into the refrigerator, poured herself some orange juice in a glass, and added some ice cubes to it. She shook the glass gently and stared at it as if in a trance. Agara poured himself some juice and sat down.

Angelina pulled herself together and addressed her husband once again. "Agara, would you please stop worrying about money. Enjoy what you have and let the fool hunt for more."

"Angelina, believe me. I have taken your advice. I'm no longer worrying about money."

She reached out and kissed him.

"But you know that there is a snake at the backyard," Agara said.

"I know the threat is there," Angelina said.

Agara dropped his head, as if in silent prayer. He looked up, picked up his glass, sipped from it meditatively for a moment, and then excused himself to go into the bedroom, where he slumped down on the bed. Angelina went and lay beside him. She knew something was weighing heavily on his mind, but he would not say what.

In a moment, he was up and dressed. "I have a meeting to attend," he said.

No sooner had he left the house than she felt a nameless dread—as if something terrible was going to happen. Before noon, she was already feeling miserable and bored.

Z-Man was a heavy financial supporter of the All Saint Churches of Oharu, Aloma, and Unaka, and of other churches around Ohadum District. He was used to people being so impressed by his wealth that they fell over themselves to do what he asked. He had the final say in many decisions of the churches. "Wealthy people spin in a different orbit from the common man," his clique thought.

Zebulon Zimako had a special corner in these churches, and his special chair was brought from his house to the church on Sunday morning, no matter which church he attended. He took his Holy Communion wine from a special cup. He was accorded all those special privileges because he had money, which he gave to the church. But they say, *"Money is the root of all evil."*

At midday, Agara was at a general meeting of the deacons of the All Saints Churches of Oharu, Aloma, and Unaka. Z-man presided over the meeting. Agara made a cash donation of a substantial amount and requested a special seat in these churches. Through the influence of Z-man, this request was turned down, leaving Z-man still the only cock crowing in those churches. Some of Z-man's supporters laughed at Agara and made fun of him for losing the bid.

Agara was mad. He went to the People's Club and stayed till late at night. Around two o'clock in the morning, Angelina woke up and found that Agara was not in bed. She was alarmed, and tiptoed into the living room. She saw him sitting on the sofa with his head bent low in his palms. She knew something was hurting him, putting him in so much pain. She wanted to know what it was.

She finally talked him into coming to bed. They made love. Early in the morning, she rose and made breakfast. They ate and sat to chat.

"Agara," she began.

"Yes, Angelina," he answered.

"Talk about it," she said. "Once you talk it out, we can try to find a solution."

He was silent.

"Agara, you are now the richest man in Ohadum District. You live in the best mansion; you are socially above all those who used to look down their noses at you. What else do you want?"

"You forgot to include that I have the best looking, sexiest wife."

She smiled. "I did not forget that. It was obvious."

They laughed.

"Angelina, my dear," he said and then paused.

"Say it, Agara. Please say it."

"The cobra is lying in wait for me," he finally said with a fury. "He will strike as soon as he sees a crack in my armor."

"We can outwit him," she assured him.

"Angelina, what would you have me do now?"

"Don't do that to me, Agara," she pleaded. "Don't shut me out like that. It scares me to see you looking so hopeless. We need to say what we feel. Whatever it is."

He stared at her. "You don't want to know."

"Yes," she said. "I do."

She started to cry. He saw her tears and her pain. He knew they were for him. He moved to her and buried his head between her breasts.

"Angelina, you are such a good woman."

He looked at her and there was no smile on her face, instead, it was worry that registered there. "Angelina, my dear," he called her again. "You are the kind of woman any man would be proud to call his wife."

The compliment stirred more worry in her. What is coming next? she wondered.

"Why are you saying these things?" she asked.

He shook his head. "Angelina, you should never have married me. I'm not meant to be a husband to a good woman like you."

"Why would you say that?"

"You asked me what I was thinking."

"Agara, you are a wonderful husband. When did you start to feel this way?"

He told her about the escalating feud between Z-man and him. He also told her about the humiliating defeat in the church.

Angelina was touched. "His defeat is mine too," she thought. She told her husband to give her a chance to think about what he said.

After dinner, she went to bed. "I'm the reason why Z-man is bent on humiliating Agara whenever he gets the chance," she thought. "I'm in the middle of the whole show. Agara has vowed that Z-man can't have me, not while he's alive. 'Not even after he is dead.'" she told herself. "Z-man has not learned that he cannot buy my love with money. I don't love him, and will never love him, and will not marry him, even if he destroys Agara."

When she was young, her aunt had advised her that whenever she was confronted with a problem that defied her solution, she should sleep on it. Her aunt said, "Through some unknown processes, when you wake up in the morning, the right solution to the problem will present itself." Her aunt believed that it was one of the reliable tools given to human beings that, when applied, helped the individual get out of trouble." While some people attribute it to the work of the subconscious mind, others call it intuition," her aunt said. With that thought, she went to sleep.

Chapter 45

When Angelina woke up, she went into the bathroom and stood beside the oversized cast iron bathtub. The tub was large and so long that she could almost lay full length in it. She loved this antique tub. The porcelain was scratched from years of cleaning, but when filled with warm water during the harmattan season, it was a place for dreaming.

She watched the maid carrying brimming buckets of hot water to pour into the tub. Another maid brought pails of cold water to lower the temperature to her liking. The tub was not plumbed for inlet of water, but for water drainage. She tested the bath water and poured bath oils into the tub, stripped off her clothes, and moved in to the sudsy water. She closed her eyes and hummed to herself as she soaked in the water, savoring the warmth that crept up her thighs and back. She let the warm water take her to another planet. Suddenly, she looked up and saw Agara admiring her. He moved closer and lay his cheek against hers. "Come into the tub for a few minutes; take a bubble bath with me, Agara," she beckoned him.

"Wow!" Agara shouted, looking at her beautiful face. "That sounds good." He couldn't think of anything better than being in that bathtub with her at that time.

"Come in with me," she said again. Then she reached her hand out of the tub to reel him in.

Agara was gorgeous in the nude and had a body that would stop a clock. They luxuriated in the tub until it got cool.

While in the tub, Agara looked into her eyes and asked, "Angelina, do you love me?"

"I love you, Agara. You excite my mind, body, and soul. You have made me feel young again."

At that point, her fingers trailed along his neck and down to his legs, and as his nature hardened, he pushed her hand away.

They dried themselves off and wrapped the big bath towel around them. They went into the house, where Agara pulled her down next to him on the bed.

"Agara," she said. "I have a plan and would like to ask that you support me. I have decided to have a meeting with some of the people who did not agree with the denial of your request for a special seat in the church. I will get their names and call for the meeting this afternoon."

"I will support you," he assured her. "What will be on the agenda?" he asked.

"It will unfold as we go along," she said.

That morning, she went into her room to do her homework. She recalled the words of her father, the late chief of Unaka: "Look back at your ancestors for strength. Prove that the blood of your ancestors is in you by making a difference in life." She resolved to show Z-man that she was the daughter of Chief Oyinatu of Unaka. After an hour of deliberation and phone calls, she came out and joined her husband.

After discussing with her husband, she sent verbal messages to ten key supporters of Agara to meet at her home. She asked her maids to prepare the conference room for the meeting.

In the afternoon, during the meeting, Angelina asked the group to support Agara in building a new church in Mbenoha, capital city of Ohadum District. The church would be called African Kingdom Seekers Church. She waited for a response.

Amos Timba, seventy-five years old, a political veteran, and the oldest in the group of church deacons, stood up. He was a well-known retired school teacher and union leader in Ohadum District. He greeted the group. He told Angelina that he would like her to step out of the room so that the group could have a chance to discuss the matter briefly. So, she and her husband left the room. Ten minutes later, the group asked Angelina and Agara to return. Amos, speaking on behalf of the group, said that the group would support her in the establishment of the new church. They would also sell the idea to all and sundry.

A committee was set up to organize the work. Angelina thanked the group and then entertained the people. In the next few days, word spread fast that a new church was to be established in Mbenoha.

The following week, four acres of land was purchased for the church. Local reputable architects, masons, carpenters, bricklayers, and handymen were assembled from the different parts of Ohadum District, and work commenced on the new church building a month later.

Every road has hills. At certain times during the building process, criticism of the project mounted very strongly. It was organized by Z-man. Z-man and his clique deplored the building of a new church as a waste of money that could be used to feed the masses and their families. But Angelina possessed an indomitable spirit. She told her husband that quitters never win, and winners never quit.

Despite all that was said for and against, the work continued until the African Kingdom Seekers Church was completed. It was big, with a towering steeple and stained glass windows, gleaming in the sun like jewels.

Doctor Paul Ezelu was a handsome man. He held a doctorate degree in theology. In his first church in the United States of America, younger single women fell in love with him. The older female members tried to marry him off to their daughters. The bishop of the church didn't like single pastors. "There is too much potential for trouble," the bishop told him.

After a church conference one day, the bishop saw the way Paul was flirtatiously chatting with a young church lady. The bishop was convinced that Paul was committing the deadly sin of lust in his heart and would sooner or later seek penitence. He advised the young clergyman to look for a wife.

While the construction work was going on in Mbenoha, Paul was in New York. He heard about the project going on in his hometown. While at home on vacation, he came to visit the new church project. Agara and his wife took him around the construction site and briefed him on the program at hand. He was impressed.

The next day, Paul went to St. Valentine Convent to visit with the nuns. While he was visiting and chatting with the head of the convent, he saw Sister Ruth passing by. Ruth gave him an affectionate glance that he could not overlook. The Holy Mother saw the look that passed between them. She smiled.

The next Sunday, Paul conducted the worship service at the convent. The choir was led by Sister Ruth, who also sang. Paul was so impressed that he thought Ruth hung the moon. As he was getting ready to go, he met with Ruth. The Holy Mother noticed again the look that passed between Paul and Ruth. She later called Sister Ruth to her office. After making the sign of the cross, the Holy Mother looked at Ruth and asked, "Was it not Apostle Paul that said 'it's better to marry than to burn'?" Sister Ruth knew what she meant. The attractive young nun later left the convent and married Paul before he went back to America.

It was time to search for a pastor for the church. The search was announced on the radio and published in local newspapers. Doctor Paul Ezelu applied for the position. The bishop of his church in New York recommended him highly. "Doctor Paul Ezelu is a very intelligent young man," the bishop wrote. "Paul has attended many seminars for professional development. His wife, Marvelous, supports him very well. In New York, where Paul has been a pastor of a small church, he is the esteemed man of God. I recommend him to any church that will need his services," the bishop concluded.

Angelina read Dr. Ezelu's curriculum vitae. After his undergraduate degree, he did a good job earning his master's and doctorate degrees, which he completed in record time. After going through the recommendation from the bishop in New York, Angelina called a meeting. As the self-appointed chairlady of the Board of Trustees of the African Kingdom Seekers Church of

Mbenoha, Angelina recommended to the board that Dr. Paul Ezelu be appointed pastor of the church. The board approved the appointment, and Paul accepted the offer. This would be his second appointment as pastor of a church since his graduation from the seminary in the United States of America.

After Paul accepted the appointment, he sat down with his wife and told her that there was just as much politics in the church as there was in other branches of the government; therefore, they would have to be on their best behavior with the authorities of the church and the rest of the communities that make up Ohadum District.

On arrival from the United States of America to assume duty in Mbenoha, Angelina and her husband gave a welcome party for the pastor and his wife. The chiefs and elder statesmen of Ohadum District, pastors of the various churches, wealthy traders, doctors, and educationists were all in attendance. Zebulon Zimako was invited, but he was conspicuously absent.

The following week, Angelina willed her power. She drew up a list of the church people to take up various church positions. She and her husband met with Dr. Paul Ezelu to discuss the list of names, which included rich traders, educators, and politicians. Some were members of the other churches, who saw the imposing church cathedral as a threat to the existence of the smaller churches. They were just ready to move to where the action was going to be.

After a brief discussion of the names, Dr. Ezelu accepted the list. In his first meeting with the church officers, Paul praised the people for their great efforts to ensure that the church was built. "Money alone could not have done the job. Your physical support is highly commended," Paul said.

When Paul took over the mantle of leadership of the church, Angelina gave him a rundown on the history of the church. He promised to uphold the tenet of the Gospel and to advance the progress of the church.

He spent his first few months studying the dynamics of the church, which could make or break the clergyman. He had to recognize where the power lay, who ran the church, and who thought they did. He studied the church workers, screening the lazy ones and those who stole anything that was not nailed down.

Chapter 46

Doctor Paul Ezelu settled in as pastor of the church. He sat with his church officials and a program was drawn for the dedication ceremony. Invitations went out to all the chiefs and dignitaries in and around Ohadum District and elsewhere.

On this morning, Angelina got out of the tub. She had been in a state of anticipation, looking forward to the dedication ceremony. Her head tie, blouse, and wrapper all matched.

"Will I do?" she asked her maid.

"You certainly will do," the maid replied.

"Do you think the shoes look all right?"

"Madam, the high-heel shoes put you in a position not to be overlooked in any crowd."

There was a big turnout. The other churches came in full support: the Baptists, the Methodists, the Episcopalians, Presbyterians, and the Catholics. Everyone in attendance was in his or her best Sunday attire. The village chiefs from the different surrounding communities were there in their full regalia.

The choir, directed by Marvelous Ezelu, stood. The ex-nun was beautiful. On a signal from the first lady, Agara stood with his accordion. Seconds later, he began to play the familiar tune, "When the Saints Go Marching In." The gospel choir took the stage; the congregation was on the floor, praising Jesus, clapping hands, laughing, dancing, and drumming. These actions were regarded as evidence of the spirit at work in the heart of man. African Kingdom Seekers Church was an apostolic church.

Doctor Paul Ezelu stood at the pulpit. The congregation sat down, sweating and fanning themselves. Marvelous, the choir director, saw Agara signal for a chance to play his harmonica. She motioned to the preacher to please allow more time. Agara picked up his harmonica and started playing the next tune,

"The Heavens Rejoice when a Sinner Repents." The congregation stood and began to dance to the tune.

The pastor finally stood again and the congregation quieted. Bishop Ezelu praised the effort of the communities in coming together to build the church. "I noticed that during the construction work, it did not matter where you came from or who you were; if you had the technical expertise, you were hired for the job. The people are happy, because the project has lifted their pride. There will be a new clergy, new deacons and deaconesses, and other church officials. The communities are impressed and hail Angelina and Agara in the highest esteem. The men and women know that Angelina is the brains behind this project," the preacher said. He continued, "We appreciate the financial support of Angelina and her husband to ensure that the project would be a success. One remarkable thing the African Kingdom Seekers Church will uphold is that there will be no special seat left for the rich. This antiquated system in the church should be consigned to the dustbin of history. The church is a place for the worship of God and not for a show of wealth." In conclusion, the pastor said, "Whether you are religious or not, you will be calmed by the music and serenity that prevail in the church. The music is good for you whether you are sad or happy. You will find peace within yourself." He urged the people of the communities to endeavor to attend church service. "To the congregation, rich and poor," he advised, "there is plenty of food and drink at the reception hall. Enjoy the good times in life, because the roof can cave in any anytime."

Zebulon Zimako battled within himself as he wondered how the dedication ceremony went. He decided that since he did not attend the ceremony, he would surprise those who attended by showing up at the reception. "What the eye witnesses requires no informant," he thought.

At the end of the dedication service, Agara proudly announced that, at the recommendation of the Board of Trustees of the church, headed by Angelina Agara Aham, construction of new buildings for the African Kingdom Seekers Church of Aloma and Unaka communities would commence the following month. Doctor Paul Ezelu had been approved as the bishop of Mbenoha Diocese. He would select the young men and women who would become the pastors of the churches. The crowd rejoiced at this, and Angelina smiled. Her plan was unfolding She would not go through this life without leaving some kind of positive mark.

At the church's Fellowship Hall, Bishop Ezelu stood in the receiving line shaking hands. Angelina turned as Z-man entered through the main door, nodding and speaking to those standing nearby. "Fire and water are not considered friends," she thought.

Z-man walked through the crowd like the chief executive of the nation. Angelina's heart swelled with gladness. It was time that this strong-willed man of Ohadum District recognized Agara as a power to be reckoned with in the communities. Z-man shook hands with Bishop Ezelu, Agara, and Angelina, and congratulated them on the success of the establishment of the church.

Amos Timba, chairman of the Deacon Board of AKS Church, laughed at Z-man's decision to appear at this reception. He thought, "A bug is a bug, no matter where or how it presents itself."

It was imperative that Angelina held herself with the utmost decorum if the plan ahead was to materialize. The assembly of the people at this function from all over the district, was an indication that the future augurs well. Never in the history of Ohadum District had so many people come together in unity.

Chapter 47

After the dedication ceremony, Angelina invited the wives of the prominent members of the church to her house for a chitchat to get to know one another. On this Wednesday night, the women came gorgeously dressed and ready to show off and have a good time.

Angelina had contacted Nnemugo, known throughout Ohadum District for her excellent catering service. She arranged for a sumptuous buffet, which was neatly laid out. You could smell the sweet aroma of the food as you entered the mansion.

Angelina welcomed the ladies and assured them of good time. Soft music was playing in the background. As the ladies gathered, they began to help themselves to the wine and champagne set out on the tables.

Gini was the first to open her mouth to talk. She was tall and voluptuous, with jet black hair halfway down her back, wearing brass earrings dangling from her ears. She was pouty-lipped, making for a sensuous mouth. There were rings on every finger of her hand. Everything about Gini was overdone. She wore too much makeup, too much perfume, and was overdressed for the weather: western pantsuit with gold necklaces and bracelets.

Gini was a "been-to"; one who has been overseas, usually just for a visit. At twenty-five, Gini fell in love with a young medical practitioner, Josiah, whom she met at the Independence Hotel during a weekend party in Lagos. She quickly became attracted to the handsome young man, five years her senior. They soon embarked on a passionate love affair, which culminated in a marriage that lasted only one year.

Initially, Gini and her husband were very much in love. Her husband sponsored her first trip to New York three months after they were married. While on this trip, Gini had the freedom to indulge in her passion for shopping for new clothes, makeup, and jewelry. She was a beautiful ebony skinned young lady—until she came back from her trip to New York. While on her trip, Gina became *Beke Akamere,* a black person who changes the color of their skin using bleaching cream. The first Sunday after she came back from her trip, Gini was in church, dressed to kill. With rouge on her cheeks, the makeup on her face was loud, and her eye shadow too thick and green. Filled with the Spirit, Gini started to shout and cry in church and as she did, her makeup began to run down her bleached face. Lord o'mercy, what a mess! And the varicose veins on her legs looked like a road map!

Soon, storm clouds gathered on the couple's romantic horizon. Although the young doctor cared a lot about Gini, Josiah devoted more time to seeing his patients in his thriving gynecology practice. Gini finally walked out on him. Her loud, extroverted personality and need to be the center of attention totally overpowered the medical practitioner, who thought being a doctor was all it took to keep a woman like Gini happy. She proved him wrong, as she later moved on to be the sweetheart of a very popular crude oil dealer, now the president of a bank in town.

"Angelina, would you introduce the first lady, Marvelous, to the group?" Gini asked. "We've heard so much about her," she said.

Angelina smiled; her face was open and friendly.

"Marvelous, would you please stand," Angelina began.

Beaming with smiles, the first lady stood up, looking very beautiful.

"Marvelous, everybody has been dying to meet you," Angelina said, introducing her to the group.

She turned to Angelina and said, "I would rather receive questions from the women than to talk at random."

"She is very smart," Gini said to Agnes, who was sitting beside her.

"Thank you," Marvelous said. "I hope what you heard is good," she added.

"I had to slap my husband in the mouth when he told me that you had a good looking butt," Gini said, looking very amused.

Hand up. "Yes, Gini," Marvelous answered.

"Angelina told us that you lived briefly in the United States with Paul. What did you do?"

"In New York," Marvelous began, "Paul attended many seminars for professional development. Most times, he insisted on my going with him. I liked that."

"I would too if I were you," Agnes said.

"Paul is a typical preacher. He conveniently ignores the part about committing adultery," Marvelous said.

"Are you serious?" Gini asked.

"You had better stop talking, or I'll be falling in love with him," Gini said.

"Gini is very good at that. You had better watch out," Agnes said jokingly.

Marvelous looked Gini in the face and said, "I'm used to women running after my husband like flies on cow manure."

"And you don't mind it?" Agnes asked.

"Nobody is woman enough to take my man," Marvelous declared emphatically.

The women started clapping for Marvelous.

"I mean it. I was a young nun in the convent when I met Paul," Marvelous said. "I had been badly burned once. It was too late when I realized that the man liked me because I was a curiosity. My mother was an Ibo and my father a Hausa. My grandmother was a Yoruba. Apart from the mixed blood flowing through my veins, my mother was a Christian and my father a Muslim. My mother believed that there is no one way to believe in God. James Kamalu, my fiancé, couldn't deal with all that integrated bloodline. He dumped me like a hot coal two months before we were to walk down the aisle. The bastard ran away with the daughter of a preacher and got married in Lagos, at the Cathedral of All the Saints. I'm not a suicidal person. The world does not stop for a broken heart. Devastated, I went to the convent, sort of straddling the fence," Marvelous said.

"She looks sexy," Rachel observed.

"When Paul came along, I prayed to hook him. Martha, another friend of mine in the convent, was also lusting for him. I knew that if you don't take advantage of an opportunity, someone else would. My prayer was stronger than Martha's," Marvelous said.

"I'm impressed with Marvelous," Agnes said. She turned to Angelina and said in a low tone, "Paul looks so pious that I can't picture him doing *anything.*"

The ladies laughed, but Marvelous had heard her and went along with the humor. "Oh yes. Paul's a wild beast in bed When we first got married, I told him that we should pray before doing anything."

"Did he agree to it?"

"He would not disagree with my first request."

Agnes looked at Gini and said, "I have wondered how often she and Paul do it."

"Looking at her beautiful hair, it may not be often, lest she might mess her hair up," Gini replied.

Marvelous heard the comment and said, "I have my hair done every Friday, and from Friday to Monday night, I'm off doing it." There was laughter in all parts of the room.

"Marvelous," Agnes called. "Angelina told us that your name was Ruth."

"Yes. In the convent, I was Sister Ruth. But after I got married and became the preacher's wife, I had to look glamorous. One day, a week after I arrived in New York, I came home from the beauty parlor and my husband took one look at me and exclaimed, 'Ruth, you look marvelous.' From that day on, I would not let anyone call me anything but Marvelous."

"That was a beautiful name to choose," Agnes said, looking at Gini.

Gini turned to the crowd of women and said, "I have known Agnes since we were young. At seventeen, Agnes was a pretty young girl, heartbreakingly lovely. Even at fourteen, there had been a hint of the beauty she'd be when she was grown. Her ebony skin, radiant with the blood of her ancestors, was flawless. She had her father's features, but her dark eyes were just like her mother's."

"Agnes," Gini said, "would you like to tell us about your life in the USA?"

"I have nothing to hide," Agnes said. "While in the United States, my husband, Solomon Idika, was always complaining about one thing or the other."

"Like most men," Gini said. "I hope he didn't make complaining a full-time job."

"In my opinion," Angelina said, "if he was complaining, you had nothing to worry about. It's if he stopped complaining that you'd have trouble on your hands."

"Amen," the ladies echoed.

"One night, Solomon came home very late," Agnes continued. "I watched him walk into the room and sit down without a word. 'Aren't you going to explain your uncertain movements this past month,' I cried out, my voice loud with pent up frustration.

"What would you have me say?" Solomon asked, his mind working furiously, trying to come up with an explanation that would pacify me without telling the whole truth. But time was a luxury that I didn't grant him.

"I don't appreciate your sitting there trying to think up those little lies," I told him. Solomon opened his mouth to say something, but shut it, because he knew that one lie leads to another. I looked at him. "Solomon, you certainly are an amateur when it comes to the game of lying. Don't you know that you are supposed to have your story ready ahead of time?"

"I'll remember that next time," he snapped.

"You could start by apologizing for your lateness home," I told him.

"Okay. I apologize," he said. I couldn't believe it. No argument, no excuses for me to vent my pent up frustration that had cost me several nights' sleep and wasted days of emotional turmoil.

"Did you go on your knees to pray? What did you do?" Marvelous asked.

Agnes looked at Marvelous and smiled. "I should have done that; but instead, I shouted, 'Say something, for God's sake.'" Solomon looked at me and slapped the lamp stand with the flat of his hand. 'What do you want me to say?' he shouted back, the edges of his mouth starting to twitch. "Ah, we are getting somewhere," I thought, listening to his loud tone of voice.

That night, Solomon prepared himself to sleep with me. I was so mad at him that I would not let him touch me.

"What did he do?" Gini asked.

"He threw a fit and went into a jealous rage. He even suspected that there was another man, and that suspicion of infidelity poured more oil into the fires of my anger. I felt like he had likened me to a woman who cheats on her husband during the day, comes home with a smile on her face, prepares the evening meal for him, and then shares a bed with him."

Agnes paused.

Angelina smiled and looked away.

"Then what followed?" Marvelous asked inquisitively.

"Stunned by Solomon's accusation, and helplessly staring at him, my hand shot out in an instinctive outraged reaction to the intolerable suspicion and struck him hard across the face."

"Did he retaliate?" Gini asked.

"No. But he looked at me and said, 'It's very much unlike you, Agnes.'"

"He moved close to me. In a moment, I felt like a dove released from its cage and soaring to the clouds. Solomon unzipped my blouse at the back and eased it over my head. He slipped the straps of my bra from my shoulder, unsnapped it, and as he freed me of it, I turned to a mass of sensations. He quickly helped me untie my wrapper and remove my panties. I gazed at him while he toured me with his eyes the whole length of my body. My eyes met him and I shied away from the stark revelation of his need. I closed my eyes momentarily. When I managed to open them, Solomon had undressed and was standing over me. He looked glorious, broad shouldered and trim waisted. We made up for the night. For the next few months, everything worked out fine. Just before I left the United States to return to Nigeria, Solomon started coming home late from work."

Angelina smiled at Agnes and her story. "What did you say to him?" Angelina asked.

"I questioned him about his coming home late, expecting me to wait for him to eat dinner."

Everybody in the room stared at Agnes, as if to say, "Come on with it."

"Solomon told me that if I didn't quit nagging him, he would be forced to shop for a newer model."

There was a frown on the faces of many in the room. Solomon had thrown a challenge to them.

"And what did you say to that?" Marvelous asked.

"I did not take it kindly at all. I fired back. 'You could even make it a different color.'"

"What did he say to that?" Gini asked.

"Solomon smiled and said, 'No difference, Agnes. One is like the other.'"

"I did not know whether he was speaking from experience. One thing was for sure; he did not stay out anymore until we came back to Nigeria and he joined the sports club." Agnes then turned to Rachel and smiled. "I met Rachel when she first came to Atlanta to meet Daniel."

"Let Rachel tell us about her trip to Atlanta," Angelina said.

Rachel took a sip of her wine and looked at the ladies who were eager to hear her story. "A couple of years after Daniel Chima registered for college in Atlanta, Georgia, his family made arrangements for me to join him. I was eighteen years old, fresh out of high school. I was ready to go to America by any means possible. At that time, a young man's future partner was decided for him by his family," Rachel Anele began. "The decision had an economic overtone—family wealth and property remained within selected families. Daniel knew nothing about me except that his parents had performed the betrothal ceremony at home and that on the day of my arrival at the Atlanta airport, he would be there to claim me. Two hours before the scheduled arrival of the flight, Daniel was at the airport, eager to meet his wife. The plane finally touched down. I was beaming with smiles, looking left and right as I cleared through Immigration," Rachel said. "She looks beautiful; black as midnight, with skin smooth as glass. At first sight, I likened her to a good book. She started pleasing right from the cover page," Daniel had told Agnes when they came home.

"Daniel drove me from the airport to his home in Atlanta," Rachel continued. "After dinner, we prepared to go to bed. I told Daniel that I would like to sleep in a separate room. He was very understanding. Considering the long trip and jet lag, he thought I had every reason to be tired. After I turned him down the second and third nights, his patience ran out."

"What did he do?" Angelina asked.

"Daniel could not understand the meaning of my visit. He took me out for dinner, and later, we went to a park. It was late in the evening. Daniel asked for an explanation. I reluctantly handed him an envelope addressed to him. He opened the mail, read the first two sentences, and looked at me. 'Rachel Anele Chima is your half-sister,' Rachel's mother wrote. 'How could you do this to me, Rachel?' Daniel demanded, almost at the point of desperation. 'I didn't do it to you, sir,' I replied. By this time, I was sobbing uncontrollably. Daniel managed to calm me down and listen to my story," Rachel said.

Continuing, she said, "Everybody in the Aloma community refers to your family as possessing noble blood. Sometimes I would do something that my mother would be proud of and she would say that she wasn't surprised, because I had noble blood. I never considered it as meaning anything until she told me at the Lagos airport, just before the plane took off, that a noble blood was going to join a noble blood. At that time, tears welled in my eyes and I let them fall. People at the airport thought I was already getting homesick. 'Be careful what you do with him,' my mother warned." She continued.

"When I saw you at the Atlanta airport, I knew what my mother meant. You are really the mirror image of our father," Rachel Chima said. "Our eye met. Nna Joseph Chima, being our father, was my mother's story. When you saw me at the airport, you probably guessed as much," Rachel told him. Daniel shook his head slightly. 'No, I didn't. I never would have thought—' Then he paused. 'Nna Joseph Chima seemed so devoted to my mother that … I …' He looked again at me. 'Our father was devoted to your mother quite all right,' I said to him. 'My mother loved him, but he didn't love her. It appears to me that all our father did was mount my mother, do his business, and move on. For him it was more a lust of the flesh,' I added.

"What did Daniel say?"

"Daniel laughed softly. 'Do you really understand what happened?' he asked. No matter what happened, it's neither your business nor mine. One thing is for sure; whatever existed between them gave rise to my being here now,' I told him."

She continued her story. "The letter did not lie. Our entire physiognomy accurately depicted our father. Daniel knew I was his half-sister. In the letter, my mother said that I was the product of the old man's uncontrolled stolen pleasures. Joseph Chima was chairman of the Deacon Board in the church, where the pastor had a reputation for being a very good preacher. When the pastor mounted the pulpit, he started with slow grunts in his speech, then progressed to a faster pace, and his voice rose louder too. Every member of the congregation adored him. No monthly meeting of the deacons was concluded if the eighty-year-old pastor did not add, 'You must be the husband of one wife, or else be expelled from the church.' He was not the kind of preacher who believed in flowery language. He meant every word of what he said. As a deacon in the church, Joseph Chima knew that to be thrown out of the church would have been tantamount to being thrown out of the world. The people knew it. My mother was so much in love with Deacon Joseph Chima that she stopped at nothing to ensure that she had something to remember him by. I told Daniel that Deacon Chima probably never thought my mother would get pregnant when he was doing his thing. I don't blame him for what happened, and my mother doesn't either. I'm glad he's our father. That's why I'm here today. As if he were out of his mind, Daniel grabbed me at this. Not knowing what his intentions were, I slapped him across the face. He released me. I was fuming. 'Don't you know that would be incest?' I asked him. 'Didn't you know that when you allowed me to spend all that money to bring you over here?' he asked me."

"Did he fight you?" Marvelous asked.

"No. He knew that when you fight with a brother or sister, you are hurting yourself, because he or she is a part of you. I looked in his face and said, 'Brother, you had better run away from the pleasure that will give you pain tomorrow.' He smiled at me and said, 'Sister, thanks for being strong.' The following day, while Daniel and I were having lunch, the telephone rang," Rachel continued. "The person asked for Rachel Anele. Daniel was taken aback. The person introduced himself as Joshua, a friend of mine. He asked if he could come over and visit with me. Before Daniel could say anything, Joshua had hung up. As it turned out, Joshua had arranged to marry me, but could not afford the money to bring me over to the United States of America. Things happened so fast that, in less than a month, Joshua and I were married in Chicago."

"What did Daniel do about it?" asked Agnes.

"Daniel went to Immigration and complained about me. The immigration authorities told him that I entered the United States with the proper documents and that I had not contravened any laws of the country. He had to grin and bear it. There was nothing that Daniel could do about it, because our elders say, 'The anger of a blood relation does not penetrate to the bone.' Like

Moses, Daniel saw the Promised Land, but could not reach it. And Joshua did."

The women laughed.

Every train has a caboose. After the party, Marvelous stayed behind to chat with the hostess. "I'm a little skeptical about Gini," Marvelous said to Angelina. "Gini, to me, is like one of those church ladies who pretend to be supportive while lying in wait for the preacher's wife to falter."

"Well, Marvelous, you will find out for yourself who the women are. This is one of the reasons for this get-together, so that you would meet with the women. Your observations will carry you far in discharging your duty as the preacher's wife. I'm here to help you make it," Angelina assured her. "Many of these ladies in the church came over from the other churches because they became dissatisfied with the dynamics of their former churches. Even after you get completely settled in, remember, just because the water is calm does not mean there are no crocodiles in it."

"Thank you for the advice," Marvelous replied.

Chapter 48

In Ohadum District, the highest office was that of the administrative chief executive of Ohadum District Ruling Council. The chief executive, Ogboso Kesa, was incapacitated the previous year and was replaced by the highest ranking New Givers Party council member, Chief Ogbo Kalu, the pro tem chief executive. The term of office would end in two months.

Attorney Kandu had been appointed Chief Justice of Ohadum District. The rank of senior advocate of Ohadum District had been conferred on Attorney Chekalu after more than ten years of legal practice. He had also distinguished himself in the legal profession.

Two political parties existed: the Old Takers Party (OTP) and the New Givers Party (NGP). Amos Timba was the chairman of the NGP and Zack Kaliba was the chairman of the OTP. According to the constitution, parties would be permitted to field candidates and make changes up to two weeks prior to the election day.

At the primary election, Zebulon Zimako, Z-man, emerged unopposed as the OTP candidate for the seat of administrative chief executive of Ohadum District Ruling Council.

Immediately after the primary election, Z-man and Zack Kaliba met in Z-man's house to discuss political campaign strategies.

"The huge turnout for the dedication ceremony of the African Kingdom Seekers Church should not be taken lightly," Zack told Z-man.

"I'm aware of it," Z-man said.

"A political campaign calls for a lot of money, you know?" emphasized Zack. He paused. "Z-man, you have what it takes," Zack added, as if to slow down Z-man's racing pulse.

Z-man knew who was talking. It takes one to know one.

"You will be on my side, won't you?" Z-man asked.

"That goes without question, you know. I'm the chairman of the party. Your success is my success," Zack spoke out, but thought to himself, *I have to feather my own nest too.*

While Z-man and Zack were talking and drinking champagne, as if victory had already been assured, Z-man's security guard walked in and announced that Simon Okafor, the OTP Secretary General, was waiting to see them.

"Send him in," Z-man said.

"Have a seat, Simon, and treat yourself to a bottle of champagne," Z-man said.

Simon opened a bottle, tipped his head back and took almost half the bottle before he rested. For him and the OTP big wheels, champagne was like water.

"What is new from the NGP camp?" Zack asked.

"The NGP has announced the nomination of Agara Aham to challenge the OTP candidate at the polls."

"It's going to be an uphill task to bring him down," Zack opined like an old, bitter politician. "I'm sure everybody is waiting to see how the two financial giants are going to fight it out three weeks from now," Zack added.

Zack sent Simon to go and invite the chief of police, Jones, and the police detective boss, Moses, to a meeting at nine o'clock that night in Z-man's house.

Jones and Moses were at Z-man's mansion at nine p.m. As the two men were drinking their champagne, Zack walked in and greeted them.

"From the information you gave me the last time we met, Agara has stopped his wharf activities," Z-man said.

"But his Agarangelina Clearing Company continues to grow unabated," Jones said. "It's a legal company, and nobody can stop its operation."

Z-man promised to reward them heavily if the two men would support his election and ensure that he won. He would, without doubt, clamp down Agara then.

The following day, Z-man received a visit from Zack Kaliba, chairman of the OTP. Over bottles of champagne, Zack told Z-man that he wanted a new car for his wife.

"What can I expect in return?" Z-man asked, looking directly at the chairman.

"My vote and the influence I will bring to bear on other voters," Zack replied.

"What influence can you possibly bring to bear on voters in a secret ballot?" Z-man asked.

"You don't think my word is good enough in the communities around?" Zack asked.

"Yes, to be honest with you."

"Would you honor my request if I should give you some dirt on Agara?" Zack asked.

"I would if the dirt you supply will stick."

"It would cause Agara to withdraw from the election. Any other candidate that the NGP will field with be a walk-over for you. You know the old saying, 'If you succeed in making love with the queen of the fairies, the rest will be no trouble at all.'"

Zack followed Z-man to the back of the yard, where a new 504 Peugeot was parked. "This will be for your wife when Agara withdraws from the race," Z-man said.

The two men laughed heartily. Zack supplied Z-man with the details of Agara's early life as a rapist, arsonist, and a fugitive.

The next day, Z-man called Agara for a meeting. During the meeting, he discussed what he held over Agara and promised not to make it a political scandal if he, Agara, should withdraw from the race.

"I will think about it," Agara said.

"I need a reply within twenty-four hours," Z-man said, happy that he had Agara by the balls.

Agara went home and called a meeting of the NGP top executives. He told them of his meeting with Z-man.

Amos Timba, chairman of the party, laughed. "The NGP should start celebrating, because victory is already ours. Z-man has dug a grave for his corpse," the old man said.

The NGP chairman immediately sent a message to the OTP chairman that Agara had withdrawn from the race and that no further information was available at that time. The OTP chairman immediately informed Z-man of the latest political news.

Z-man called his top executives to come and party with him. Immediately, Zack collected the keys to the 504 Peugeot and drove away, laughing loudly. "Z-man should be careful not to claim victory prematurely," the old politician thought.

Amos knew the constitution of the Ohadum District council front and back. Two weeks and one day before the election day, he summoned a top level executive meeting of the NGP at Agara's mansion. In an inner circle party meeting, with champagne being consumed as if it were bottled water, he called the members to order.

"Ladies and gentlemen of our party," he began, "I want to introduce the most hard-working lady of this district, Angelina Agara Aham, whom you all know. In her youth, Angelina had been courted by numerous admirers, as she was considered not only the most beautiful, but also the brightest girl in Unaka. As the daughter of the most powerful chief Ohadum District has ever known, she has shown that the blood of her ancestors is in her. She had a good start in life and went on to become a teacher and a graduate of New State University. She is a mother and the force behind the founding of the African Kingdom Seekers Church of Ohadum District."

There was clapping of hands for Angelina.

"Agara has stepped down for good reasons," the chairman continued. "At this time, I want someone to nominate Angelina Agara Aham as the NGP candidate for the office of the Administrative Chief Executive of Ohadum District Ruling Council."

After the nomination process, the NGP unanimously endorsed Angelina as the candidate to challenge Z-man. She accepted the nomination. The party chairman filed the nomination two hours before the deadline, and the NGP campaign started.

After the party meeting, Angelina went into her room and shut the door. She tried to recollect the last pieces of advice that her father gave her: "Keep your ancestors alive in your heart. Your past family history is one part of your life that you cannot change. You can make a difference. Success and failure are the two hardest things to handle in life." She wondered if this political adventure was what she really wanted to embark upon; then she realized that she had to face Z-man squarely. "Men and women are different, but they are equal," she thought. Her inner voice said to her, "Don't quit before the finish line. You can do it." She knelt down and prayed for guidance from the Supreme Creator. She was going to face a tough and ruthless adversary.

When she came out of her room, she felt happy.

The news of Angelina's entry into politics spread like wildfire in the harmattan. In no time at all, the elite women of Ohadum District were at the front yard of the Agara mansion chanting, "We support Angie! We want Angie!"

Angelina came out to meet them. Gini, the spokeslady, said, "Angelina, since the creation of Ohadum District, no woman has been known to head the district. Men think they are the privileged ones to hold the office. If you would think back, that seat has been occupied only by men—Chief Okonkwo, Chief Okeke, Chief Okoye, Chief Okoafor, and Chief Ogboso Kesa. None of these people ever vacated the office voluntarily. The last ruler would have still been there if he had not been forced out by fate. Today, everybody in Ohadum knows that you are the brains behind the establishment of the African Kingdom Seekers Church of Ohadum, the largest church congregation in Ohadum District. Angelina, the women have voted to support you in the race for chairman of Ohadum District Ruling Council."

Angelina thanked the group for their confidence in her.

The news of Angelina's entry into politics in Ohadum District took Z-man by surprise. He sent for his party chairman, Zack, who took his time to come and see him. In the presence of the chief of police and the police detective boss, Z-man arrogantly declared that he could not imagine a woman ruling Ohadum District, the wealthiest district in Africa.

Moses smiled. "Gentlemen," he said, "history has it that even as far back as the sixteenth century, women like Elizabeth the First and Isabella of Spain ruled their entire nations."

"We have to resort to any available means to stop her from winning," Z-man declared, and asked the people to work with him.

At 11:00 p.m. this night, a week before Election Day, Amos Timba was in the conference room of the NGP political headquarters. He had summoned a meeting to share his political plans with the inner circle party executives. Moses, Jones, Bishop Ezelu, Angelina, and Agara were there. Champagne bottles were opened and small chops served.

"Most of the voters are susceptible to bribery," Amos started. "This has been my observation in politics. Angelina, do not forget that you have an advantage over your opponent in this coming election," the old man warned.

"What is the advantage?" Angelina asked.

"There are four major towns in this district: Aloma, Mbenoha, Oharu, and Unaka. Through the establishment of the AKS Church, you have come across many of the voters on a personal basis," the old man said.

"That's true," Angelina agreed. "But Z-man has been popular in this district for a long time," Angelina said.

Amos laughed. "That's nothing to worry about. Only few politicians rely solely on popularity to get elected," he assured her. "If popularity was the basis for being elected, many of the world's leaders would be out of office," the seasoned politician said.

Doctor Ezelu told Angelina that church and politics were somehow inseparable. God desires for a good leader to shepherd the flock. He prayed for Angelina to successfully ride out of the political storm ahead.

Angelina stood up and greeted her supporters. She thanked them for the trust they had in her. "I feel confident in my entry into the political arena. I'm now part of Mbenoha, and will bloom where I'm planted," she declared.

Agara gave her his approval and vowed to do everything he could to put her on that seat. "If someone can do it, you can do it," he assured her. It would be a shock to Z-man not only to lose the election, but to lose it to a woman who had given him the bitter pill to swallow when she refused to marry him," Agara said.

Sunday morning, Angelina's running was announced at the African Kingdom Seekers Church and other smaller churches around. It took Z-man by surprise that the announcement was made at the All Saints Church without consulting him. It was a slap in the face. He was livid, and threatened with abusive words to fire the pastor of the church. The deacons of the All Saints Church overruled him.

"Spoken words can't be recalled," the pastor told him after he calmed down and apologized.

This was the beginning of his crises in the church. His power was fast eroding. Many had already decamped to the AKS church. The future of his authority in the churches hung in the balance.

Z-man wasn't helped by the fact that Dr. Paul Ezelu, bishop of AKSC, the largest congregation in Ohadum District, didn't hesitate to make it clear who the church's preferred candidate was.

The political campaigns of the two candidates were fast growing. Angelina and Z-man campaigned vigorously. Z-man employed every form of persuasion possible: distribution of money, bales of dried stock fish, bags of rice, and car-tons of beer.

Days passed. Whenever his political analyst briefed him on how many votes he expected from each area, Z-man still didn't feel confident that he would have the majority. There was absolutely no way of telling how anyone would cast their votes in a secret ballot.

On that last day of the campaign, Angelina went to the market square of each community and addressed the people. She mounted the stage and greeted the people. "As we approach the new era of the government of Ohadum Dis-trict," she began, "if elected, I will see that attendance at the finest schools of Ohadu District should be available to any child of proven academic ability and not decided simply by to which rich parents the child was born. This is a legacy we owe our children. Such fine schools should be staffed with highly qualified academicians."

She paused as the crowd shouted, "We want Angie! We want Angie! We want Angie!"

Angelina told the crowd that Zebulon Zimako was a rich man and that he had been chairman of the All Saints Churches of Aloma, Oharu, and Unaka for many years. "What has he done to improve the lot of the people?" she asked. She paused. "You know what I have achieved for you in a short period of time—" She was interrupted by shouts from the crowd, "We want Angie! We want Angie!"

"Zebulon Zimako has invested his money in buying expensive homes overseas, but my husband and I have built our home here in Ohadum Dis-trict."

More shouts from the crowd, "Angie will lead us! Angie will lead us!"

"Tomorrow, you will decide who will lead you," she said. "Who will lead you?" she asked in conclusion.

While the crowd shouted, "Angie! Angie! she exited from the stage.

The candidates campaigned until midnight. Aloma, the home of Z-man, was the last place Angelina campaigned. People turned out en mass to cheer her. This last lap was the hardest. Z-man's supporters in his own territory wanted to fight for the son of the soil, but the chief of police and the director of the detective squad were on hand to control the situation.

At the end of the day, Angelina was exhausted. She came home and met Bishop Ezelu, his wife, Marvelous, Agara, and Amos. As they were chatting over champagne, Jones and Moses joined them.

"What is new, Jones?" Amos asked.

"The situation is under control," the police chief informed, adding, "you have Abraham as the Godfather!"

The people burst into a hearty laugh.

"What does the other camp look like?" Amos asked.

"Uneasy," said Moses.

"Angelina," the bishop called her by name. "You have done so much for the community. The Lord is going to take care of the rest. Members of the African Kingdom Seekers Church and the rest of Ohadum District are behind you now."

"Thank you, Bishop Ezelu," Angelina said.

Chapter 49

As the people went to the polls the next morning, Angelina sat at home while Agara took over; he was at the Angelina Campaign headquarters.

Z-man met with his top level campaign team. At this meeting were the COP, Jones Sanuwo, the police detective, Moses Nduka, and the campaign manager, Simon Okafor. The campaign manager briefed the team on the arrangement made to ensure victory for Z-man. Simon, a seasoned politician himself, had been burned before. From experience, he knew that he who digs a pit for another may fall into it himself.

The manager reported that ballot boxes filled with fake ballots had been assembled from Aloma, Mbenoha, Oharu, and Unaka at an undisclosed area. Only Zack, Jones, and Moses knew about it, since they were part of the scheme for Z-man's victory. Z-man was happy.

Simon told the team that he watched the enthusiastic response of the crowd while Z-man was making his last appeal for votes in the Ohadum communities. The crowd was for him, and victory was expected.

Jones told Z-man that while all looked good, he should not forget that voters are the most untrustworthy of crowds. Many a time, what they say in front of a candidate is different from what they do when casting the vote.

"Be prepared for the unexpected. A politician has only temporary friends," Moses warned with a smile on his face.

"But you are with me?" Z-man asked.

"To keep the peace," Jones answered.

Z-man thought about his dealings with the people of Ohadum District; how he had thrown his weight around until Agara rose to financial fame. "If you do evil, expect to suffer evil. Could this be what Moses hinted?" he wondered.

By 6:00 p.m., the polling booths closed and the ballot boxes were on their way to the central counting station. During the first hour of the election returns, Z-man was leading but Angelina was gaining rapidly. In the last hour of the counting, Angelina was leading by a wide margin.

Wisdom is seldom used during troubled times. Simon immediately told Z-man that he would lose the election unless the fake ballots were moved in quickly. Z-man became wild and uncontrollable. He hollered and screamed and asked for the fake ballots to be moved in without delay.

Pandemonium broke out. In the confusion that ensued outside the central counting station, Moses asked Jones to declare a state of emergency. On the order of the COP, tear gas was fired to disperse the crowd.

Z-man continued to scream, and Jones ordered him taken to Mbenoha General Hospital for examination. Motives are behind everything we do. The medical director, Dr. Rufus Dibia, was there waiting. He had turned the volume of the radio high.

As Z-man came out of the car and was being led to the emergency room, Radio VOD, Voice of Ohadum District, announced that Angelina Agara Aham had won the election by an overwhelming margin.

Z-man shouted crazily. Dr. Rufus Dibia examined him and diagnosed him with temporary insanity. He was committed to the lunatic asylum, where he was tranquilized. When he woke up, he told Dr. Dibia how he had suffered in life.

"Do not look forward to the day when you will stop suffering, because then you will be dead," Dr. Dibia told him.

On the day of Angelina's installation ceremony, Z-man was released from the asylum.

"Do you plan to attend the installation ceremony?" Dr. Dibia asked him.

"I do not plan on it," he replied, unhappy with the doctor for declaring him insane.

"It would be good if you gave it serious thought to attend. Do not dismiss a good idea just because you don't like where it came from," Dr. Dibia said.

Z-man smiled. "Seeking revenge prevents the wound from healing," Zack Kaliba said. He was reading Z-man's mind. "Stop blaming others for your failure," he advised.

Simon Okafor came to visit Z-man. He, too, had been through political baptisms. Each kind attracts its own. He saw the anguish in Z-man's face and reminded him that no one goes through life without suffering. "Let go of anger," Simon said. "It hurts you more than the person with whom you are angry."

"I agree with Simon," Dr. Dibia said. "Please, Z-man, listen. No matter how far one has gone along the wrong road, it is better to turn back. Life is too short to nurse animosities."

Z-man smiled. He was taking in the advice from his sympathizers. "I will think about all that has been said to me," Z-man said, believing that time heals all wounds.

Chapter 50

The election campaign had taken its toll on Angelina. Her sun had come up after the political storm. Seated at the stage with her were Agara and Sochima.

At the appointed time, Angelina stood at the center of the stage, surrounded by top political members of the NGP. The Honorable Kandu, chief justice of Ohadum District, swore her in as the first woman administrative chief executive of the Ohadum District Ruling Council. In his advice to Angelina, the chief justice said, "Do not try to rule the people forever. You will not succeed. The men before you tried it and got no where. You are on this seat because of the trust from the people. A good deed is never lost. Watch out. Power can corrupt."

SAO, the senior advocate of Ohadum District, Mr. Chekalu, rose in his legal regalia. "Angelina Aham," he began, "congratulations on your achievement I would like to tell you the story about your predecessor, Ogboso Kesa. When he first thought about running for the executive office, he started telling the public how corrupt political and government officials were. He went very far in substantiating his accusations and won the admiration of many followers, who crowned him 'Champion of the Poor.' When election time came for the Office of the Administrative Chief Executive of the Ohadum District Ruling Council, he won with a landslide. He was sworn in with unprecedented fanfare. Many looked up to him as the hope of the people. During the first two years of his office, Ogboso built for himself the best home in the community, purchased houses in the principal towns of Ohadum, and overseas. Only a small fraction of fund-voted for community development projects trickled down for executing the job. Reporters sought interviews with him, but could not reach him. Eventually, one of his inner circle advisers helped to corner him for a news commentator. But Ogboso cunningly turned to the newsman and said, 'You cannot talk while you are eating.' With that, he left his office and drove away. It was not long after that he became incapacitated and was forced out by fate."

As Angelina was sworn in, Dr. Rufus Dibia smiled. He boldly told the reporters that Angelina knew where she was going and how to get there. She charted the course very brilliantly and left no stone unturned. She knew she was going to soup with the devil and had to provide herself with a long spoon.

Z-man watched the installation ceremony with tears in his eyes. He recalled his own words: *"Famous men have power. If you try to work against them, they will use every means in their power to stop you. Powerful men play dirty; the more powerful, the more unscrupulous and ruthless. He has the money and the power to ensure that things are done his way."* He sighed. "Power does not reside in one's hand forever," he thought.

When Angelina came outside and saw Z-man, she smiled. As the head of her government, she could not afford to isolate anybody. She went to him. Looking at her, Z-man said, "Mrs. Angelina Aham, chairman of Ohadum Ruling Council, I bow to your superior intelligence. You are truly the chief's daughter, the daughter of the most powerful chief Ohadum District has ever known."

She smiled.

"After what you've been through," Z-man continued, "you deserve to be happy." He gave her the victory sign and embraced the woman he could not have. At the moment of embrace, his manhood moved. Angelina looked at him and said, "Give it up, ol' man." Z-man smiled at her, but he was not yet ready to give up his atrocious plans against her.

After the installation party was over that night, Agara pulled his wife close. He kissed her and assured her of his love for her; then he got up to answer the knock at the door. It was the maid, who had brought two plates of goat meat pepper soup and a bottle of chilled wine. She set them on the table and left.

They moved to the table to enjoy the soup. Agara opened the chilled wine expertly, so that it only burped loudly, without spewing. She looked at him and smiled at his expertise. He poured the wine into two glasses. Her hand trembled slightly as she reached for the stem of her glass of wine. She broke the spell when she moved toward him. She calmly took a sip of the wine and watched him give her a sexy smile.

She picked a piece of the meat from her soup and put it close to his mouth. He bit into the succulent piece of meat.

"Hm! It's delicious," he said.

She put the other piece into her mouth. "It's nice and juicy," she said. She realized that he was looking at her mouth. His eyes were as unblinking as a cat's. She felt vulnerable beneath the steady gaze of his eyes. No longer pretending to be eating the pepper soup, they abandoned the bowls, because another kind of hunger had set in. There was no sense in denying it. She had emptied her glass of wine. The wine went straight to her head and to her thighs, which had turned rubbery.

He led her to the bedroom. It was dimly lit. "Do you want me turn the lights on?" he asked.

"Actually, I would prefer it as it is," Angelina said. The dimly light room was having a dangerous effect on her. She was ready.

Early in the morning, she looked out through the window. Bright sunlight was already filtering through the leafy branches of the trees and casting wavering patterns against the closed glass windows in the bedroom. Birds were chirping happily from the branches of the frangipani. Squirrels chased each other through the upper branches of the mango trees. Butterflies flitted from the flowers of the hibiscus plants to those of the bougainvillea.

Angelina was happy. Her life was shining brightly.

Chapter 51

Agara came home from the clubhouse one day, and parked his car. It was a beautiful afternoon. Angelina had gone to the campus of New State University at Mbenoha to visit with her daughter, Sochima.

There was a perfunctory knock on the door.

"Who is it?"

"Blessing," the voice said.

He went to the door and opened it. He was taken aback.

She stared at him. Time stood still. She was back in time, back in bed with him, many years ago. She gave him a tantalizing smile and said, "May I come in?"

Agara stepped aside and she went in and sat down.

"How have you been, Blessing?" he asked.

"Fine."

"What brought you back? I was told you went to live in Lagos after I fled the village many years ago."

Blessing was now older, but she still looked very beautiful.

"Agara, I have missed you since the last time I was with you before you fled. Did you miss me?" she asked.

"I'm married now," he told her.

"So I heard," Blessing said.

"Tell me about yourself since you left the village," Agara prodded her.

"After you fled the village many years ago, I went to Lagos and got married to a young, enterprising man, Tunde. Agara, you should see him. He's a business man, handsome and sexy."

"Where is he now?"

"He's in Lagos. After three years of marriage, we got a divorce because I didn't want any children. We still see each other, only when it is convenient for both of us. He pays my house rent in Lagos."

"Why are you here now?" he asked.

"I still like you, Agara." She got up and held his hand. Blessing rubbed against him like a she-cat in heat. "This time I'll make sure you don't carelessly get me knocked up. I love my freedom from men," she said.

"You said you were pregnant before I fled. What happened?"

"Three months after you fled, I had a miscarriage. I would have loved to carry the pregnancy to full term."

"What else?" Agara asked.

"After you fled, I heard you met an attractive young lady in Unaka and got her knocked up too. When the news reached the village, most women in the area, at that time, knew you were in a perpetual state of arousal. So no one was surprised to hear it. You probably wanted to ease yourself and move on but got hooked by extreme lust. That was okay. You didn't have to pay any dowry. You had free sex for the time you were with her. After you got tired of it, you took off again, leaving her wondering who next would fall victim to your insatiable lust."

"Shut up, Blessing."

"I forgive you, Agara, for running away from me the first time. I have mellowed down since that time. I knew you as a very virile man and irresistible to the women."

"God almighty," he shouted. "Blessing, will you please shut up!"

"I will when I'm through."

"Now that you have told me all the information you have gathered regarding my relationship with my wife, Angelina, what do you want? What is the price for getting you off my back? Sexual favors?"

"Agara, I'm not asking you to give Angelina up; she is your wife. The only thing I want is for you to recognize me as your mistress. I know you love free sex. Let's enjoy lovemaking as we did before. Send for me when you want. I'm not asking for money. Tunde takes care of that for me. You see my car outside, Hassan bought it for me. He takes care of my travel expenses."

On walking into the house and seeing Agara and Blessing talking and laughing, Angelina felt like she couldn't breathe. It felt like no air could enter her body. She pictured Agara and Blessing having sex in the bedroom. The thought pierced her, and she let out a moan. She wished she could die at that moment.

Suddenly, Agara looked up and saw Angelina standing at the door. She moved her gaze from Blessing to Agara.

As if she did not see the woman at the door, Blessing looked at Agara and said, "Tell me you loved me, Agara."

"There is nothing to tell," Agara said. "It was a meaningless affair."

"Meaningless? You loved me, Agara," she cried.

"I never loved you," Agara repeated.

Angelina walked closer to watch the drama.

"You know you did," Blessing shouted.

Looking at Angelina, Blessing said, "He couldn't get enough of me."

"I'm not interested in knowing that," Angelina said.

Angelina thought about their time together at the Potompo celebration night, the way their bodies met, heart and soul. She shook with anger at his succumbing to the caprices and whims of this whore. Tears welled in her eyes and she let them fall.

"Angelina, this isn't what it looks like," Agara said, surprised to see her. He did not hear her drive up.

"Tell me what it looks like, Agara. You are standing there holding that whore close, your manhood bulging as if its hat will push through the fly of your trousers and go straight through her panties, if she is wearing any."

Angelina turned to look at Blessing, who was assessing the situation. Blessing knew that Angelina was up to something. She took off for the gate, shouting, "Z-man where are you?" Angelina heard her and smiled. She would finish with her husband first.

Blessing ran to her car and drove away. She made a bee-line to Z-man's compound and got her cut for the job.

"Can you listen to me Angelina?" Agara asked.

"Go straight to hell, Agara. You are a two-faced, despicable, hypocritical bastard," she spat out. She turned to move and Agara said, "Hold it, Angelina." She turned back and faced him.

"Why are you so hard on me, Angelina? You haven't even heard from me yet."

"What do you want me to hear? How you and your ex-lover were caught in a compromising position? Tell me this, Agara, has this been going on behind my back since you came back to Mbenoha?" Angelina asked.

"No," he answered. "I have not betrayed you, Angelina, and will never do so," he said. "It was my fault that you met me with her holding my hand. I'm asking that you forgive me."

She looked at him and smiled at his words.

"Have you slept with her since you returned?" she asked again.

"No," he answered. "It was because of Blessing that I fled Oharu years ago. I put her in the family way then and fled. Since I returned, today is the first day I have had a talk with her."

"I see. Both of you were trying very hard to make up for lost time? Your arms were around her when I walked in."

"She took me by surprise, Angelina."

"You expect me to believe that, when I saw the happy expression on your face? If you claim to be so innocent, why didn't you order her out of the house? Agara, you take me for a fool to have waited so long for you and then surrender myself back to you as if we parted on friendly terms. I have loved you since the first day I laid my eyes on you."

"So have I," he said.

As she moved away, her thoughts were on Agara holding Blessing in his arms. Now that she had calmed down, she remembered hearing Blessing shout, "Z-man where are you?" Her thoughts went back to the warning from

Chankola, concerning her husband: *"He has led a fast life with women and he is trying very hard to distance himself from them, but they keep coming back, since he now has a promising financial future. His enemy plans to get to him through one of his old women, Can you trust him?"*

More than ever, she was determined not to let Blessing or any woman ruin her marriage. Agara tried to make her believe that what she saw was not of his doing. Could she trust him at this time?

Agara held her and they kissed each other. He looked into her face and smiled. Their life had not been perfect.

"Angelina, from the very beginning, you have been the most fascinating, sexiest woman I have ever met." He took her in his arms and led her to the bedroom. "Angelina," he whispered, I'm sorry that you found me in that position with Blessing. I could have ordered her out of the house, but I did not."

"Agara, I forgive you," she whispered, pulling him close. "As long as you keep trying, we'll make it.

The words touched Agara like a gentle, calming breeze after a turbulent storm. He smiled at her with devastating sexiness.

Chapter 52

Two months later, Agara and Angelina agreed to have a formal wedding. Angelina sent a message to her daughter, Sochima, who was in school at New State University. On the weekend, Sochima came home to help her mother plan the wedding.

Nnemugo, Director of Cheggs Event Planners, was contacted. She came and joined the family in the planning. Bishop Paul Ezelu and his wife were present. At the end of the meeting, invitations went out to all the Ohadum District chiefs, members of the Ohadum Ruling Council, and the surrounding churches. The announcement was published in the daily papers. Important men and women of Ohadum were accorded special invitations.

"Oh, Agara, what about a maid of honor and a best man? We need them, don't we?" Angelina asked.

Agara didn't consider this long. He knew exactly whom he would choose, and he could already hear him laughing. "Zebulon Zimako will stand for me," he said.

"I will ask his mistress, Joy, to do the same for me," Angelina said.

Nnemugo contacted Z-man at his mansion. His mistress was there. Z-man felt as if it was a trap set to embarrass him.

"Let bygones be bygones," Nnemugo told him.

Joy said, "Z-man, give peace a chance. It is stressful and a lot of work to hold a grudge."

"It sounds like I'm a coward," Z-man said.

"You do not have to be a coward to want peace," Nnemugo told him.

Nnemugo asked Joy to stand for Angelina.

"It would be an honor for Z-man and I to do so," Joy said.

Angelina and Agara met at the African Kingdom Seekers Church for their marriage vows. Bishop Ezelu, thirty-two, was the officiating minister. The church was filled with flowers. When Angelina saw the whole arrangement, she smiled. She was happy.

The ceremony was informal and brief. "Twenty two years ago, Angelina and Agara were married by the gods at the Unaka Sacred Forest during the traditional Potompo festival," Bishop Ezelu began. "Everyone goes through trials to get to where they are. This couple has gone through turbulent trials. It is true that life goes in cycles between sadness and happiness. Through Angelina's steadfast love, Agara has turned out to be a faithful lover," Bishop Ezelu said. He finished with the preliminaries, followed by a promise from Angelina and Agara to honor and respect each other as long as they are together. He then charged them to "sin no more." The rings and kisses were exchanged.

Agara and Angelina had become the wealthiest people in Ohadum District. An elaborate reception was planned. Cheggs Event Planners took charge. Nnemugo, known for her planning and culinary skills, prepared a sumptuous buffet. The smell of the food made the mouths of many guests water. Silverware tinkled as guests began to visit the buffet table, laden with rich African food, including rice with stew, pounded yam and soup, pepper soup, fried plantains, beef patties, and much more. People took their food to small tables, where they sat and chatted about the huge success of the wedding party.

Auntie Mary delivered the multi-tiered cake.

The reception hall was beautifully decorated. The gathering was festive. Only Agara and Angelina, plus a few invited highly placed friends sat at the special table. There was no formal sitting arrangement for the rest. Dignitaries were there to wine and dine and rejoice with the couple. Many of the guests here had skipped the church ceremony and moved to the reception, where they knew there would be plenty of food and drink. Waiters went around with trays of champagne. Beer, soft drinks, palm wine, and hot drinks were passed around freely.

When the Newtime Band boys started playing their popular high-life music, Angelina and Agara took to the floor. Soon, Z-man and his mistress, Joy Nneoma, joined in the dance. Soon after, a crowd of people surged to the floor, shimmying and shaking their hips.

At one corner was a mountain of wedding gifts from wealthy traders, top level government officials, and contract-seeking chief executives of various companies. Angelina was thrilled at all the thoughtfulness. These people cared about them. She had been aware of their support in building the African Kingdom Seekers Church and their political support. The cards, the flowers, and their presence—she cherished them.

Champagne bottles were placed on every table. When the cork popped out of the bottle, Angelina jumped. Some of the dignitaries sitting nearby burst into laughter. Angelina was happy. The glasses were filled and passed around. Agara handed her a glass. "To us," he said as they clinked glasses together and each took a sip. Agara kissed his wife.

Jacob Ikonne got up and said, "I'm happy to be here today. I feel that I was the matchmaker for you two."

"You were," Agara said. "You said things to her and to me that made us come together at the Potompo celebration, during which we were married."

"More than that, the two of you have demonstrated that no one should underestimate the power of love," Jacob said. "No matter how many years elapsed, Agara found his way back to you, and you took him back. Now that both of you are together again, remember that when both people work at a marriage, it becomes twice as good. A good marriage gets better with time," Jacob concluded.

A guilty conscience needs to confess.

Z-man got up. The crowd clapped for his change of heart. "One of the greatest lessons I have learned in life is that I should be happy without the things I cannot have," he began. "Some people have to be burned before they learn." He paused and smiled and then, looking at Angelina and Agara, said, "I heaped insults on both of you. I know that insults last longer than injury. Even when I sent Blessing to mar Angelina's marriage, I could not succeed; what is well planted cannot be uprooted. The gods married you for life," he said as he paused again.

There were smiles on the faces of the crowd.

"Agara and Angelina, I'm asking that you forgive me," Z-man said. "I have learned not to underestimate the power of a woman. I have also learned that one cannot buy a woman's love and love cannot be forced. I thought I was better than Agara because he came to Angelina poor, but I have learned that no one is better than anyone else," he concluded.

The crowd cheered and stood for him. At this moment of standing ovation, he took his seat happily.

Agara stood up and thanked Z-man for his confessions. He assured Z-man that he and his wife had forgiven him.

To record the day, Moses got out his camera. Angelina and Agara smiled for the picture.

After the reception, Agara came home feeling completely refreshed. He found his wife slumped on their bed, tiredness evident in every wilting line of her frame. "Are you tired?" he inquired.

"It's been a long day," she said.

The bathwater is lovely and moderately warm, if you want to take a bath."

She got up and went into the bathroom. Settling into the warm bath, Agara pulled her close.

"Agara, I love you! I love you so much. Please don't leave me again!"

"I love you too," Angelina. I always will," Agara said. His voice vibrated with tenderness and longing. He opened his arms and she eased into them. They clung to each other as if they would never let go. A tide of happiness engulfed them.

"Angelina, when I made those wedding vows at the altar, before Bishop Ezelu and the guests, I said them from the bottom of my heart. I love you."

Agara angled his head and lowered his lips to hers. When he withdrew, he whispered softly in her ear, "I love you, Angelina, you are my one and only wife."

In a moment, her body accepted him. If there had been anyone nearby, Angelina could not have cared less. When it was over, she felt fearless. Nothing mattered now. She loved Agara and he loved her. They had the rest of their lives for their love to grow.

She searched for the bed sheet, drew it over them, and drifted into dreamless sleep. Beside her, Agara lay sleeping, his arms across her waist. His face looked peaceful.

Suddenly, his eyelids fluttered and he looked around with momentary confusion. When he realized where he was, he smiled. He couldn't think of any better way for God to have used Adam's rib.